DROWN MY BOOKS

PENNY FREEDMAN

Matador
9 Priory Business Park,
Wistow Road, Kibworth Beauchamp,
Leicestershire. LE8 0RX
Tel: 0116 279 2299
Email: books@troubador.co.uk
Web: www.troubador.co.uk/matador
Twitter: @matadorbooks

ISBN 978 1785893 018

British Library Cataloguing in Publication Data.
A catalogue record for this book is available from the British Library.

Printed and bound in the UK by TJ International, Padstow, Cornwall
Typeset in 11pt Book Antiqua by Troubador Publishing Ltd, Leicester, UK

Matador is an imprint of Troubador Publishing Ltd

MIX
Paper from
responsible sources
FSC® C013056

This book is for the people with whom I have read and talked about books over the past thirteen years:

For Mary, Janet, Jane, Sue, Robert, Sarah, Rosie, Jonathan, Joyce and Jan.

For Chris, Jan, Rose, Judy, Sally, Ann, Joan, Shelagh, Gloria, Celia and Jill.

And for Jan Dawson and the Warwickshire Super-readers.

My thanks, too, to the volunteers and readers in Studley, who introduced me to the pleasures of the community library, to Jan Sewell, who set me thinking about a murder in a book group, to Mary Wells for research trips and to Melinda Wells for willingly modelling Freda.

PREAMBLE

The events I record here happened early in 2014. You will be reading about them later, through the prism of events of 2015, the daily horror of thousand upon thousand would-be immigrants – many from Syria – dying in the seas of southern Europe. These deaths produced a change, of sorts, in the UK government's attitude to Syrian refugees. In the first half of 2014, however, only 24 Syrian refugees were admitted to Britain under the government's programme for the relocation of vulnerable refugees. In that competition, my student, Farid Khalil, stood very little chance.

Gina Sidwell

Chapter One

THE SEA

Tuesday 28th January 2014

When people ask me – and they certainly do ask me – how I come to be living here, I tell them that in the course of a single week I lost my mother, my job, my lover and my home. That usually shuts them up. My answer is disingenuous, of course. I did lose my mother; she died, quickly and quietly, while sitting in her chair one summer afternoon. The job, the lover and the house, though, were less straightforward: the job was a question of jumping before I was pushed, and the lover likewise, really. As for the house, well, with everything else gone, there really seemed no point in holding on to that.

I don't tell people all this, nor do I add that when your life is all washed up, there is nowhere better to find its concrete metaphor than in a scabby little house so close to the sea that when I step out of my front door my mobile phone sends me a message welcoming me to France.

I had an image of the home I was seeking – the Platonic ideal of a seaside refuge – but I've had to lower my sights, of course. I have the sea-bound cottage I was looking for but without the picturesque isolation I had envisaged. My gimcrack little house sits squeezed into the middle of a cliff-top terrace in which one house or another invariably sports overbearing scaffolding. The economical and ecological driftwood fire I saw casting its soft, flickering glow has been downgraded to an electric one since a surly chap called Gary told me my chimney would need a *total rebuild – arm and a leg job* if I wanted to do anything as reckless as light a fire in my grate. I am too much of a snob to go for coal-effect so mine is an uncompromising two-bar fire with no flickering glow, soft or otherwise.

The dog and the cat don't mind, anyway. They are stretched out on the hearth rug now, as the rain hurls itself at the window and the sea boils beyond. I promised myself a dog as part of my new life and I've been as good as my word, though I don't really like them much; their neediness gets on my nerves. Fortunately, Caliban doesn't ask for much and doesn't pretend to any great affection for me. He is a lugubrious, heavy-jowled beast whose default manner is weary acceptance of whatever life throws at him; the occasional gesture of affection from me is met with wary indifference. Having started on the *Tempest* theme, I had to call the cat Ariel, of course, though she is no airy spirit. In the course of sixteen months, she has gone from being a weightless ball of fluff to a solid beast with the shoulders of a wrestler and the facial markings of a gangster's mask. The dog is terrified of her.

If they don't mind the two-bar fire, nor do I. I'm happy enough with my experiment at living poor. When my daughter, Ellie, first saw this house she looked round in open dismay and asked what I was punishing myself for. Annie, my younger daughter, won't come here at all; she has not forgiven me for selling her childhood home, even though she is living in London with her boyfriend and has no need of said home. Freda, my granddaughter, reacted best. 'It's like a caravan, Granny,' she said, 'only with an upstairs and no wheels.' You can trust Freda to get to the heart of the matter.

I don't think I'm punishing myself; testing myself maybe, yes. I was shocked, you see, after my mother died and I sold her London flat and took 'voluntary' redundancy from my job and sold the family house in Marlbury, which had appreciated absurdly in value with the introduction of a fast rail route between Marlbury and London. I was shocked to find myself rich, the possessor of wealth in the region of a million pounds. The discovery was deeply unsettling. I didn't know what to do with it. It was not that I feared I would run amok and fritter it all away on yachts and designer shoes, but that I feared becoming a different person. I had always been short of money: a job in the public sector and two children to bring up alone meant that life was always a bit hand to mouth even if we were some distance from the actual breadline. An eye for a bargain and the feeling of not being among the privileged has always been part of my sense of identity, so faced with all this money I had an insane urge to give it away to a good cause and pretend it had never happened. I was stopped, of course, by the girls, who cornered me and demanded to know my plans. Forced to admit to my confusion, I was marched off by them to seek help from a most unlikely source.

They took me to see the Rev Peter Michaels, the vicar of St Olave's church, Lewisham, who conducted my mother's funeral. The girls got to know him and like him when they were organising the service, and they were convinced that he was the man to help: spiritual enough to understand my qualms but worldly enough not to let me throw away their inheritance in a quixotic panic. They were quite right, as it happens: he sent me in the direction of ethical investments and I deposited the lot once I had forked out the peanuts required for my current hovel. I still worry that one of those ethical companies will turn out to be employing trafficked children or keeping slaves in mines but I have done my best.

And since interest rates are at rock bottom, I get very little income from my money. I am quite satisfactorily poor.

I have found it surprisingly easy to be poor. Without children, who grow out of their clothes, need three square meals a day and require endless handouts for sports equipment, school trips, dental treatment and the latest *must have* without which teenage life is insupportable, without a job that requires respectable clothes and regular haircuts, it is amazing how little one needs. I have turned the garden over to vegetables. They are not a great success since the ground is chalky and the produce salty and windblown. I have done quite well with root vegetables, though, even if my parsnips seem to have taken their inspiration from Hieronymus Bosch. I buy up bargains in the Co-op and drink cheap plonk. I brought with me only clothes for slobbing about in (except for one silk suit which will have to do for any remotely smart occasion – there have been none as yet) and I have no intention of buying more. What makes it easier is that everyone in St Martin's-at-Cliffe is poor, really, so expectations are low. The name is deceptive. I know – it's that 'e' on the end of 'Cliffe' that does it, evoking a quaint Agatha Christie charm that it entirely lacks. It is, in fact, nothing more than a bedraggled outpost of Dungate, a seaside town going rapidly to seed with the decline in popularity of the windbreaks-and-sand-in-the-sandwiches English holiday. It is a straggle of battered dwellings, clinging to a crumbling clifftop, with a hinterland of boxy 1980s housing, one shop, an unwelcoming pub, a primary school that teeters on the edge of closure and a library abandoned by the county library service. So you can see that it suits my purpose admirably.

In keeping with my new austerity, I brought the minimum of furniture with me but my living room still feels crowded since I weakened in the matter of books. I brought about two thousand with me and they throng my walls. My intention was to have shelves put up but Gary – he who advised against an open fire – also advised against overtaxing my flimsy walls, so freestanding IKEA bookcases jostle for space all round the room and I am supposed to be living up to my intention of rereading every book I own. This has turned out to be quite the most difficult thing about my new life, though, because I had reckoned without my need for the simple excitement of wondering what is going to happen. I started off all right, singling out books the plots of which I had actually forgotten, but then the need for novelty became urgent and I was rescued by the library. It was closed by the local authority three years ago but it is run now by a team of devoted volunteers, including me, and it is in some ways the hub of my new life. It will loom large in the story I have to tell you, so more of that later.

This afternoon the book on my lap is *The Tempest* because soon the doorbell will ring and Theodora will sidle in for her twice-weekly session of A level English coaching. These sessions, and those I do with one other student, constitute the only paid work I have and you may be wondering why, as a well-qualified and experienced woman of fifty, I don't get myself a proper job. You have a point and I can only say that I have worked all my adult life, even when my children were babies, and I am enjoying the break. I shall work again when I feel like it. I hope that will do as an answer, and while we are addressing the questions you might like to ask, I will add that if you are wondering why, with the world my bivalve mollusc, I opted to settle hardly thirty miles from Marlbury, the town I was escaping from, my answer, quite simply, is Freda, and I am not prepared to say any more.

Dora, as she is generally known, is punctual to the minute, as usual, and slips into the house with an apologetic duck of her head like a nervous cat. She contrasts nicely with Matt, my other student. She arrives on time and anxious, wearing her school uniform and carrying annotated texts and a neatly labelled file of notes in a rather old-fashioned leather briefcase; her latest essay will be presented to me in a clear plastic folder. Matt appears anything up to fifteen minutes late, panting and cheerful, in a sweaty tracksuit and toting a huge sports bag on his shoulder, from which he will rummage a suspiciously pristine text; his essay will often be produced, folded and damp, from a pocket of his tracksuit. He is a county-level athlete and he wants to study Sports Management. He needs a pass in A level English to go with his C in Business Studies. It is hard going. Dora, on the other hand, wants to do European Studies at Marlbury University and needs a B; she could do this easily if only she was not so afraid of expressing an opinion. She knows the texts inside out but resorts to immaculate retellings of the plots in her flight from the dangerous possibility of getting something wrong.

Today I usher her in and offer her a cup of tea, as I always do, and she declines, as she always does. She is the daughter of a Greek Orthodox priest and I assume that she thinks builders' tea with milk is a barbaric concoction. The presence of a Greek Orthodox church and priest in St Martin's is a touch of the exotic quite at odds with the blandness of this dull little Anglo-Saxon settlement, but here they are right on my doorstep. The church, you see, is actually in this row of cottages, just three doors along from me, an English seafront cottage with two pillars and a pediment bolted onto its façade and its upper window given an ecclesiastical arch. Perhaps that was what brought me here: I came to the church once for the baptism of a Greek student's baby and it stayed with me as a surreal experience – the salty wind and grey northern sky and wailing of the gulls outside and the deep, rich, guttural roll of the language, the candlelight and the heady scents of the Aegean within.

The church is here, I gather, because it was once the home

of the chairman of the committee that decided that a place of worship was needed for the Greek Cypriot restaurateurs and café owners who were beginning to gather along this coast. Originally they simply met in his front room but, as the congregation grew with the influx of Greek students at Marlbury University, he moved out and the whole building, small as it is, became the church. Dora and her father don't live there; they have a flat on the estate behind us, as bland and characterless as those around it. Disappointingly to me, there is talk of a move. Negotiations are in hand to buy a small church in Dungate which the Methodists have given up on. The Orthodox congregation has been swelled of late by Romanians, Bulgarians and some Poles and Ukrainians working in the hospitality business, so the little house can hardly contain it. What is more, it has become quite famous. It has, for years, held a Theophany ceremony on the beach at Dungate, attended colourfully by Orthodox bishops, and even the odd archbishop, as well as lay dignitaries of various kinds and an enthusiastic crowd of the faithful. The archbishop throws a cross into the sea and hardy young men hurl themselves in to retrieve it. I went to watch it last week and couldn't help worrying about them in a mother hen sort of way. It is January, after all, and though I know there are hardy Brits who swim on Christmas Day, they are the products of generations of sinewy, leathery types, inured to the cold over many lifetimes. These young Greeks, I felt, don't have the genes for this kind of enterprise; they have sunshine in their DNA. Their mothers really ought to stop them.

Dora certainly feels the cold. She looks pale and pinched and is regularly dressed, as she is today, in an oversized school jumper with the sleeves pulled down over her hands and a scarf wound several times around her neck. My two-bar fire, it seems, does little for her. I have been teaching her since

September but she is still not relaxed with me. She is quiet, polite and attentive, she writes down almost everything I say, she smiles dutifully at my jokes but she isn't enjoying herself and she's not comfortable. I have tried to modify my usual teaching style. My normal approach is to bounce quiet students into life by relentless good humour and jokes. If they won't express opinions, I put forward opinions of my own so outrageous that they have to argue with me, but that just terrified Dora. She became paler and quieter until the point where I said that the problem with *A Passage to India* is that it's all about sex but Forster has to do it in code, and her eyes filled with tears. After that I reconsidered and we have been taking things very gently ever since.

I have some hopes for *The Tempest*. After all, she is an only daughter, living alone with her father; she must have some views about Miranda, stranded with her father on a desert island, mustn't she? I don't care for Prospero myself. The play has been in my head a lot since I moved here. I quite fancied myself as Prospero, betrayed and rejected, brooding here in my cave, looking out over the lonely sea and plotting my revenge. I even have a beguiling role model in Helen Mirren, who plays a fetching 'Prospera' in a 2010 film version, but aspiring to be Helen Mirren is, frankly, asking to be disappointed – especially when one can't afford a decent haircut – and, to my surprise, I find I can't do the revenge. Even the vice-chancellor of Marlbury University, who engineered my losing my job, can't stir me to vengefulness. Partly, I can't be bothered; partly, I know that some of the fault was mine. And this is where I part company with Prospero. Of course it was wicked of his brother to usurp his dukedom and put him out to sea with his daughter in a leaky boat, but Prospero was a bad duke: he spent all his time in his library and didn't do his job. He ought to think about that and not fixate on getting his revenge. What is more – and this is my real beef about him – he never really forgives. He has shipwrecked his brother and the brother's cronies, terrified, tantalised and tortured them, but that is not enough for him. He cannot give us the moment of forgiveness, the heart-filling moment that Hermione, Cordelia and even Isabella give us. He says the words, *I forgive*, but they are words only. He is obdurate and cold-hearted to the very end. I can't believe that Shakespeare intended us to like him.

And then there is the way he treats Miranda, his daughter, and that's what I want to discuss with Dora this afternoon. In place of forgiveness in his heart, Prospero has a plan to marry Miranda to Ferdinand, son of Alonzo, King of Naples, who helped Prospero's brother to usurp his throne. Miranda and Ferdinand conveniently fall in love at first sight, as soon as he is washed up on Prospero's island, but is Prospero happy? No. He puts obstacles in their path, as well as harping unpleasantly on the possibility that Ferdinand intends to ravish this girl whom he obviously worships. I won't suggest to Dora that Prospero is a cold-hearted, vengeful, controlling bastard because that will make her cry, but I would like her to think about it.

The results of my gentle probing are surprising. Dora actually argues with me. When I ask whether she thinks Prospero enjoys power for its own sake, she says no, he always has good intentions. 'Even when he clicks his fingers to make Miranda fall asleep?' I ask. 'Just because he wants to have a private conversation with Ariel?'

'He does everything in care of her,' she says firmly. 'In scene two he says so. *I have done nothing but in care of thee. Of thee my dear one.*'

She does know the text – I can't fault her there.

'But he treats Ferdinand badly, doesn't he?' I suggest. 'He threatens him and makes him carry piles of logs as though he's punishing him for loving Miranda, when all the time his plan is that they'll get married.'

She has an answer for this, too. 'Prospero says he doesn't want it to be too easy for Ferdinand to get Miranda. She doesn't know to hold back,' she says, 'and be modest. She has no experience so she tells him right away she loves him. Prospero has to make difficulties or Ferdinand won't value her.'

She looks so earnest sitting there that she almost persuades me but I have one more go. 'But he says he'll hate her if she speaks up for Ferdinand. He's always threatening people – Caliban, Ariel, Ferdinand and even Miranda. He does like his power trip, doesn't he?'

She turns tragic dark eyes on me. 'He didn't want to be cruel to Caliban, but he had to protect Miranda. Caliban would...assault her otherwise. Prospero has to make him very afraid. He is a father. He must protect his daughter.'

I am so delighted by her eloquence that I decide to leave it there and let her enjoy the feeling of making her point. We'll come back to the unengaging soliloquies and the unsatisfactory forgiveness another time. We spend the rest of the lesson on the less contentious themes of masque and magic.

As I open my front door to let Dora out into the gusty, rain-laden evening, I find that there is a man standing on my doorstep. He looms so surprisingly out of the dark that I give a foolish little squeak of surprise before I see his face in the light from the hall and recognise him as one of my students from my other job, the one I don't get paid for.

Dover, just along the coast, teems with asylum seekers. After God knows what travails to get here, they find themselves a precarious toehold there, crammed into decaying B&Bs, forbidden to work or earn, prey to all kinds of violence and corruption, waiting for judgement: the dubious paradise of staying or the predictable hell of returning. They meet with plenty of resentment from the local population, but one redoubtable couple has been moved to action on their behalf. They have persuaded their local church to let them have its hall a couple of days a week. There, asylum seekers can come for the traditional British comforts of tea, biscuits and talk. The couple help with form-filling and interpret the language of officialdom, as far as they can and, just recently, they have started offering English classes. Which is where I come in. They called for volunteers, in an article in the local paper, and I put my hand up.

It is the hardest teaching I have ever done – harder, far than strong-arming the trainee criminals who made up the D and E streams at Marlbury's least-favoured secondary school, where I taught for ten years. There are technical difficulties because the level of English they already have varies hugely, so this is mixed-ability teaching to an epic degree, but these are nothing to the issues of motivation and commitment. Most of them turn up sporadically, don't do homework and fall asleep in class. Sleeping six or seven to a room, always on the alert against being robbed, knifed or raped, how can they possibly muster the energy or concentration to sit in a classroom for two hours, learning a language they have only the slimmest of chances of putting to use? The Immigrant Removal Centre, a bleak stone fortress with walls topped with barbed wire, stands on the skyline and lowers over the town, sending out a clear message: one way or another, in the labyrinthine process of asylum-seeking, a reason will be found to send them back.

Farid, the lad who looms on my doorstep this evening, was secure here until last summer, a student from Syria, studying medicine at one of the London colleges. In June, though, his life collapsed. After a rocket attack by government forces on a suburb of Damascus near his parents' home, his father, a doctor, went to help the injured and was killed by a sniper, positioned, presumably, precisely for the purpose

11

of punishing such blatant acts of humanity. So Farid lost not only his father but his right to be here. There was no one now to pay his fees so he was out on his ear, his student visa cancelled despite his being a model student. Universities, it seems, do not engage in blatant acts of humanity. His immediate reaction was that he should go home to look after his mother, but she – a strong-minded woman – has insisted that he should stay, so he has applied for asylum, planning to work his way through the remaining years of his medical training.

You would think it was a simple enough case but it is not so in the eyes of the Border Agency. The stumbling block is that Farid can't prove that he would be in danger if he was sent back home. A raging civil war in which, at a conservative estimate, 200,000 people have already been killed, and a father shot on his own doorstep for doing his job are not sufficient indicators of peril, it seems. I don't know how Farid manages to keep his temper with these people; I would have battered someone over the head with a box file by now. As it is, he has to be content, for the moment, with being my star student. He doesn't actually need the classes; he is well beyond the English language level he needed to study medicine here – a score of 7.0 in the International English Language Test System. He says it helps to be learning something, though, and he doesn't seem to mind the boredom of sitting through others' struggles. I find him more challenging stuff to do, bring him books and newspapers. We shouldn't have favourites among our students, of course, but I can't help liking Farid.

And now, here he is on my doorstep, looking anxious.

'I'm sorry,' he says. 'This is rather rude, I'm afraid, and I wasn't sure about knocking.'

'How did you get here?' I ask – ungraciously, I realise as soon as I've said it.

'I walked,' he says.

'But it's thirteen miles!'

He smiles. 'I have time on my hands,' he says.

I usher him in and he and Dora perform one of those little dances as each tries to make way for the other in the narrow hallway. Then she ducks past him and almost runs out of the house. He watches her go.

'One of my A level pupils,' I say and show him into my living room.

'Are you in trouble, Farid?' I ask.

He looks startled. 'No. Oh no, nothing like that.' Then he shrugs. 'Well. No more than usual.' He looks round the room. 'So many books,' he says, 'just like you told us.'

'Did I?'

'Yes. Last week. You described your unusual house.'

'And you thought you would come and see it?'

'I – I like to walk. It gets me out of the hostel. When I'm walking I can think. So this afternoon I thought I would try to find your house. You told us how it is along the coast, right by the sea, and about the Greek church right by, so I thought I would walk until I found it.' He smiles. 'You can't get lost walking along by the sea.'

'It must have taken you hours.'

He looks at his watch. 'Nearly four hours,' he says.

'Cup of tea?' I ask.

'Please don't trouble. A glass of water will be fine.'

'It's no trouble. You need a hot drink. Have a seat by the fire. It's a pathetic thing but it will warm you up.'

When I come back with tea and some rather punitive flapjacks I made with jumbo oats, he is looking through my copy of *The Tempest*.

'Very hard work,' I say as I pour tea. 'You might find this more accessible.' I pick up my copy of Carol Ann Duffy's *The World's Wife* and hand it to him. Then I attack a flapjack and

13

watch him as he leafs through the poems. If you don't know the book, it's a series of poems written from the point of view of the wives and girlfriends of famous or legendary men: Queen Herod, Mrs Midas, Frau Freud, Anne Shakespeare née Hathaway, Queen Kong, the Kray sisters, and so on. I love it and I've gone out on a limb a bit to set it as the next book to be read by our book group – more of which later.

Farid asks, 'These are real people?'

'Some of them are – the men, at least. Or legendary. A lot of them come from Greek myths.'

He shakes his head. 'I don't know them.'

'No reason why you should. Have a look at *Mrs Darwin*, though. That might make you laugh.'

He finds it and reads it while I finish the demolition job on my flapjack. He hands the book back to me.

'British humour,' he says, 'is hard to learn.'

When he has drunk his tea and crunched his way through a flapjack with apparent enjoyment, I offer him the use of the loo and the bus fare home. He accepts the first but adamantly rejects the second.

'In that case, borrow my bike,' I say.

'But you will need it.'

'Actually, not,' I say.

I am embarrassed to admit this but my bike, which used to take me everywhere, has languished here. I either walk the few hundred yards around St Martin's or I get the bus into Dover. I don't go anywhere else. I had good intentions of cycling to and fro to Dover but you're going East on the way there and you're nearly always going into the teeth of the wind. There should be compensation coming back but I found the vigour of the wind behind me quite scary so, after a couple of attempts, I gave up and the bike is rusting, despite its plastic cover, among the vegetables in the back garden.

'I don't use it,' I say. 'Keep it if you want to, or you can bring it back some time when you feel like an outing.'

'It would be stolen,' he says mournfully. 'Everything is stolen.'

'I don't think any self-respecting thief would want it,' I say. 'I'll give you a padlock but if it does get stolen it really doesn't matter. It's had its day, I'm afraid.'

He is resistant but when I take him out into the garden and run a torch over the bike he can see that this is not a great treasure I am handing him and he accepts. I find him a new battery for the back light, which isn't working, and he raises the seat, which is set for my stumpy little legs. I stand with him in the garden, holding the torch for him. With his face turned away in the dark, he asks, 'Your student who was here, is she English?'

'Greek,' I say. 'Her father is the priest at the church along here.'

'Oh, really,' he says.

I wave him off from my front door and watch him go. Do I feel a niggle of misgiving about what I may have set in motion? I think perhaps I do but it is momentary, forgotten as soon as he disappears from sight.

Chapter Two

THE GOD OF SMALL THINGS

Tuesday 11ᵗʰ February 2014

My morning ritual is invariable; I find I have to impose discipline on this life that is so free of external constraints. This morning is no exception, though life has been a bit bumpy in the two weeks since I introduced you to Dora and Farid, and gave Farid my bike. Caliban and I are, as ever, out for our walk by eight-fifteen. As ever, as I close the front door behind me and cross the road towards the sea wall, my phone gives its chirpy little signal of an incoming message and I ignore it. It will come from Orange and it will welcome me to France. I can't tell you how irritating I find this. It is not just that I am so clearly not in France, with the whole of *La Manche* spread out between me and it, but that I don't find the French connection at all exciting. I am, at heart, a Francophobe. I refuse to do the British cultural cringe about their wonderful food, their glorious wine and their oh-so-chic fashion; in my view, their food is fussy, their wine overpriced and their fashion chic only on women who are intensely slim and chic to start with. Italy does all three better – and Italians don't shrug. The French language is wonderful, of course, but it's not enough to make me want to be there.

I could avoid the irritation of the morning message beep by not taking my mobile with me, but I have a superstitious fear that the day I decide to do that will be the day I fall down the steps onto the beach and need to summon help. The steps are steep and made of unforgiving stone. I worry for Caliban, who is an ungainly beast, as well as for myself, but they are the only route onto the beach. Once down there, we lollop over the pebbles or gambol along the sand, depending on the tide. My practice is to walk into the teeth of the wind first so that we get aerodynamic propulsion on the way home. This usually means walking east first; on the odd occasions when I turn west first Caliban gets flustered and tries to head me off. He doesn't seem to understand about the wind. When we have both had enough, I put him on his lead, we climb back up the steps and we walk away from the sea, inland, to the village shop to collect the newspaper.

Kelly Field, who runs the shop, is the reason why Caliban and I don't go onto the beach until eight-fifteen, although we have been awake for some time. Kelly swims every morning, without exception, come fog, tempest or blizzard. She comes past my house at half past seven, without fail, and the slap-slap of her flip-flops under my bedroom window rouses Caliban to noisy outrage. (Yes, I admit it, he sleeps with me. Not on the bed – that is understood between us though he still gazes yearningly at it from time to time – but in his basket. He sleeps quietly. He is less trouble than most sleeping companions I have known.) I dare not take him down to the beach until I am sure that Kelly has gone, because he hates her. I'm not sure that he knows that she is the owner of the slapping feet, and it would be uncanny if he did, but he growls at her in a way he does at no one else. Even the postman gets a better reception from him.

So, I don't attempt to take him into the shop, but tie him up outside, where he slumps down, a picture of reproach, and I have to admit that he does have a point about Kelly – she is not terribly likeable. She is mid-thirties, I suppose. She used to run the shop with her father, who was already in the early stages of Alzheimer's when I moved here, and has now gone into a nursing home, leaving Kelly with the shop and the flat above it. It can't be much fun for a young woman, I suppose, and she certainly doesn't seem to enjoy it. She has recently dyed her hair purple, which ought to make her look funky, but it just accentuates her bad skin and the sour droop of her mouth. Although I come into the shop every morning and we are both members of the village book group, she greets me, as she always does, with barely a flicker of recognition. Well, two can play at that game. It would be natural for us to discuss the harrowing thing that happened yesterday, but if she's not going to mention it, neither am I.

'Guardian, please,' I say.

She hands it to me and takes my money without a word, and that would have been that if there had not been, suddenly, the rush of heavy feet on the stairs and the arrival from the flat above of a young man toting a large sports bag and in the process of zipping up his tracksuit top. It is my A level student, Matt O'Dowd. The implications are obvious and neither of them attempts to deflect me from the obvious. I knew that Matt delivered the papers for her in the mornings but not about the bonking afterwards. They look at each other; the colour rises under her sallow skin. Matt grins and hands her a book. It is a copy of *The World's Wife*

'You were looking for this,' he says. 'I found it under the bed.'

He turns to me. 'I didn't look at it,' he says, 'but I guess it's one of those women-getting-their-own-back books, right?'

'Not exactly,' I say. 'Never judge a book by its cover.'

'OK,' he says, hitching his bag higher onto his shoulder. He pushes the door wide open, startling Caliban.

She calls, 'See you tomorrow.'

'Maybe,' he calls back as he starts to jog away

She runs to the open door. 'Fucking better,' she yells to his back. He doesn't turn round.

'Nice lad,' I say as she turns back into the shop.

'That's all you know,' she says.

I untie Caliban and walk round to the library.

A visit to the library is not part of my regular morning routine and when I do go there I don't normally take Caliban with me, but I have something I need to discuss urgently with Lorna, who runs the place. The library is attached to the primary school, both built in the optimistic sixties. Three years ago it fell victim to the first round of local government cuts and Lorna started organising a band of volunteers to keep it open. I joined them as soon as I realised how necessary the library was going to be to my new life of austerity and I'm on duty most Saturdays, having no family here in the bosom of which to spend my weekends. A year ago, I proposed starting a book group based on borrowing sets of books from the county library service, and it's the book group I need to discuss with Lorna this morning.

We are an eclectic bunch in age and background, which makes for wide-ranging, if somewhat shapeless, discussions (I have had to abandon all ambitions for critical rigour). Until recently there were eight of us, ranging from eighteen-year-old Dora to eighty-year-old Eva Majoros, who came to England with her husband in 1956, escaping the consequences of the failed anti-Soviet revolution in Hungary. After some years in London, leading the precarious lives of émigré intellectuals, they moved here, where her husband, a semi-successful writer by this time, could find remoteness, quiet and a cheap house a two-hour train ride from London. She established herself as a translator, specialising in translating English Golden Age crime novels into Hungarian. He died some years ago but Eva lives on amid the mementos of her literary and European past. When it is her turn to bring refreshments to a meeting of the group, she brings almond cakes and strudel.

The other members of the group, besides me, are Lorna, Kelly Field, a nice woman called Lesley, who used to work for Dover Council, was made redundant in her early fifties and now has plenty of time for reading, and Alice Gates, a neighbour of mine, who teaches at the primary school. We had an eighth member but we have lost her, and this is the crux of what I need to discuss with Lorna, and the thing I have avoided talking about to you while I wittered on about dog-walking and the possible sex life of our village shopkeeper.

Lily Terry was our eighth member. I bullied her into joining, I suppose, because I wanted Dora to join and I didn't think she would unless we had someone else young in the group. Lily and her husband, Jack, lived in the end cottage, next door to the Greek church. *Lily and her husband* makes them sound staid and respectable but they were just kids, really. Lily was twenty-two I learned yesterday, as I sat with the rest of the group in St Martin's Church and looked at her dates on the front of the order of service: *Lily Charlotte Terry 18th September 1991 to 5th February 2014.* Jack is a few years older, I guess. They were married for about eighteen months and getting married was pretty much at odds, I suppose, with the rest of their lifestyle, but they seemed blissfully happy in the way only the young can be. They ran a window-cleaning service – in demand around here, where the windows get salt-caked in no time – and they were cheery in even the vilest weather. But that was just the day job; what they wanted was to be rock stars and what they loved was their band, Bad Lads. Jack was quite a bad lad, I've been told, until Lily came along to audition for the band and everything changed. Everything must have changed for the band, too, I think, because Lily's pure, true voice became its trademark sound.

Lily died a week ago in an accident that was both predictable and utterly shocking. As she and Jack were cleaning the windows of the pub – he at the front and she at the back – her ladder slipped and she fell, hitting her head on a low stone bollard that marked the edge of the car park. Jack heard the fall and rushed round there. He called an ambulance and sat with her, talking to her, as a small, silent crowd gathered. She was dead by the time she reached the hospital.

I have been more upset by her death than I would have thought possible, to the extent of sudden floods of tears and bursts of rage that have had me stomping around the house, kicking the furniture and demanding of a God I don't believe in why He thought killing Lily off was a good idea. I have wanted to help Jack but he looks so wild in his grief that I can't begin. I think I am actually afraid of him.

I'm worried about next week's meeting of the book group. I'm uncomfortable about going ahead with it as though nothing has happened. In fact, I rather dread it, but I think that's because I'm not sure that I shall be able to keep my feelings under control. So I need to talk to Lorna. I like Lorna, and I think she likes me. If so, it is an attraction of opposites: she is quiet and calm where I am noisy and turbulent. She has a soft, musical Scottish accent while I am all bossy Home Counties. She is a person who considers and weighs her words where I frequently don't know what I'm going to say until I've said it. We share a sense of humour, however, and hers is quietly subversive in a way that I love. She was a school librarian for thirty years and we bond from time to time by rerunning scenes of horror from our teaching pasts. She took early retirement (she has a heart problem) just at the time when our library was threatened with closure, and she offered to run it on a voluntary basis. It is she, really, who keeps the book group going. I run the meetings, insofar as they are 'run', but she does all the ordering of books and the chasing up, with quiet persistence, of those that don't get returned.

This morning, as I step inside the library, she greets me with an unexpected hug.

'How are you doing?' she asks.

'I don't know what to do about next week's meeting,' I say. 'I don't think we can just carry on as if nothing has happened.'

She leads me over to the staff desk, where we pull out chairs and sit down. As usual, she looks as though she has dressed to play the part of a librarian in a 1950s play. Her hair, which is hardly touched with grey, is cut in a neat bob and she favours slim skirts of modest length, low-heeled court shoes and pastel twinsets – where can you buy those these days? – sometimes accessorised with a string of pearls. Occasionally her skirt is a kilt – a tribute to her Scottish origins, I assume. Perhaps she gets the twinsets too on her annual holiday in Scotland. I have never asked her about her style choices because I could find no way of doing it politely, but, knowing her as I do, I am pretty sure that they are ironic, a private joke about other people's stereotypes.

'I was worried about you yesterday' she says.

'Why me particularly? We were all upset.'

'Oh, come on.' She smiles. 'You were such a mother to Lily.'

'*A mother?*' I protest. 'No! She was very bright and she'd given up on her A levels, and I just felt – it was more of a teacher thing, if anything.'

She has taken off her glasses, which hang on a chain round her neck, completing the librarian motif, and she is looking hard at me.

'If you say so,' she says.

'I do say so.'

She gathers up some request slips from the desk and pats them into a neat pile. Then she looks at me again, smiling but intent. 'So your feelings for Lily had nothing to do with the fact that her own mother is in Australia and you have a twenty-two-year-old daughter whom you hardly ever see?'

'I do!' I protest. 'I see her. We talk on the phone.'

'But you saw Lily nearly every day.'

'Of course I did. We lived three doors away from each other.'

'I think that's my point.'

'That she was a daughter substitute?'

'One you could have a much easier relationship with because you weren't her mother.'

'Well,' I say, 'perhaps we should go through into the office and I'll lie down on the couch and you can psychoanalyse me properly and I'll pay you three hundred pounds.'

I mean this to be light-hearted but it comes out sounding sour and hurt. She puts her glasses back on.

'How about going into the office and having a cup of coffee?' she suggests.

'I've got the dog outside,' I say ungraciously. 'I can't leave him out there forever while we discuss my pathological need to mother.'

She looks around. 'Well, there's nobody here,' she says, 'and he's house-trained, isn't he?'

Caliban shows more animation about being admitted to the library than I have ever seen him show about anything, except, possibly, for the unwary rabbit he once hunted down among my cabbages. I suspect that the reason for his joy is the same in both cases – a pleasure in the illicit. He has intuited that rules are being bent here, and that delights him. We settle in the office, which used to be the staff common room and has two easy chairs and a lumpy sofa, and Caliban's cup runneth over when Lorna gives him a Rich Tea biscuit.

'He really shouldn't,' I say.

'Peace offering,' she says. 'For you, not him. I really didn't mean to suggest that there was anything pathological about your feelings for Lily. I just meant that you will take it harder than the rest of us. You were close to her, you knew her in a way the rest of us didn't. You shouldn't feel you have to bottle up your feelings but you should try not to get angry with the rest of us because we're not grieving in the same way.'

'So you think we should go ahead with the meeting?'

'I think we should. It won't get any easier if we leave it.'

And there it is. No flailing about and going round in circles; just a quiet decision. In my next life I'm going to be Lorna.

If you are a worrier by nature, the removal of a worry affords only the briefest moment of relief. In the mind of the compulsive worrier, anxieties line themselves up in strict priority order and as soon as the first is dismissed, the next steps up smartly to replace it. Thus it is that, on the walk home, I start worrying about Farid and Dora. I have been very slow to spot the problem here. I'm not blind – I could see that Farid was interested by Dora in that brief moment of meeting in my hallway. Why wouldn't he be? He sees no one except fellow asylum seekers, who are traumatised, guilt-ridden, damaged in all kinds of ways, and hardened to an uncaring world. Dora is the most innocent eighteen-year-old I have ever come across, a butterfly just stretching her damp, new wings, untouched by the world. I don't mean to imply that Farid wants to despoil her; I trust him to behave well, but I can see how he would want to breathe in that innocence. As for Dora, well, Farid is good-looking, charming and clever, and she doesn't get to meet boys like that in this village – or at her Dover convent school.

So, it shouldn't surprise me that they have started meeting. I hoped that I had stopped Farid in his tracks by telling him that she was a priest's daughter, but I reckoned without the drive of the young to the forbidden, the attraction of being star-crossed lovers. What I have been slow to catch onto is the way they have managed to meet, given the eagle eye that Dimitris Karalis keeps on his daughter. When I found my bike back in my garden, neatly wrapped in its plastic shroud, two days after I gave it to Farid, I was puzzled. Had he not understood that it was a gift, or at the least a long-term loan? I asked him about it the next time I saw him in class and he said he was worried about its being stolen from his B&B but would like to borrow it again if I didn't mind. 'Feel free,' I said and noticed, vaguely, that it came and went over the next week. Once, I looked out of the kitchen window at seven-thirty in the morning and noticed him returning it. I offered him some breakfast but he declined and hurried away. Then, the day before yesterday, I caught an early bus back from Dover after the English class. Going in twice a week, I usually take the opportunity to go to the Co-op before getting the bus but it was the day before Lily's funeral and I didn't have much appetite. At the bus stop, I witnessed the happy meeting of the young lovers and I understood how they were managing to use Dora's only unchaperoned time. Farid would travel on the bus with her and return on my bike. And then do the opposite in the morning. I doubt he did it every day because he couldn't afford the bus fares, but they had developed a little routine and I was a facilitator in this – if not Juliet's nurse, at least Friar Lawrence. They didn't see me and I waited for them to get on the bus and move to the back before I got in and sat at the front. There would be a chance, I thought, for me to talk to Farid as he walked round to collect my bike. I wasn't sure what I was going to say but we would at least have things out in the open.

As it turned out, however, whatever I was going to say was superseded by what Dimitris Karalis had to say. As the bus drew in to its stop opposite the village shop, he emerged from the shop and swept across the road in all the magnificence of his black robe and patriarchal beard. He did not shout or threaten; he simply stood on the pavement waiting, and when Dora dismounted he just said, 'Dora', and put out a hand to her. She didn't take it but she walked away with him without a backward look at Farid, who came down the step behind her. Farid watched them go and I watched him watching. Then he turned and noticed me. We stood and looked at each other, and he looked baffled and angry and desolate all at the same time. I just looked stupid, I imagine. Certainly what I said was hardly adequate to the occasion.

'Would you like a cup of tea?' I asked.

He refused the tea but he came back for the bike and rode away. I watched him disappear into the evening gloom and I have been worrying about him ever since.

Chapter Three

OFFSHORE

Tuesday 11ᵗʰ February 2014

Kelly

Stupid bloody woman. Smug, patronising, know-all. Typical teacher. Kelly Field stood at the door of the shop, watching Gina whatsername untie her nasty dog and walk away. 'Nice lad,' she had said, as though Kelly needed her approval for a bit of recreational sex on a cold morning. Thought she knew everything, didn't she? Thought Matt was actually a boyfriend. Didn't know that he was nothing to the real man in her life. Know-all didn't know it all. She allowed herself a smile. Wouldn't they all be surprised when it was out in the open?

She went back to her till and her hand went to her phone, lying beside it, but she pulled away as though it might electrocute her. Not yet. She had promised herself that she would wait, and she would. Maybe tonight, though. If she didn't hear from him, maybe tonight. In the meantime, there was the day to get through: a few people in for papers, then the old people tottering in around eleven, taking an age to buy nothing much, and then just the odd stay-at-home mum until the after-school flurry – whiny little kids wanting sweets and crisps first, and then a few kids off the Dover bus – light-fingered, some of them, needed watching – and people on their way home from work. *Boring, boring, boring.* She could remember how her father used to chat to everyone and actually seemed to like it, until the Alzheimer's got too bad and he got embarrassing. Thursday she would go and see him as usual. Close up early and go and have tea with him. Sometimes he knew her, sometimes he didn't. Either way, she didn't know him any more.

She went to the door and stood, looking out. She could see the Greek priest coming up the road for his paper. Well, she was glad she had told him about his precious daughter and that Arab boy. It turned her stomach seeing the two of them at the bus stop there, all love's young dream. Time they got real. Time everyone got real…

Chapter Four

BRING UP THE BODIES

Thursday 13ᵗʰ February 2014

Caliban and I sleep late this morning and I would like to be able to say that this rings alarm bells for me, but I have to admit that it doesn't; I am too preoccupied with the vileness of the weather that is revealed when I open the curtains. Under the blackest of skies a ferocious wind is whirling rain around and flinging it at the window, and as I pull on my clothes I ask myself aloud – living alone does this, I find – why the hell I thought becoming a dog-owner was a good idea. I munch a couple of slices of toast while Caliban paces and whines, and then, booted and anoraked, I step out with him into the full fury of the gale.

I negotiate the slippery steps down to the beach with care, clinging to the handrail; it is twenty feet, I guess, from top to bottom. When I step onto the beach and turn into the teeth of the gale, I am blinded by the rain and the breath is knocked out of me by the wind, but Caliban goes galloping off, undeterred. The tide is high, so we are forced to walk on the pebbles and I am making very slow progress as I see, through my dripping lashes, that he has found something high up near the sea wall. I can't see what it is from here but I do see a blur of bright pink and deduce that it is something man-made – something washed up high on the beach by the boiling sea, I assume. Caliban doesn't like it; he is barking in short bursts and making little runs at it, as though to try and drive it away.

I toil over the pebbles with the breath beginning to burn in my chest as I push against the wind. As I get closer, Caliban runs to me and then runs ahead of me, urging me on. I can see now what it is, though not yet who, and my mind is doing all sorts of refusing in the face of the evidence that what my dog has found is a body. Not necessarily dead, my mind tells me, but not lying there voluntarily, not in this weather. So, injured or unconscious? I feel in my pocket for my phone. An ambulance. I shall ring for an ambulance. And then I get close enough to see the hair. I stagger the last few yards and kneel down beside her. She is lying face down and I neither want nor need to turn her over. The chemical purple of her hair and the bright pink anorak tell me that this is Kelly Field. Even then, I am desperate to normalise this. Hypothermia, I think. Swimming in this weather. Ridiculous. She must have staggered out of the sea, put on her tracksuit and then collapsed. Queasily I reach for her hand and try to feel for a pulse. I can't feel anything but my fingers are so numb with cold that they're not much good. Then I see the blood. It was quite obvious; I just wasn't seeing it. It spreads out from under her head into the pebbles, diluted by the rain but indisputably blood. I haul myself to my feet and get my phone out. On my screen Orange is welcoming me to France, of course, and it occurs to me to wonder if I shall be charged at the international rate for making a 999 call. I am impressed by how calm I am on the phone, though I am breathing rather hard. I tell them where Kelly is to be found and who I am. Then I look around. No one else is stupid enough to be on this beach this morning. I am on my own. In spite of the blood, the hypothermia idea stays with me and I wonder if I should take off my sweater and anorak and spread them over her. Or should I lie down beside her and try to impart some of my body heat, such as it is, to her? The fact that I don't do either of these things tells me that I know, in fact, that she is dead.

I turn to go back home. I gave my details in my phone call; they can find me. I am shaking so hard now that they may find me collapsed on the pebbles, too, if I don't get inside. Caliban is reluctant to leave so I lean down to put him on his lead, and that is when I see the book, lying open, face down, on the far side of Kelly's body, her copy of *The World's Wife*. I shall be rebuked for this later, by the police, but I can't leave a book – a library book at that – lying out in the rain. I pick it up and take it home with me.

Back at the house, I rub Caliban down with a disgusting old towel kept for the purpose, put the kettle on, change out of my wet trousers and look for something alcoholic to put in my coffee. This is not easy. I don't mind becoming a weird, scary, cliff-dwelling woman but I won't become a sad old drunk. I can see the temptation of the comforting glass or three in the evening, when my own company begins to lose its charm, so I don't keep spirits in the house and I buy wine sparingly, one bottle at a time. I have some cooking brandy, though, left over from making the Christmas cake, and I slop some into my mug, surprised to see how shaky my hand still is.

As I start to feel better, I take a look at Kelly's book. Why on earth did she take it to the beach with her? This has been nagging at me: a woman lying on a beach, book and beach towel beside her. It is like a grotesque version of summertime normality. What was she thinking, and what went wrong? I spread the book out on the kitchen table. It was lying face down, so the sticky-back plastic coating that the library service puts on its books has saved it a bit from the rain, but the inner pages are sodden from the wet pebbles. I insert sheets of kitchen paper between the wettest pages so they don't stick together, and I see, as I do so, that the book has been defaced. Someone has drawn a circle in red felt pen round the title and opening lines of the poem *Medusa*. Did Kelly do that? Medusa was a gorgon, with snakes for hair, who could turn a man to stone just by looking at him. And haven't we all wanted to do that from time to time? It would certainly be my superpower of choice – far more useful than being able to fly or mind-read, in my opinion. Was that what Kelly was after with her alarming hair?

I hear sirens approaching and go upstairs to look out of my bedroom window. The one interesting feature of the front facades of these otherwise unremarkable houses is that the upper front windows are angled outwards – two windows, meeting at an angle, with a triangular sill inside, just big enough to make a window seat. Looking out of the left-hand window, I can see an ambulance and a police car. Two paramedics come running along past the house and disappear down the steps. I have no view of the top of the beach from here because the sea wall is in the way. All I can see is some milling about around the police car and another car that has now arrived. I think about getting an injured person up those steps; they would surely have to winch her up over the sea wall, like Cleopatra hauling Antony up into her monument. Easier to bring up a body, of course. The paramedics return; they are not running now.

I go downstairs to consult the kitchen clock; one of the affectations of my new life is that I don't wear a watch. It is not yet ten o'clock but I would like to crawl back into bed. I consider this as an option but I need to plan what I'm going to do with my asylum seekers this afternoon, so I get out my work bag and consider once again what one really needs to be able to say when living on borrowed time in an unfriendly foreign land. I have hardly got started when my doorbell rings and I find a young man on my step, waving a police identification card at me.

He is DC Aaron Green and he looks extremely young. I don't comment on this, though, as I do like to avoid clichés. I sit him down, provide him with coffee and answer his questions. He does pretty well with his questioning. Personally, I would have taken things in a different order, but he covers the ground in the end. In the course of our interview, I tell him who Kelly is and how I came to find her. I tell him that she runs the village shop, lives alone and has no relatives that I know of, apart from her father, now wandering far in the wilderness of dementia. I suggest that Matthew O'Dowd (phone number supplied) might be able to give him more information. Asked about the nature of their relationship, I reply that I really couldn't say, but he delivers her newspapers. I tell him that she swam every morning without fail, and it is only when he asks whether other people knew about her morning swim that I realise that the police suspect unnatural causes.

When DC Green has gone, I look again at Kelly's book. I should have handed it over to him, of course, but I wanted a chance to look through it when it is dry, to see if she marked anything else. If she marked it at all, of course. That circle could have been made by any borrower, at any time, I know, but the Medusa image fits Kelly too well for me to discount its being her work. Kelly is Medusa until someone tells me otherwise.

I decide to record the BBC news for my class this afternoon. One of the things I discovered early on with these students is how isolated they feel from the wider world. The B&Bs some of them live in are not the sort that boast TVs in every room; they can't afford newspapers and if they once owned smart phones they have, without exception, had them stolen in the course of getting here. They are desperate for news, hungry for information, so I persuaded Ruth and Ernest, who organise these classes, to invest in a combi TV/DVD player, which I found in a charity shop, and install it at the hall.

There is no aerial there, so they can't watch live TV but we can watch recordings. The BBC news is their favourite, and listening and arguing is excellent language practice. They frequently know more than I do about the background to foreign news stories, so I am learning quite a bit, too, and it's good for them to be telling rather than asking.

It feels odd to be going off to teach as usual after the day's dramatic start, but there is nothing I can do here and work, I have always found, is a great distraction from life. My teaching session starts, as ever, with organising the canteen-style tables and folding chairs in the hall. At the beginning, I had the tables arranged conference fashion, pushed together so that we could all sit round like the adults we are, but I realised that a lot of the women were uncomfortable with that sort of proximity and now we have the tables set out in lines, facing me, with two students to a table. The men and the women sit on different sides of the room, as they will generally in any classroom, actually, whatever their cultures or religions. The women seem fairly content to sit two to a table, but the men will claim a table to themselves if they get the chance, and I don't notice friendships developing, people regularly sitting together or working together. I take an informal register at the start of the class but if I ask where an absentee is I get no response. In my past life, teaching overseas students in a British university, I was used to rapidly developing friendships, love affairs, group solidarity, the emotional energy of young people settling in for a two-, three- or four-year experience, eager for friendship, open to newness, excited by life. If my asylum seekers were ever eager, open or excited – as no doubt some of them were – those dangerous emotions have long been knocked out of them. These students are watchful, anxious and mistrustful at best, traumatised and suicidal at worst. They are not making social connections for their projected future; they barely know where they will sleep tomorrow night. And they are not really students, I have to remind myself. Ask any of them to describe him or her self and 'student of English' would come very far down on their list.

I have eight students this afternoon. This is an average catch; there can be as many as twelve and, occasionally, when I sense that there is some sort of crisis but nobody is willing to talk about it, as few as three. Farid is here, I am glad to see, and most of my regulars.

There are three men besides Farid: Hassim, a hyper-voluble Iraqi who is, I think, acutely post-traumatic and given to unnerving fits of laughter; Hani, a gentle, silent Saudi lad, who is here, I conjecture, because he is gay, and Jing Wei, whose story Ruth has told me. Tricked by traffickers, he was shipped here from China and locked in a house where his job was to tend cannabis plants. He managed to escape and has applied for asylum because he fears the retribution of the traffickers if he is returned to China. He fears them here, too, but touchingly believes that the law will protect him here.

Among the four women is a pair of teenage sisters, Yaema and Aminata, from Sierra Leone, fleeing from forced marriages to men three times their age. I asked Ruth how they managed to finance their journey and she told me that they stole the money their father had been given as their bride price. They haven't yet had the optimism of youth knocked out of them but I don't think they stand a chance: in the eyes of the UK Border Agency they are thieves, and they will be happy to send them back to face the consequences. The other two women are older: one is Soraya, an Iranian English professor, who has privately told me her story. She fell foul of the authorities through her teaching of English Literature, spent six months in prison, was released only after her parents raised the money to pay an enormous fine, and came here in conditions of such horror she still can't talk about them. Her English is excellent but she comes to classes because she finds the atmosphere of a classroom soothingly familiar. And after all, as she says, what else is there to do? Ivy, from Zimbabwe, doesn't really need the classes either. English is her second language, after Shona, but she comes, I think, because she would go mad on her own. When her husband was brutally beaten by the police at a political meeting, they knew that it would not be long before he was arrested. They made their way to Britain in a series of container lorries but many people got sick and their two small sons died on the journey. Her husband is being held at the Immigrant Removal Centre, threatened with deportation to Zimbabwe since the bureaucrats see 'no credible threat' to him there. Ivy's own case is still under review since she is a year older than her husband, born in 1981, before the British Nationality Act, which may make all the difference. She says nothing; I don't know how much she understands; sometimes she rocks herself in silent grief. I would say that this is the saddest story I have heard, but in this business another will always come along to trump it.

I start this afternoon's session by telling them that my dog found a dead body on the beach this morning. This may seem a bit unorthodox but I often start by telling them what I have been doing. I have been used, with more privileged students, to getting them to talk about what they have been doing: *Did anyone do anything interesting over the weekend?* It is good speaking practice, shaping a narrative and holding people's interest. It is not a strategy for these students, though: anything out of the way that happens to them is likely to be bad and, anyway, they have learnt that anything they say may be used in evidence against them. So I tell them things instead: the doings of my cat and dog, the occasional anecdote about my grandchildren, things I have seen in my walks along the beach, small domestic dramas. It is not exciting, my life, but I do my best with it. Perhaps I want to remind them about normality, to make them believe that there is the possibility of a dull, uneventful life once they get off the precarious cliff face that is their current existence.

So I tell them my story. 'An extraordinary thing happened to me this morning,' I begin, and off I go. It occurs to me that my experience may not seem so shocking to them, that some of them – maybe most – will have seen dead bodies before, casualties of conflicts at home or of the brutal journeys they have made to escape, but they actually look disturbed. Looking at them, seeing how the mood of the class has tensed up, has shifted from mild interest in what I may have to offer to an unsettled, edgy alertness, I realise that this is the last thing they want to hear. Despite the hostile natives and the heartless bureaucracy, the UK is their place of safety, their asylum. The last thing they want to hear is that one's neighbours can turn up as dead bodies here, casually dumped on beaches. And Farid looks horrified, white-faced and intent. *He thinks it might be Dora*, I think. Of course he does. 'The body of a young woman, someone I knew,' I said, but nothing more. It feels disrespectful to say any more about Kelly; the purple hair, the daily swim, these seem like tittle-tattle. I can put Farid out of his misery, though, even if I can't dispel the unease of the rest of them.

'The young woman,' I say, catching Farid's eye, 'ran our local shop. Everyone in the village knew her.'

His face changes but does not relax. He puts his head in his hands. I abort my blundering anecdote and busy myself with the TV. I have recorded three news items: a first meeting of officials from China and Taiwan after sixty-five years, which I put in for Wei, although he doesn't seem to be much interested, the Winter Olympics under way in Sochi and a second round of UN-brokered negotiations in Syria between the Assad government and a consortium from the US, Turkey, Saudi Arabia, Russia and Switzerland, undermined by the

Syrian government's decision to put the names of members of the opposition on a list of wanted terrorists.

We start with Sochi. The teenage girls, who are usually bored by the news, quite like the snippets of athletes in action, and when the BBC's pundit on the spot reflects on the difficulties that have emerged in the run-up to the games – corruption among officials, legislation threatening LGBT athletes and supporters, and the danger from Jihadists – everyone except Hani and Ivy has something to say. I let the two of them be: I don't want to embarrass Hani by challenging him, and Ivy is in some unreachable place that even I won't blunder into. We move on to the item on Syria. Anything about the Middle East, let alone Syria, usually gets Farid talking but today his mind is only half on it, and the others accept the story with weary cynicism. *That's how governments are*, their faces tell me. *What else do you expect?*

I wrap up the desultory discussion and move on to a vocabulary exercise. Form filling. This is an activity that looms large in their lives, as you can imagine, and it is one of the ways in which the bureaucrats set out to break them. I try putting it this way to them in an attempt to rouse some fighting spirit, but I get anxious frowns in response, so we buckle down to *domicile* and *abode* (definitions of and distinction between), *marital status* and *dependants*, *eligibility* and *validity*, *registration* and *extension*, *tenancy agreement* and *sole occupancy*. When we have been through these, they have some other queries: Hani says he has been called for *screening* and asks what it involves. I realise that the medical associations of the word are alarming and assure him that no intrusive physical examinations will be involved – just a bout of unfriendly questioning. Soraya asks whether the lawyers on the list she has been given of *regulated advisors*, work for the government, and I tell her that the *regulated* bit means only that their qualifications have been checked and they are not frauds. I don't add that, though not frauds, they are unlikely to be any good, asylum work being the least well-paid legal work and those doing it – barring the occasional saint – forced into it for want of anything better. What is the point of discouraging her, after all? Finally, Ivy, who is applying for a British passport, rouses herself to ask what a *Crown Dependency* is, since coming from one of those seems to make life easy. I tell her that I'm sure Zimbabwe is not one, though I'm not sure which places are. Gibraltar? The Falkland Islands? Maybe just the Channel Islands?

I would like to find something upbeat to finish with but nothing comes to mind. They drift away until only Farid remains.

'I'm sorry, Farid,' I say, as I extract the DVD from its slot. 'I gave you a fright. Did you think I was talking about Dora?'

'Her father,' he mutters. 'I thought her father...'

I stop my fussing with the DVD player and turn to look at him properly. 'He would never hurt her, Farid,' I say. 'He's not that kind of man. He just wants to protect her.'

'He doesn't feel his honour is harmed?'

'Well, it's embarrassing, you must admit, if you're an Orthodox priest and you find that your daughter is seeing a Muslim, but Dimitris Karalis is big enough to cope with that.'

'I haven't heard from her since yesterday. I send her text messages but she doesn't answer.'

'Well, she may have promised her father not to contact you. Or he may have taken her phone away. I did that once or twice when my daughters were teenagers.'

'Because they were seeing boys you didn't like?'

'Actually, I usually liked the boys. It was more a question of the money. Long calls to a boyfriend who was on holiday with his family in Morocco. That sort of thing.'

He looks around. 'Can I pack up these tables?' he asks.

'That would be great.'

39

Released by not having to look at me, he says, as he stacks a folded table against the wall, 'I feel I made her die, you know, by wishing.'

'Kelly? Why?'

'She was the one. She told Dora's father, when he was in the shop. She saw us together at the bus stop one day. She said she would tell him.'

I am really not surprised. There was always an edge to Kelly, a sour resentment of a world that wasn't treating her well. The years of looking after her father must have been hard; maybe Dora was a particular annoyance to her, loved and secure under her father's wing.

'You know that's irrational, don't you, Farid?' I say. 'If wishes were knives to the heart, there would have been a lot of dead people in my life by now.'

He manages a smile. 'So what do you think I should do?' he asks.

'About Dora? I guess she would like you just to give up.'

'No!' He bangs a table into place. 'You don't understand how it is between us. It is – important.'

There are tears in his eyes and I can feel an answering welling-up in mine. *Why shouldn't he have this,* I think, *when he's lost everything else?*

'Leave it with me,' I say. 'We've got a meeting of the book group tomorrow night. I'll try and find out what she wants. If she knows, herself.'

There is an unfamiliar car parked outside my house when I get home. This is quite usual in the summer, when people park here and haul their stuff down the steps onto the beach, but it is unexpected on a February evening. The light is on in the car and its occupant is reading. She doesn't look up but I recognise her: she is an ex-colleague of my ex-lover and she dislikes me quite a lot. As I get out my key I hear the car door slam. Refusing to turn round, I unlock the door and switch on the hall light. Then I turn to greet her. 'Hello, Paula,' I say.

I have the advantage; I saw her first. She peers at my unmade-up face and weird hair.

'Bloody hell, Gina,' she says. 'What are you doing here?'

'I live here.'

'Mrs Virginia Sidwell?' she asks. 'Is that you?'

'It is.'

She peers at me again. 'Have you got married?'

'Nope. I just got more unmarried. Maiden name. Do come in.'

I lead the way into the sitting room and switch on the fire.

'But you haven't told me who you are,' I say. 'Aren't you going to do your thing with your ID?'

She produces her card. *DI Paula Powell. Marlbury Police.* I am impressed. It seems no time since she was made DS and David was so pleased with himself for getting her promoted in the face of opposition from some men who didn't like to see a mouthy young woman being fast-tracked. She doesn't like me because I got involved in one or two of David's cases and that irritated the hell out of her. Also, I was convinced that she fancied him. I quite like her, actually, or at least admire her. That doesn't mean I'm prepared to make things easy for her, though; when I admire people, I generally get competitive.

'So what brings a Marlbury DI here?' I ask. 'Surely not the body on the beach. This is Dover's pitch.'

'Dover police are swamped,' she says, sitting down unbidden. 'They've asked us to help.'

'Really? What's swamped them?' I sit down, too.

She looks at me. 'It's confidential.'

'Terrorism?'

She lets a pause fall, and then says, 'Let's concentrate on this, shall we? Tell me exactly what happened this morning.'

'This is a bit below your pay grade, isn't it, Paula? A DI for an accidental death?'

'An unexplained death. At present.'

'Well, the Dover police already have my statement. Haven't they passed it on?'

'I'd like to hear it directly from you.'

'OK.' I speak very fast. 'At approximately eight-fifteen this morning my dog found the body of a young woman on the beach about fifty yards from here. I recognised her as Kelly Field, who runs the village shop. I called 999.'

'How was Kelly lying when you saw her?'

'On her front.'

'How did you recognise her, then?'

'She dyed her hair purple. And I recognised her tracksuit.'

'Did you touch her?'

'I felt for a pulse.'

'Anything else?'

'No.'

'Did you wait on the beach for the paramedics to arrive?'

'No.'

'Why not?'

'It was freezing cold, blowing a gale and pouring with rain.'

'Did you see anyone else on the beach?'

'No.'

'Is that unusual?'

'Not in the kind of weather we had this morning.'

'You walk the dog there every morning?' She glances at Caliban, who is pacing uneasily, disturbed by this unknown visitor.

'I do.'

'Did you see anything at all unusual or different this morning?'

I make an effort to visualise the scene. 'I didn't see

anything much, to be honest, with the rain driving into my face.'

A silence falls. She sits looking at me, as if willing me to come up with something more.

'There was one thing,' I say. 'Not something I saw but something I didn't hear. Or, rather, that Caliban didn't hear. It is, in fact, a case of the dog that didn't bark in the night-time.'

She makes a sort of growling noise and says, 'Let's assume, shall we, that not being a professor of English, I don't get your clever literary references. What didn't you hear?'

'Kelly. We didn't hear Kelly. She comes – came – running past the house at about seven-thirty every morning, come what may, and went down the steps for a swim. Every morning she woke Caliban and he barked and woke me. This morning, he didn't bark, so I assume she didn't come by.'

'Presumably there are other steps down to the beach.'

'Some way along in either direction, but why use them?'

We look at each other. We are both thinking the same thing, I'm sure, so I decide to say it.

'If I were the police,' I say, 'I would be thinking that either she jumped from the sea wall or she was pushed.'

She stands up. 'Why are you always there, Gina?' she asks. 'How do you always get involved?'

I stand up, too. 'I'm not an ambulance-chaser, Paula,' I say. 'I'm there because I notice things and I think about them, and I get involved because I feel responsible. You could do with more people like me.'

'You think?' she says.

As I'm escorting her to the door, I glance into the kitchen and I see Kelly's copy of *The World's Wife* lying on the table. A hot wave of embarrassment sweeps over me. At the time when I picked it up and brought it inside, I thought Kelly had died of natural causes and I couldn't bear to leave a book out to be ruined. Now I see this is a proper police investigation and I have tampered with evidence. As usual when I know I'm in the wrong, I try to brazen it out.

'Ah!' I cry, picking up the book and shaking the sheets of kitchen paper out from between its leaves. 'I meant to give this to DC Green this morning. I found it on the beach and I just had to bring it in out of the rain.'

Paula's face goes still and her mouth goes into a very straight line. With what seems to me to be ostentatious care, she takes gloves out of her pocket, dons them, takes the book from me and drops it into an evidence bag, also taken from her pocket.

I think of telling her about the highlighting of the *Medusa* poem, but she doesn't give me the chance.

'What the fuck were you thinking, Gina?' she asks. 'Removing evidence from a crime scene? I could arrest you for this.'

'I didn't know it was a crime scene,' I protest. 'I thought it was hypothermia. It was cold enough and I thought —'

She flips. Completely.

'It's a crime scene!' She yells. 'Someone pushed Kelly Field over the wall and then battered her head repeatedly against the stones. It doesn't matter what you thought. You're not supposed to think! You're an arrogant, superior know-all and you need to stop thinking you know best. You need to stop thinking full stop. Just leave the thinking to us.'

I stand and watch her as she gets herself under control. 'We shall need your fingerprints,' she says very quietly, 'for elimination purposes. First thing tomorrow morning.'

I panic. 'In Marlbury?' I ask. 'Do I have to go to Marlbury?'

I can't go to Marlbury. She needs to understand that. It is my past and I've shut the door on it. Marlbury is the one place in the world I can't go to.

'Dover,' she says. 'I'm working out of Dover station.'

'OK,' I say, and then, 'I'm sorry, Paula.'

44

'You'll come in and get your fingerprints done,' she says, 'and then you will keep right out of this investigation. If I find that you have been getting your nose into it in any way I shall arrest you for obstructing a police investigation. Are we clear?'

'We're clear.'

I watch her go back to her car. There was a time when a warning like that would have had me determined to muscle in on the investigation in any way I could, but this is my new life. This is my life of detachment and retreat where the world can go hang. Paula can have this all to herself. Count me out.

Chapter Five

THE GATHERING

Friday 14th February 2014

Lorna

Lorna Dering started her morning by driving into Dungate to buy a local paper. It was usually delivered, along with their daily copy of *The Independent,* but the village shop had closed with its proprietor's sudden death and she and her husband had agreed that he would buy the morning paper on his way to work. She wanted the local paper right away, though, both because it would have the story of Kelly Field's death in it and because she liked to take it into the library. The small grant they got from the local authority to keep the library open did not stretch to daily newspapers but she was happy to provide the local one.

Parking in front of the library, she let herself in and savoured the reassuring library smell – wood, paper, dust, and people, she supposed – some particles of sweat, saliva, breath – that had accompanied her working life. Now she was working for nothing, but where else would she rather be? There was another smell, too – something lemony. Whoever had been on duty the previous afternoon – Lesley, she thought – had spritzed the tables with spray polish, as well as hoovering the carpet. She looked at her watch. There was time to reshelve the books that stood waiting on the trolley before she opened up. She switched on the computer at the issues desk and took the trolley on its short tour of the little library.

Then she went to turn the notice on the front door to *Open* and found Jack Terry waiting outside. She ushered him in, trying hard not to show her shock at the look of him. He had looked bad enough at Lily's funeral, but his young face this morning seemed all bones and she thought he probably hadn't shaved since then. He fished in the pocket of his parka and pulled out – the last thing she was expecting – a copy of *The World's Wife*.

'Returning Lily's book,' he said, holding it out to her. 'I know you're having a meeting tonight. It's on our calendar.'

The pathos of this – the picture of Lily's writing on the calendar, her plans for the coming weeks neatly recorded – caught Lorna so sharply that she had to keep her head down as she reached out for the book, so that he would not see her sudden tears. She turned away from him and headed for the office. 'Cup of coffee?' she called over her shoulder. 'I was just going to put the kettle on.'

'Oh, no,' he protested, 'there's no need – I just, you know, brought the –'

'Nonsense.' She had her tear ducts under control now and turned back to face him. 'If you're working this morning, you can do with some coffee. It's perishing out. Take one of the comfortable chairs over there. I won't be a minute.'

When she came back with coffee and biscuits, he was reading the local paper. Kelly's death was not the lead story. This was a Dover-based paper, and the headline was about a Dover planning issue, but her story was on the front page, occupying a long column down the right-hand side, complete with a photo. Not knowing how to talk to Jack about Kelly's death, which was a tragedy, but somehow nothing like

47

Jack's tragedy, Lorna busied herself with milk and sugar and pressing him to chocolate digestives. He was not up to small talk either, so they ate and drank in silence. *Companionable silence,* she reassured herself, but as soon as he had drained his coffee, he got up, mumbled thanks and shambled away, hands deep in his pockets. Lorna returned the tray to the office and put Lily's book into its box, where it nestled beside hers, unread and unneeded.

A trickle of library users arrived in the next half hour: two mothers with toddlers, who headed for the children's section, an elderly man who regularly spent mornings in the reference section, a middle-aged woman wanting a session on one of the library's two computers, and Simon Gates, who taught at the primary school next door and was picking up a new book on crustaceans, which he had ordered for use with his class of ten-year-olds.

Then a young man arrived who, Lorna saw immediately, was not after library books. He did not look around, nor savour the atmosphere, but headed straight for her as she sat at the issues desk.

'DC Aaron Green,' he said, displaying a card. 'Dover police.' Lorna had stood up as he approached; now she sat down heavily. *Don*, she thought. *It has to be Don. Car accident? Heart attack?* She forced herself to speak. 'My husband,' she said. 'Has something —?'

He held up a hand. 'No, no,' he said. 'Nothing like that. I've got a query about a book.'

Lorna was not a woman who shouted but just for a moment she had a strong inclination to shout at him. This was a library, however, and there were readers in it. She kept her voice low.

'A book?' she asked.

'Yes.' He looked around. 'You are the librarian, are you?'

She decided not to explain to him about the community-run status of the library and said instead, 'I'm the person on duty at the moment.'

'Right. Well what I need to know is whether you issued a certain book and if so who to.'

'All right.' She turned to the computer. 'I'll need the book. Or the barcode.'

He looked startled. 'The book's evidence. I can't carry it around with me.'

'Evidence for what?'

'This is in connection with the fatality on the beach here.'

'This is to do with Kelly?'

'Yes.'

'And where does the book come in?'

He looked around and then lowered his voice.

'A county library book was found at the scene.'

'Well, if you can get me the barcode, I can tell you if it's one of ours and, if so, who we issued it to.'

'What if I tell you the title?'

'It's highly unlikely that it's the only one in any of the county's libraries. What is the title?'

He took out a notebook. 'It's a book of poems,' he said. 'It's called —'

'*The World's Wife,*' Lorna said.

'You've been talking to Mrs Sidwell, haven't you?'

'To Gina? No.'

'Then how — ?'

She stood up. 'Come with me,' she said.

He followed her into the office, where she produced the county library box with the two books in it. She explained, briefly, about the book group and about reading group sets. 'So the books aren't issued individually,' she explained. 'I wouldn't be able to tell you who had that book, even if I had the barcode. We had eight books issued to us this month. Tragically, we've lost two members, one in an accident and one – well, you know better than I do, I expect. The rest of the books will be returned at our meeting this evening.'

He pointed to the books in the box. 'So one of those books was Kelly Field's'.

'No. One of them belonged to Lily, the girl who died in an accident, and the other is mine.'

'So the one on the beach would be Kelly's?'

'I suppose so. Though it's hard to imagine why she would take a book onto the beach in the pouring rain, isn't it?'

'I shall need the names of the rest of the group. And I shall need to know from you if anyone fails to return their book this evening.'

She took a piece of paper from a desk drawer and started writing. 'I can tell you the roads people live in,' she said, as she wrote, 'but I haven't got house numbers. And I've only got one or two phone numbers. We use email to arrange meetings.'

He was not listening but looking at the box containing the two books. 'Why does it say that on the top?' he asked. '*Broomstick Brigade*?'

'Oh, it's the name of the group. It's a sort of joke. We used to be called just boring *St Martin's Book Group*, but Gina – the person who started the group – decided we should change it to *The Broomstick Brigade* because that's what the men call us.'

'Which men?'

'The men in the pub. The old codgers who go in there every night. We used to go in for a drink after our meetings – all except our youngest member,' she added, conscious that she was talking to a police officer. 'We used to walk her home first and then go into the pub, and they didn't much like it. At first they called us *The Mothers' Meeting* or *The Knitting Circle* but then the landlord called us *The Broomstick Brigade*, and that was the one that stuck.'

'Why? Why did they call you that?'

'Oh, you know, a group of women getting together, saying they're talking about books. Don't believe a word of it. They must be up to something. Something dodgy going on. They didn't mean it. It was just a dig at us, but it was annoying, so we stopped going in the end and we take it in turns to bring a couple of bottles of wine here.'

She stood up and took the piece of paper to him. 'These two,' she said, 'Gina Sidwell and Alice Gates, are neighbours, both in Overcliffe Cottages, down on the front. And Eva Majoros and Lesley Harper are neighbours, too, both in Marine Drive, but I don't know the numbers. Then Theodora Karalis lives in Larkspur Close, and this is me, Lorna Dering, and my address.'

He folded the paper and put it in his pocket, then gave her a card. 'My number,' he said. 'Let me know right away if anyone doesn't bring their book back.'

'All right. But it will turn out to be Kelly's book, won't it? That's the only thing that makes sense.'

She watched him go, returned to the office and wondered about phoning Gina to tell her about this latest development. They had spoken briefly since Kelly's death and agreed that this evening's meeting had to go ahead. They would have to talk about the future of the group – six people were really too few. She was surprised to realise how important the survival of the group was to her, how much she had tied it to the survival of the library, how she depended on it to keep the place feeling busy. Her strategy of getting people to drop into the library to collect the next book for discussion, for example, instead of handing out the next set when the previous ones were returned, as most groups did, had meant seven extra people coming in, perhaps taking out other books, and the opportunity for a bit of book chat at the issues desk, making anyone else in the library feel that books were live things, to be thought about and talked about. She had even thought about getting a local author to come in and talk one evening. If everyone in the group could guarantee to bring one other person with them, and if they advertised it well, it would be an event, would give a buzz to the place. She wasn't ready to give up. She needed Gina to be positive tonight, too. She phoned her number but her phone was switched off.

She was back in the library by seven, having taken a break to go home and give Don his dinner. She laid out wine glasses and napkins on the table where she had sat drinking coffee with Jack Terry that morning. It was Eva's turn to bring refreshments: the wine would be something rich and red, and there would be little canapés with pickles and sour cream, as well, no doubt, as strudel.

Gina arrived early and flustered. 'Sorry, Lorna, I can't put my hand on my book. I had it on the coffee table for weeks but I hadn't looked at it for a while, and then I sat down this afternoon to make some notes and pick out my favourite poem, and it wasn't there. I've turned the place over but it's not in the house. I can only think Matt or Dora has taken it. They put their books and stuff on the coffee table when they come for their lessons, and one of them must have picked my book up by mistake. I tried ringing Matt and left him a message, and I can ask Dora this evening.'

She paused for breath and took off her coat. 'What makes it even odder,' she says, 'is that when I found Kelly, there was –'

'A copy of the book lying on the beach,' Lorna finished.

Gina stared at her. 'Have the police been talking to you?' she asked.

'This morning. And I'm sorry, Gina, but I've promised to tell them if any book isn't returned this evening.'

52

'Do they think the one I found on the beach wasn't Kelly's then?'

'They want to be sure, I suppose.'

'Bugger!' Gina said. 'She's just dying to arrest me and now she's got her chance.'

'She?'

'Detective Inspector Paula Powell, in charge of the case. She's been brought in from Marlbury. We have history.'

"And she's dying to arrest you?'

'She threatened me.' She heaved a sigh and plonked herself down on a chair. 'When I found the book on the beach I took it in out of the rain, and then I forgot to tell DC Green about it. I'm guilty of tampering with evidence.'

Lorna sat down, too. 'I think I would have done the same,' she said. 'Leaving a book lying out in the rain – it goes against all one's instincts, doesn't it?'

'But you'd have given it to DC Green right away,' Gina said gloomily. 'Your good intentions shine from you, whereas mine – mine get obscured.'

There was a silence, and then Lorna asked, 'Do you think the book could have been your copy? Could you have had it in your pocket? Maybe it dropped out when you bent over the – over to look at Kelly.'

'No. I don't carry books in pockets. In handbags, yes, but not in pockets. Besides, I know for certain it wasn't mine.'

'For certain?'

'Yes. Someone had defaced that copy – a big circle in red felt pen round the title and first few lines of *Medusa*. It could have been done any time, I know, but I felt sure it was Kelly who'd done it. Anyway, it certainly wasn't my book.'

'Well, if they don't find a copy at Kelly's house, they'll know that one was hers.'

'Not if I don't find mine.'

The door opened and Dora came in. Gina jumped up.

53

'Dora!' she said. 'You haven't by any chance got my copy of the book, have you?'

Dora looked alarmed – *her default expression*, Lorna thought.

'Your copy?' she asked.

'You didn't pick it up at my house by mistake?'

'No.' She displayed her copy. 'I just have this one.'

'And you're sure that one's yours?'

'Yes. It has my bookmark in it.'

Seeing her distress, Lorna said, 'Not to worry, Dora. Gina's copy's gone walkabout. It happens. I'm sure it will turn up. Have a glass of juice.'

As she reached for the carton, there was a flurry of noise at the door and Eva burst in, laughing, with Lesley following behind, carrying a bag of clinking bottles and a platter. They presented the contrast they always did: Lesley, plump and comfortable in a padded anorak that did her figure no favours, and Eva, slim and immaculate in a black coat with a fur collar, and a matching hat. She called out as she approached, 'My dears, I thought I was getting to be a daft old lady, but Lesley is not old so she has no excuse. We have both lost our books! Can you believe it?'

As Lorna glanced at Gina's stunned face, she knew her own must be looking much the same. Eva raised her hands in protest. 'It is not a tragedy, my dear book-lovers. We shall find them or pay for new ones. We shall not be drummed out of the service.'

'It's not our standing with the library service that we're worried about, actually, Eva,' Lorna said, helping her off with her coat and going to hang it in the office. The others were happy to sling their coats over empty chairs but Eva liked hers to be treated with care.

As she went, she heard Gina say, 'Come and sit down and pour us some wine and we will tell you a tale. And then

54

we will see if we can work out the answer before the police do.'

She was suddenly much more cheerful, Lorna thought, now that she wasn't alone as an object of police suspicion. As she came back from the office, Gina was splashing wine into glasses. 'I'm too agitated,' she was saying. 'I shall tell the tale vilely. Lorna can tell you all about it while I recover my wits.'

So Lorna told the tale as briefly and undramatically as she could: the visit from DC Green, the book found on the beach near Kelly's body, the request from DC Green that she inform him of any missing books.

'But the thing is,' Gina chipped in as soon as she had finished, 'the book on the beach had distinguishing marks; someone had drawn a circle round the first part of *Medusa*. Does that ring a bell with either of you?' As they shook their heads, she said, 'Nor me,' and flopped back in her chair.

'So the book must have been Kelly's,' Lesley said. 'But why take it onto the beach when she was going swimming in the rain?'

'And what has happened to our books?' Eva added.

'Well, there's an answer to the first question,' Lorna said. 'She must have had it in her pocket and it fell out when she fell. What was she wearing, Gina?'

'That pink anorak she usually wore.'

'So, she had taken it with her somewhere in her pocket and it was still there. It's only a small book, after all. You could easily forget it was there.'

'I'm not sure Kelly was someone who took a book with her everywhere she went,' Lesley objected. 'You and Gina, maybe, but Kelly was usually doing something active.'

'She had the book by the till in the shop one day, I noticed,' Eva put in.

'And she might have taken it if she had a doctor's appointment,' Lorna persisted, determined to carry her argument. 'Or the dentist's – somewhere where she thought she might have to wait. She didn't like being bored.'

'OK,' Gina said. 'Let's say for the moment that Kelly might have had her book with her, then there's the other question. What's happened to our books?'

'It could be coincidence,' Lorna said slowly. 'As I said, it's a slim volume – probably the smallest book we've read – more easily mislaid…' She tailed off.

'Come on, Lorna,' Gina said. 'You don't really —'

She stopped as Alice Gates came flying in, panting hard.

'So sorry,' she gasped. 'It's my fault, letting the house get to be a tip. I've shouted at the boys and I've shouted at Simon, but —'

'You can't find your book,' Gina said.

Alice waved her empty hands. 'Obviously not,' she laughed. 'Well deduced, Sherlock!'

'Join the club, Alice,' Gina said. 'Fortify yourself with a drink and we'll explain.'

Lorna went to lock the outside door now that the group was complete, and returned to find that the job of explanation had again been allocated to her, but as soon as she had finished Gina took up her earlier question. 'So what we were considering, Alice,' she said, 'was, assuming it was Kelly's book on the beach, who has taken our books and what the hell for?'

Nobody was in a hurry to answer the question. They sipped their wine in silence and looked at Gina, waiting for her to answer it herself.

'I think it's someone's idea of a joke,' she said. 'Someone who knows the group and knows what we've been reading, obviously. They've heard somehow about the book on the beach and they thought it would be funny to get us all questioned by the police.'

'Not all of us,' Dora said quietly. 'I have my book and so does Lorna.'

'That's true,' Gina conceded. 'Well, you two are the quietest and best behaved of the lot of us. Perhaps he decided to let you off.'

'He?' Eva queried.

'Well, it's got to be a man, hasn't it? They don't like us, they think we're witches and if they took a look at this book it would confirm their worst fears. The review extracts on the back alone would do it.' She picked up Dora's copy. *'subversive, a feminist classic, a swipe with a dishclout at the famous men of history,'* she read. 'He wouldn't even need to read the poems to be affronted.'

'But you're thinking about the old codgers in the pub, Gina,' Lorna objected. 'They couldn't possibly know what we're reading. It would have to be someone who knows one of us well.'

'By which I think you mean someone who is married to one of us,' Eva said with a wry little smile.

'Well, it's not Don,' Lorna said. 'He's probably more of a feminist than I am. And he's got nothing against the book group – he's used to sharing me with books. Besides, I've still got my book.'

'Simon doesn't like the group much, if I'm honest,' Alice said. 'I think he does suspect that we spend our time slagging off men, but there's no time in his life for plotting elaborate practical jokes, breaking into people's houses and stealing books. Two kids, a full-time job and a working wife just about leave him time for football once a week, and that's it.'

'Well, Peter's bad leg rules him out as a cat burglar,' Lesley said. 'And actually he's been away at a conference all this week, so I think he's in the clear.'

'And I've still got my book so it's not my dad,' Dora said,

producing a small burst of laughter as they each pictured the dignified patriarch breaking and entering.

'And Gina and I live in blessed singleness,' Eva concluded. 'So that's that.'

In the pause that followed, there came a thunderous knocking on the outer door. Lorna went to answer it, speculating on a second visit from DC Green and pushing aside fanciful thought of the ghosts of Lily and Kelly demanding entrance. A large male figure stood outside. It was not DC Green but a big raw-boned lad whom she remembered as an occasional library-user, generally in search of Coles notes on his A level texts.

'Is this the book group?' he asked.

She told him, warily, that it was and let him in. He fished a book out of his pocket. It was, of course, a copy of *The World's Wife*.

'I'm just bringing this back,' he said.

Lorna could hear Gina behind her, talking as she came towards them. 'Oh my God! Is that my book, Matt? Am I reprieved?'

As she stretched out a hand for the book, he pulled it back. 'It's not yours,' he said. 'I got your message. That was what reminded me that I had this. Kelly lent it to me. She said I ought to read it. Can't say I have but you said you needed the books tonight so I brought it round.'

He looked round at six pairs of horrified eyes, hesitated for a moment and then fled. *Straight round to the pub to tell them he's been hexed by the Broomstick Brigade*, Lorna thought as she locked the door after him.

She and Gina sat down again.

'Back to the drawing board, then,' Gina said, looking at the book. 'This is a whole new thing, girls. Now we're in an Agatha Christie. Just up your street, Eva.'

'Well, if we're going in that direction,' Eva said carefully, 'there is something I thought of saying but had decided not to, because, of course, I made my living translating Christie and Sayers and Allingham and the rest, and I was afraid you would think I was letting my imagination run away with me, but —'

'Oh, say it, Eva, do,' Gina broke in. 'Imagination is what we need right now. Speak, do!'

'Well, Jack Terry had tea with me this afternoon. He came to clean my windows and I invited him in. He didn't say much. He is not an articulate young man at the best of times, but it was clear to me that he does not believe that his Lily's death was an accident. So it is possible, isn't it, that the police should be looking for a serial killer and that we are the potential victims?'

Chapter Six

SOMETHING TO ANSWER FOR

Saturday 15th February 2014

I am not really surprised to find DI Paula Powell outside my house at eight-thirty this morning. Well, I suppose I had hoped to have time to walk Caliban before she came thundering on my door, but conscientious Lorna must have rung DC Green at first light to report the missing books and now here is his boss stepping out of her car just as I emerge from the house, pulled by an eager dog with important things to do. I play stupid.

'Paula!' I say. 'You just can't keep away from the seaside, can you?'

She slams the car door and comes very close. 'This isn't a joke, Gina,' she says. 'I am this close to arresting you.' She raises thumb and forefinger a couple of millimetres apart and pokes them at me, narrowly missing my right eye. Caliban, alert to aggression, growls threateningly. He is not, I suspect, really fond of me, but I am his source of food and shelter and he is programmed to defend me.

'Sorry, Paula,' I say. 'There's nothing I'd like better than a chat at the police station, but Caliban's bladder waits for no woman. You can either go into my house and search for clues while I take him down to the beach, or you can come, too.' I look at her nice leather boots. 'But take care on the steps in those heels,' I say, and head across the road.

On the beach and off his lead, Caliban does his own thing, while keeping a wary eye on us, and we stand in the shelter of the sea wall. It is too cold for standing still, really, but Paula will ruin her boots if we walk on the pebbles. We hunch into ourselves and keep our hands in our pockets. I am better prepared for this in my padded anorak and woolly hat; Paula is incongruous as well as cold, bare-headed and in her town coat. We stand side by side, not looking at each other; we could be a couple of spies in a Le Carré novel. We ought to have cigarettes.

She doesn't speak immediately so I take the initiative. 'I don't suppose you've heard from David at all, have you?' I ask, nudging pebbles with the toe of my boot.

'Nope.' She says, shortly. I don't look at her but I can hear that she has gone pink. 'You?'

'Oh no,' I say airily. 'But I took steps to go off his radar.'

'What sort of steps?'

'Sold my house, changed my email, threw my mobile into the sea.'

'Oh well, that should do the trick,' she says. She is actually laughing at me. 'I mean, he's only a DCI with the Met,' she says. 'Without your address or email or phone number, what can he possibly do?' And then before I have time to recover from being wrong-footed, she asks, 'Why didn't you tell me that book was part of a set? What stupid game are you playing now? The problem with you is you think we're stupid – you always have – but we're not – I'm not – and you're not getting away with anything.'

I put my resentment at being laughed at into sounding righteously injured. 'You didn't give me a chance,' I say. 'As soon as I gave you the book I found on the beach you went ballistic. You swore at me in a quite inappropriate way, ordered me to stop thinking and threatened to arrest me if I tried to make any contribution to your investigation. So I did as I was told. I went and got finger-printed and then I shut up, as instructed.'

She is very cross. If she had Caliban's vocal equipment she would growl at me. She opens her mouth to speak but I add, 'And that was in spite of the fact that I think I may be in personal danger.'

'Ha!' She throws back her head with a noise that is somewhere between a laugh and a yell of fury. 'So it's actually all about you, is it?' she asks. 'Of course it is. Why didn't I think of that?'

'Not just about me. The whole book group may be in danger.'

'Oh, spare me, please!'

'Think about it, Paula. Two women in the group have died in the past three weeks – both in 'accidents'.'

'The first one – Lily Terry – was an accident. We've checked it out. There was never any doubt about it.'

'That's not what her husband thinks.'

'Grief does that. People need someone to blame.'

'All right. But you must admit that Kelly's death wasn't accidental. You wouldn't be here if you didn't think she was killed. And a copy of *The World's Wife* was found beside her body. It's a feminist book. It's subversive. It mocks men and celebrates women. The men around here don't like our group as it is. They call us *The Broomstick Brigade*. Now one of us is dead and someone put a copy of the book beside her body. It wasn't her copy and it wasn't mine, so —'

'I only have your word for it that it wasn't yours.'

'It had been defaced. You must have seen that if you've looked at it properly. Someone took a felt-tip pen to it. Ask anyone who knows me and they'll tell you I'm incapable of defacing a book.'

'And you ask our forensics expert and he will tell you that the only fingerprints on that book are yours.'

'Well, that's suspicious in itself, isn't it? It's a library book. Lots of people have handled it. People don't generally wear gloves to read a book, do they? Whoever put it there wiped it clean and wore gloves, didn't they? The point is, that book was left as some sort of message – presumably by Kelly's killer – and then our books disappeared – four of them – and –'

She breaks in. 'They haven't disappeared, Gina, have they? One of you left that book there and now you're all playing the 'I am Spartacus' scene to cover up. I don't know yet what you're doing, but I will find out and –'

'They were taken, Paula! Someone got into our houses and took them. Maybe they just wanted to get us into trouble but maybe it's more sinister than that and you won't know that until one of us turns up dead with a book lying beside us.'

I am shouting by this time and Caliban comes racing up in anticipation of canine gallantry. Paula turns away and makes for the steps. 'I'm not listening to this, Gina,' she says. 'This isn't a TV drama. I'm investigating one death and some stupid game that you and your friends are playing.' She starts to mount the steps and then pauses and calls down to me, 'And I'll tell you how I know there isn't some sort of serial killer stalking your book group. If he was, wouldn't he have started with the most completely bloody infuriating person in it? And that would have been you.'

I watch her climb the steps and listen for the sound of her car driving off before putting Caliban on his lead and going home.

I have no time for worrying about Paula today. It is half-term and my granddaughter, Freda, is coming to stay tomorrow, so I am engaged in some last-minute embellishments to my milieu. Freda has been kinder than the rest of my family about my decision to live in a hovel but even she finds it less than ideal. At six, she is a serious reader and her expectations of the world derive largely from literary stereotypes, so in her world it is fine – appropriate, indeed – for a granny to live in a cottage, but the granny should wear her grey hair in a wispy bun and have spectacles on the end of her nose, and her cottage should stand in the middle of a wood with a garden round it and a cosy fire, home-baked cakes and a cat inside. The bun and specs are not an option, not even for Freda, and I can do nothing about my house's seabound state, but I can offer a cat, I can bake a tin of ginger flapjacks and I will, I have decided, produce the cosy fire. For Freda I have broken my vow of austerity, paid out two thousand pounds, and expect a slick young man to arrive at any moment to install a woodburning stove in the fireplace condemned by Jason the builder as unusable but declared by the slick young man (Will, by name) to be no problem for woodburner technology. 'We just stick a pipe up the chimney,' I was informed, 'and you're cool.'

'Or warm?' I suggested.

He smiled but I'm not sure he took my point.

So now I'm waiting for him to arrive and perform this piece of magic. *Two hours max* I am assured. Actually, I'm terrified now. I have no faith in my ability to manage burning wood, even if my chimney can stand the strain. Never mind serial killers, I'm quite capable of incinerating myself and Freda with no malice aforethought.

Will is reassuring, however, turning up on time with his sidekick, Chas, both wearing Aran sweaters and corduroy trousers, as though they were away on a shooting weekend. If they hadn't decided to start up this business, I feel, they would be working in merchant banks. They aren't based on this dingy bit of coast, of course – we're more food banks than merchant banks down here. My internet trawl found them in upmarket Tunbridge Wells; they are slumming it today but are too well-bred to let it show. They do turn down my offer of the obligatory cup of tea, however, not wanting to embarrass me by asking for Earl Grey, I suppose, though they explain, charmingly, that they want to 'crack on' and 'get out of my hair' as quickly as possible. They are done with time to spare, don't ask to use my loo and depart, leaving me feeling, in spite of the cheque they have taken with them, that I have been the beneficiary of kindly youthful voluntary service.

I devote the rest of the day to getting to grips with the fire-breathing monster I have let into my house. I test the humidity of my bag of logs, using the implement I have been sold for this purpose, I experiment with the air-flow control and try the doors closed and open. Open is a bad idea: air rushes in and flaming splinters of wood fly out. I burn holes in the hearth rug and spend a good deal of time on my hands and knees with a wet j-cloth, neurotically chasing down the sparks which I imagine will smoulder away, only to burst into flame later and barbecue me in my bed. Only when I feel I have the mastery of the monster do I eat a cheese sandwich and go to bed to dream of infernos.

Chapter Seven

IN A FREE STATE

Monday 17th February 2014

Well, we have not been incinerated. Freda arrived yesterday, escorted by her family – Ellie her mother, Ben her stepfather and Nico her brother. I cooked lunch like a proper grandmother and we sat round the woodburner while the rain lashed the window panes. Freda is gratifyingly delighted by the woodburner, insisting that it is like the witch's stove in *Hansel and Gretel*. She is seriously into witches at the moment, arriving with two *Harry Potter* DVDs and three volumes in the *Worst Witch* series. She confides to me, after the rest of the family have left, that she has told her friends at school that I am a witch. I take this to be a response to the untended state of my hair but she says, 'No, Granny. Because of your broomstick!' I had forgotten about my besom broom, bought in my new spirit of austerity off a market stall. I don't actually use it because it turned out to be pretty ineffective and the hoover is quicker, but it stands in a corner of the kitchen and I am very much afraid that, if it ever stops raining, Freda will want me to fly on it. So far she has been satisfied with a viewing of *Harry Potter and the Chamber of Secrets*, a witch's brew supper of minestrone soup and a chapter of *The Worst Witch Strikes Again* as a bedtime story. She has her eye on Ariel as my familiar, I can see, but the cat is staying firmly by the fire, looking ostentatiously earthbound and unmagical. I know how she feels.

This morning, I am taking charge of our agenda. We walk Caliban in a light drizzle and then set off for a trip to Dover Castle. This, I think, offers excitement without witchcraft, though it turns out to have its drawbacks. I had forgotten what a long climb it is up to the castle's cliff-top eminence; Freda starts protesting before we are halfway up. Neither had I anticipated the French invasion. Perhaps unwisely, I showed Freda the *Welcome to France* message on my phone as we left the house, so when the first flock of French schoolchildren chatters past us, she tugs my hand and says earnestly, 'Granny, I think we ARE in France.' What are they all doing here when the sole purpose of this castle, for hundreds of years, was to keep out our despised Gallic neighbours?

Whatever their teachers' reasons for dragging them here (surely not by ferry?) in the icy blasts of February, they are here *en masse* – from little ones in bright high-vis tabards to sullen teenagers glued to *ses téléphones portables*. So Freda and I play Dodge the Frogs, heading for anywhere that looks quiet before the place gets overrun and we beat a retreat.

Freda likes a cartoon version of the history of the Plantagenet kings. She doesn't follow the history – who does? – but she likes the way defeated kings fall over flat on their backs with their crowns on. She also finds a throne that she can sit on while I take a photo of her on my phone. Then, when a French advance party arrives, we head for the Saxon church and the Roman lighthouse, the Pharos. Freda knows about the Romans. You can hardly grow up in Marlbury without knowing about them; they are there from its solid city walls to the mosaics and coins in its museum, to its gates, north, east and west. She is much less sure about the Saxons, which only goes to demonstrate the truth of Orwell's observation that history is written by the winners. (I know Churchill is supposed to have said 'History is written by the victors' but no one seems to be able to say when or where he said it, so I'm going with Orwell, who definitely wrote his remark in *Tribune* in February 1944.)

Freda likes the Saxon church, though, because it has intricately tiled walls, which fascinate her, and the Pharos is pleasantly spooky without overdoing it. Then it is time for lunch. My vow of poverty does get a bit wobbly when Freda comes to visit, so we do not eat sandwiches on a bench in the face of a biting wind that carries the taste of the Siberian steppes on its breath. Instead we treat ourselves to soup, bread and cheese, and flapjacks in the warmth of the castle's café. We are virtually the only clients – the French children, it seems, are doomed to freeze with their sandwiches. This is all very satisfactory and I feel that we are doing well as we make a few educational purchases in the shop and scamper down the slope to the exit, though I am disconcerted when Freda spots an ice-cream sign at the bottom and cannot be persuaded that ice creams in February are inappropriate. She selects chocolate and raspberry in a cone and licks it happily as we walk into the town. One advantage, I have to say, of eating ice cream when the temperature verges on freezing is that it doesn't make a mess. Freda consumes the whole thing without getting drips on her gloves.

After this, life gets tedious for her because I have to take her with me to my asylum seekers' class. I can't cancel the class because we are never quite sure where people are to let them know, and though Alice, my neighbour, offered to have her for the afternoon, the noise made by her two sons racing round the garden this morning made Freda wobbly about going there, so there is nothing for it but for her to sit with her freshly purchased book about castles while my students and I work on verb tenses. I did convince myself that, in some way, seeing Freda would be good for my students, on the principle that a small child is always a cheering thing, a reminder about renewal and hope, but I did also think to warn them that Freda would be here today and I am not surprised that Ivy has stayed away, needing no reminder of her lost sons. What does surprise me, though, is that Farid is not here. He never misses a class and his absence makes me uneasy.

We work on the difference between the simple and progressive forms of verbs, the *aspect* of the verb form, as it is called: *Where do you live?* (simple) as opposed to *Where are you living?* (progressive) for example. Does anyone ever ask my students where they live? No. They ask where they are living, because that covers the temporariness of their arrangements. Asking someone where they live implies a settled state, with all the accoutrements of legal entitlement; asking where they are living acknowledges the temporary, includes the unspoken phrases, *at the moment* or *for the present*. We mull this over for a bit and I get them to tell the bits of their recent travels they can bear to relate in progressive terms: *I was travelling for x weeks; While I was travelling y happened; I have been waiting to hear about my asylum application for z months.*

At the end of the class, they want to hear from Freda, and I do understand the fascination of hearing a small child speak effortlessly a language that one is struggling to learn. I have stood staring at French infants as they rolled their guttural '*r*'s with no trouble, their lips already poised in the perfect pout. Freda, I must say, acquits herself well, getting over her initial shyness and demonstrating, at the end of the session, a flawless mastery of the perfect progressive tense with her answer, 'I have been staying with my granny since yesterday.'

Freda is tired by the time we arrive home, so I get the fire lit and we sit in front of it to eat cheese on toast with crispy bacon (her choice) and watch a quiz show that neither of us quite understands.

Upstairs, as I'm giving Freda a bath, we hear shouting from next door. I can't hear what they are saying, but Alice is mostly yelling at Simon, with aggrieved burbles from him in response. Freda looks surprised. 'Is their TV upstairs?' she asks. I am momentarily nonplussed by her question, and then I am so delighted that I have to sit down on the laundry box to compose myself. You can't know, really, the state of your children's relationships; Ellie and Ben seem happy and fond when I see them together, but they are juggling jobs and children and not enough money and it could be that it gets on top of them from time to time. God knows Ellie and Annie heard enough shouting when they were growing up. It was much like what we are hearing from next door, I suppose: me yelling and Andrew infuriatingly calm and quiet, turning me into a two-year-old in a tantrum. But Freda thinks if there is yelling in a house it must come from the television and I bless her innocence.

Chapter Eight

TROUBLES

Monday 17th February 2014

Alice

Alice Gates lay in bed, luxuriating in idleness so unusual for her that it felt almost criminal. Outside in the garden she could hear her boys playing; Simon, she knew, was out there with them and she could relax. She arranged her pillows, sat up and took a sip of her tea. She looked round the room, greyly lit by the north-facing window. It was pathetic really, this room: a wall of fitted cupboards and the bed and barely room to move round it. It had been the right decision to give the boys the bigger room at the front, looking out to sea, because, with the bunk beds in, there was room for it to be a playroom as well, and that meant they could keep some of the chaos out of the sitting room downstairs. What was really pathetic, of course, was that they had to live in this poky little two-bedroom place at all, both of them full-time teachers, and Simon a deputy head. But Simon had Paul to support; Heidi wasn't going to let him off the hook there, even though she had remarried and the new husband was some sort of whiz in the city. Simon had been taken for a ride over the divorce and he knew it; that was one of the reasons why the black moods came over him. Heidi had got the house, as well as maintenance for Paul until he was eighteen. She had produced medical evidence that her health was *too fragile* for her to work. Not too fragile, it seemed, for keeping a horse and holidaying in St Lucia.

Enough. She took a deep breath and drank her tea. She would not be sour. Not today. She would bless half term and a husband who didn't mind getting up early even on a non-work day, and two bright, healthy, noisy boys and a new book to read. She had just yesterday picked up from the bookshop in Dungate a copy of *May We Be Forgiven*, which won the Bailey's prize and was promisingly puffed as being about sibling rivalry and murderous rage. Life was not at all bad.

This thought got her out of bed, ready to go downstairs and warm up one of the *pains au chocolat* she had bought as a half-term breakfast treat. She looked out of the window. The boys were bouncing on the trampoline and Simon was leaning on the fence, talking to Harry, their neighbour. Harry gave her the creeps a bit, and he had had a UKIP poster in his window for the local elections, but she knew she ought to think of him as a vulnerable old man and she did keep an eye open for milk piling up on the doorstep and curtains not getting drawn. She just didn't want to have to talk to him, so she was glad that Simon seemed happy to do it.

As she was eating her *pain au chocolat* and savouring the first pages of *May We Be Forgiven*, Simon came in from the garden and took his car keys off a hook above the sink.

'Where are you going?' she asked.

'Just a quick trip into Dover.'

'Are you taking the boys with you?'

He glanced out of the window. 'They'll be fine out there. You'll only need to look out for them now and then.'

'No, I won't!' she protested. 'We agreed, Si. This is my

morning off. I'm on duty this afternoon. Why can't you take them with you?'

'They'll be bored. They'll be fine here.'

'No, they won't. The minute you're gone, they'll be in here moaning about being bored and demanding this, that and the other, and bang goes my morning off. '

'Have you any idea how whingey you sound?' He was jiggling his keys, dying to be off.

'I don't care! We had an agreement. Take them with you or go this afternoon.'

'I can't. I'm taking Harry with me. He's got something he needs to do.'

'Harry? Why? Why can't he get the bus like he always does?'

She saw his face relax as he spotted a chance for self-righteousness; he almost smirked. 'Listen to yourself, Alice,' he said. 'He's an old man and it's freezing out there. The least I can do as a neighbour is give him a lift.'

'So take him this afternoon.'

'What he has to do is urgent.'

'Is he ill? Are you taking him to the hospital?'

She saw the blood surge into his face, the warning signal she had got used to, the tremor of an imminent explosion. 'Why can you never leave anything alone?' he growled, and she could see the effort it cost him to keep his voice low. 'If you must know, he wants to go to the police station, and, before you ask, he thinks he has some information about Kelly's death.'

'What sort of *information*?'

He was moving towards the door now, desperate to be off.

'He saw someone hanging about,' he said as he moved down the hall. 'Young guy, foreign looking.' He had the door open now. 'I shouldn't be much more than an hour. You can manage that, can't you?'

'This is crap, Simon!' she yelled, and slammed the front door after him.

She stood for a moment, taking some deep breaths, before going back to the kitchen and finishing her breakfast. She would not – *would not* let the day be spoilt, As she cleared her crockery into the dishwasher, she felt, rather than heard, something outside. She looked up to see her sons' faces flattened against the panes of the window. Both of them, she noticed, had runny noses. She opened the door.

'What are you doing?' she asked. She saw that they had dragged upturned plant pots across to stand on.

'We're cold,' Sam said, wiping his nose on his sleeve.

'Really, really cold,' Joe added.

'Well, come in, then.'

'Dad said we had to stay out here and not disturb you,' Joe said, jumping down from his pot and coming to bury his face in her anorak.

Guilt. Great waves of it. As was intended, of course.

'How about some hot chocolate?' she said.

The morning passed perfectly pleasantly, if she discounted getting no chance to read her book. They baked biscuits, the boys watched some TV and, at lunchtime, when Simon returned, she decided not even to comment on the three hours he had been away, nor to ask what he thought he was doing encouraging Harry's xenophobic paranoia. That could wait. She dished up sausages and chips and kept her counsel. *Play happy families*, she thought, *and you might even convince yourself.*

She felt she had been rewarded when Simon got the boys to help with clearing the table and then took them upstairs to work on the chemistry set that Sam had been given for his birthday, but was forbidden to use without supervision. She settled herself on the sofa with her book, feeling mildly virtuous.

The knock on the front door came almost immediately. At the door stood a smartly-dressed young woman whom she took to be selling something until she pulled out a warrant card for her scrutiny.

'DI Paula Powell,' she said. 'Attached to Dover Police.'

'Is this the library book again?' Alice asked. 'Because I've already talked to a police officer about —'

'It's not about the book,' DI Powell said. 'Can I come in?'

Alice showed her into the sitting room but did not offer tea or coffee. She returned to the sofa and ostentatiously marked her place in her book and closed it. 'If this isn't about library books,' she said, 'then I suppose it's about our neighbour's phantom foreigner.'

DI Powell looked at her sharply. 'Phantom? Why do you say that?'

'Because Harry sees dangerous terrorists behind every garden fence. He thinks boatloads of them come across in the night and land on the beach down there.'

'So you haven't seen any young men hanging about here in the past few weeks?'

'No.'

'Although your husband has?'

'My husband?'

'Yes. He didn't tell you?'

'No. He didn't.'

She could hear, above their heads, the bumps and creaks of Simon and the boys at work with the chemistry set.

'Look, he's just upstairs,' she said. 'I can call him down and we can —'

'No.' DI Powell stood up, as though she might need to block her path. 'We have your husband's statement. It's you I want to talk to.'

'OK. Well, I don't know when Simon is supposed to have seen this guy, but I should tell you that this time of year we're hardly here in the light to see anything. Simon and I both teach at the primary school in the village, and the children go there as well. We bundle out of here at eight-fifteen in the morning, and we're not looking around for enemy aliens at that point. It's a good day if everyone has the right shoes on and we've all remembered our packed lunches. And in the evening, after we've sorted out our classrooms, we're not back usually until four-thirty, and it's getting dark. We're into the house, fire on, curtains closed.'

'What about the shop?'

'What about it? Anyway, it's closed at the moment, since — '

'Before it closed. Did you never stop off there on your way home?'

'Not if I could help it. It'd mean fighting off demands for sweets and comics. We do a weekly supermarket shop, and that's it.'

'What about your husband? Does he make a habit of stopping off at the shop?'

'Not as far as I know.'

'You don't know? Doesn't he come home with you?'

'He's the deputy head. He quite often has more stuff to deal with.'

'But you never ask him to pick something up from the shop? If you've run out?'

'I do my best not to run out.'

'And he didn't tell you that he had seen a young man – not a local – having an argument with Kelly Field in the shop a few days before she died?'

'When you say *not a local*, I assume you mean not white?'

'Well – yes.'

'He'd have been keen to tell you that.'

'But he didn't tell you?'

'He didn't mention it.'

'Is that usual? Don't you share that sort of thing with one another?'

Alice felt her face grow hot. She could just come out and say it; what did it matter what this woman thought about her marriage? *My husband is a racist,* she could say, *and we don't like each other very much.*

'We're busy,' she said. 'And when we're at home we're focused on the children. There's not much downtime.'

'You said your husband would have been keen to tell us that the young man was from an ethnic minority. Why do you think that?'

'He's not comfortable with people who are different from himself. Let's put it like that.'

'But you are?'

'I am what? Different from him?'

'Comfortable with people who are racially different?'

'Yes. I didn't grow up round here, unlike Simon. I grew up near London.'

DI Powell stood up. Alice suddenly felt as if she was an actor in a TV crime drama. At any moment, she thought, DI Powell would say, *There is just one more thing,* and that would be the killer question.

'As a matter of interest,' DI Powell said, 'If you had seen a young, foreign-looking man hanging around near your house, what would you have thought?'

Alice stood up, too. 'I would have thought how miserable it must be for him to be hanging around in this freezing, sorry arsehole of a place,' she said. 'I'll show you out.'

She went back to her book but could not settle to it. The afternoon was spoilt. She would not tackle Simon until the boys were in bed but she was not letting this go. The thought of Simon and Harry in cahoots with each other, running off to the police with their tales of a dodgy foreigner made her feel sick, and the leaden weight of the knowledge she tried so hard to avoid pressed down on her. She had made a terrible mistake. She had married a man she despised now, and was afraid of, she had two children with him and she couldn't stay with him. It was going to be a mess at best, and very ugly at worst. She jumped up and went to the foot of the stairs.

'I'm just popping out,' she called. 'Shan't be long.'

Without bothering with a coat, she put the door on the latch and, hunched against the wind, hurried round to Gina's house. There was no answer to her knock and she remembered then that Gina had taken Freda into Dover with her. Reluctantly, she walked across the road and stood looking at the sea. What had made her let Simon persuade her that there was something romantic about living here, facing this endless, grey turmoil of water? She thought about the young Arab lad. Could he have felt more displaced anywhere than here, on this seafront? She knew who he was, of course, though she was damned if she was giving the police any more information. He was Theodora Karalis's boyfriend. She had seen them together at the bus stop one morning, when she had gone into school early, ahead of Simon and the boys, because her class was performing in morning assembly. They weren't holding hands, or even talking to each other, just standing side by side, but the look on Dora's face said everything. And another time she had looked out of the bedroom window and seen him wheeling a bike along the alley behind their houses. She assumed that father Karalis didn't approve but she was glad for Dora – *time for her to get away from his suffocating attention*, she thought.

She paced up and down for a few minutes, trying to keep warm, but gave in eventually and went back home.

Over supper, Simon did not ask who their visitor had been, but he had looked out of the window and seen her, Alice felt sure. There was something false about him: he was too eager to please, overacting the fun dad, avoiding her eye.

When they had finished, she told the boys they could watch a DVD before bed. 'Half-term treat,' she said. They sped out to the sitting room and, without looking at him, as she loaded the dishwasher, she said, 'We need to talk about my visitor this afternoon. I suggest upstairs.'

He went on the defensive as soon as she closed the bedroom door. 'I would have told you the police might want to talk to you if you'd only given me the chance, but you were so keen to get back to your bloody book – couldn't wait to get the boys off your hands –'

'Shut up, Simon, and listen to me.' She was shaking, she realised, with the rage she had been storing up all day. And she was afraid. He had never hit her but she had always known that he could. The only thing that held him back was that he knew she wouldn't hesitate to go to the police. She sat down on the bed. 'Don't tower over me like that,' she said. 'I don't like it. Sit down and we can talk properly.' She kept her voice low and even. *Low and slow* – the mantra for teachers dealing with angry children.

There was nowhere to sit in their cramped little bedroom but on the bed, so he sat on the floor under the window and scowled at her.

'I don't care about having to talk to the police,' she said quietly. 'What I care about is you sneaking off to the police with fascist Harry to sell them poisonous gossip.'

'Well that shows how little you know. There's no gossip involved. I told them what I saw and what I heard.'

'And what was that, exactly?'

'I saw a young guy – Arab, Middle-Eastern – whatever the PC term is – threatening Kelly Field.'

'What with?'

'What do you mean?'

'What did he threaten her with? Knife? Gun? Suicide vest?'

79

'It wasn't like that.'

'Oh, just words, then?'

'He said, *I warn you, if you say anything to him I will make you sorry.* And he repeated it – *I will make you sorry.*'

'So that lets him off the hook, then, doesn't it?'

'What are you talking about?'

'Well, you seem to think that threatening to make her sorry is evidence that he killed her, but I'd say it's the opposite. You don't make someone sorry by killing them, do you? Because they'd be dead and wouldn't be able to be sorry.'

'You're splitting hairs.'

'No. I'm not. Haven't you ever told a child at school that you'd make them sorry if you ever caught them doing whatever again? But you didn't mean you were going to kill them, did you?'

'This is ridiculous.'

'No!' Her voice was rising now; she couldn't do low and slow any more. 'You're ridiculous – running off with a crazy old bigot to make trouble for a young guy who's been hanging around here simply because he's got a girlfriend here.'

'Who?' he laughed. 'Who's the girlfriend?'

'I'm not telling you. But that, I imagine, is what he didn't want Kelly to tell.'

'So, then.' He stood up, sensing triumph, she could tell. 'He wanted to shut her up, didn't he?'

'You watch too many bad crime dramas,' she said.

'Don't be so bloody superior,' he growled, standing over her now. 'You never used to be like this. Not till weirdo woman came to live next door.'

'Weirdo woman?'

'Yes. With her bloody book group, so you've got snotty about what I read, and her horrible vegetables that you insist on us eating, and her smart remarks that we have to hear about. *Gina says, Gina thinks* – You know what they call that group of yours, don't you?'

'By *they* I suppose you mean your charming friends in the pub? Well, they've come up with some really clever names, but *The Broomstick Brigade* is the one we like best.'

'And how do you think that makes me feel, hearing my wife called that sort of thing?'

'Pretty stupid, I imagine – pretty stupid to be spending your time – and your money – with Neanderthals like them.' She stood up now. 'But I'll tell you how I feel when I'm with my friends at the book group. I feel that here, at least, I can have an intelligent, truthful conversation about things that matter, that I can have a discussion – a disagreement, even – without anyone shouting or name-calling. It's a great feeling and it's one I certainly don't get at home.'

And then he hit her.

Chapter Nine

THE INHERITANCE OF LOSS

Tuesday 18ᵗʰ February 2014

My day starts with an eight o'clock phone call that has my heart thumping in panic. The call is bad news, though not of the kind I fear. Paula Powell is on the line.

'I tried to see you, yesterday,' she says, 'but you weren't there'. She says it accusingly, as though I were under house arrest.

'No,' I say. 'I've got my...' and then I stop. Why the hell should I explain myself to her? 'You're right,' I say. 'I wasn't there.'

'What can you tell me about a young Arab man who's been seen hanging around near your house?'

'Seen by whom?'

'By your neighbours. And by you, too, I imagine. Only you didn't think fit to tell me about him.'

'You told me not to interfere.'

'Don't start with me, Gina. I'm not in the mood. Have you seen him?'

'I think,' I say carefully, 'that you may be talking about a student of mine. A medical student. He borrows my bike sometimes.'

'Why?'

'Why what?'

'Why does he borrow your bike?'

'Well, to be honest, I don't use it much these days, what with the dog to walk and there's the bus, you know, and – '

'You know what I mean. Why does he want your bike?'

'To ride it, Paula,' I say.

'Why,' she asks, and I can hear her teeth gritting as she speaks, 'doesn't he have a bike of his own if he needs one?'

Well, I wasn't going to be able to stall forever, was I? I don't want to tell her that he's an asylum seeker; I want her to hold the image of *medical student* in her head for as long as possible. 'He's a bit short of money,' I say.

'What's his name?'

'Farid Khalil.'

'And where is he studying? You're not still teaching at Marlbury Uni, are you?'

'He's not at Marlbury. He's studying in London but he's... taking a break at the moment.'

'What sort of break?'

'Look, he's from Syria, Paula,' I say.

'So?'

'So, they're having a bit of trouble over there at the moment. You may have heard.'

'Are you telling me he's not a student, in fact?'

'He is. He's done two years in London – and been a model student – but his father was killed and there's no more money. He's taking a break while he finds a way to support himself.'

'If he's not actually studying, he has no business being here.'

And then I have to say it. 'He's applied for asylum.'

There is a silence. Then, 'Where can I find him?' she asks.

I am tempted to say I don't know – which is, strictly speaking, true – but that will only send her off to the Border Agency to track him down and probably make matters worse. 'Try Ruth and Ernest Cartwright,' I say. 'They run a drop-in centre at St Saviour's Church hall. They may have an address for him.'

'Right.'

She is about to ring off but I stop her. 'He's not a killer, Paula. Really he's not. This is a wild-goose chase.'

She rings off.

I take Freda to Folkestone for the morning. There we career down the zigzag path to the beach. It is an odd time of year to be doing it but we find other families desperate enough for half-term entertainment to be doing the same. We return in the Victorian cable car and finish off with excellent hot chocolate in a rather charming arty café. It is a satisfactory morning and I am distracted from worrying about Farid but on the way back, on the train, I start to fret. I am quite sure that he didn't kill Kelly, but there is something I know which I have no intention of telling Paula. It was three days before Kelly's death that Dora's father strode across the road and carried her away from Farid. He took my bike and rode off back to Dover. I was worried about him and kept an eye open during the next two days, for his returning it, hoping to have the chance to talk to him. There was no sign of him, though, and I concluded that he was keeping it for the time being, even though it was no use for assignations with Dora any more. On Thursday morning, though, the day Kelly died, as I paced about the house waiting for the police to come and talk to me, I saw the bike, in its plastic cover, in my garden. Some time between Wednesday night and Thursday morning Farid had been back.

Freda brings me back to the present, enquiring what our plans are for the afternoon, and the truth is that there are none. That is to say, I have plans: I shall be teaching first Matt and then Dora. I was hoping that Freda might conquer her fears and go to play with the Gates boys.

'Do you feel brave enough to play with Sam and Joe?' I ask.

She considers the matter seriously. 'I think so,' she says.

When we get back to the cottages, I ring at Alice's door. No one answers for a long time, although I can hear faint sounds of television inside. I ring again and eventually the door is opened not by Alice, but by Simon. He looks terrible – unshaven and red-eyed. He is not welcoming. He regards me not just with annoyance but almost with fear.

'Oh, it's you,' he says.

'Yes. Hello Simon,' I say brightly. 'I was hoping to have a word with Alice.'

I can hear that the children are watching some kind of cartoon programme. There is smell of burnt toast in the house.

'She's not here,' he says.

'Will she be back this afternoon?'

'She's gone away.'

'Away?'

'For a few days.'

'How nice for her. Brave of you to hold the fort,' I say cheerily, but I am puzzled. Alice said nothing to me about plans for going away this week and we had a vague arrangement to go to see *The Invisible Woman* in Dungate later in the week. 'Has she gone somewhere nice?' I ask.

'London,' he says, and starts to close the door.

After lunch, I make various suggestions to Freda about what she might do while I'm teaching but she has a plan of her own. She will spring-clean the dolls' house, she says.

I am impressed by this idea, largely because the concept of spring-cleaning must be something Freda has got from a book. Cleaning of any kind has never really been my bag; just enough to prevent the place from becoming a health hazard has always been my guiding principle and to judge from the state of Ellie's house, I would say it was hers, too, so Freda has experienced only virtual spring-cleaning. *The Wind in the Willows* is my guess for her inspiration. I always had a soft spot for the proletarian Mole and I see no reason why Freda shouldn't feel the same.

Bringing the dolls' house here was against the William Morris rule that I applied for selecting what to bring with me: *Have nothing in your house that you do not know to be useful or believe to be beautiful.* I was more stringent than that, actually, interpreting *useful* as *essential*, and I was mortified to discover how little of my domestic paraphernalia I believed to be beautiful. Well, the dolls' house is not beautiful and I could hardly claim that it was useful until today. Now I can claim that I showed remarkable foresight in bringing it with me for just such an occasion as today. Actually, though, sheer sentimentality drove me to bring it. My father made it for me for my sixth birthday. It has not worn well and it was never intended to be beautiful. My father eschewed the romantic fancies of most dolls' houses; there were never roses round the door. It was, in fact, a faithful copy of our house – a 1960's box of a house which my mother liked because it was efficient and she didn't have to think about it very much. The dolls' house furniture, though, was my choice and I spent my birthday and Christmas money on the romantic and fanciful, from Swedish pastoral flower-painted to French chateau white and gold. And I filled the house with people – not just Mummy, Daddy and children but an elderly retainer in shirt-sleeves, a cook in an apron, a governess with spectacles, a visiting vicar and several grandparents. These provided me with a cast for creating high-voltage domestic dramas that occupied me for hours. It was the perfect toy for an only child.

When I haul it down from the top of a bookcase in Freda's room, it is covered in dust and its interior is chaotic – furniture scrambled and upended and the dolls lying prone in attitudes of extreme distress. In fact, I am a little disappointed, now, that Freda wants to do anything so mundane as to spring-clean this richly suggestive scene; there is so much potential for drama here in what is obviously the aftermath of some apocalyptic event. She is adamant, however.

'I'm going to make it all smart,' she says, 'and then they can have a party.'

I don't say that it looks to me as though they've had the party already; I fetch her a damp sponge and leave her to it.

Matt arrives for his lesson looking more subdued that I have ever seen him, and without the sweaty glow of recent exercise that usually accompanies him. He flops down in a chair and says he is sorry but he hasn't written his essay.

'So much hassle,' he says. 'Man, you wouldn't believe the hassle.'

'About?' I ask.

'About the thing – you know – about Kelly. I was really going to get down to it – the essay – this morning, and then that policewoman turned up. Again. Wanted to know about the Arab guy Kelly had a row with.' He looks sheepish. 'I had to tell her about the guy and Dora.'

He closes his eyes and runs a hand over his face. His hands are huge, I notice suddenly.

'The thing is,' he says, 'she's got it in for me. She thinks I know more than I'm telling. *You were in a relationship with her*, she keeps saying, and I keep telling her it was like – you know – just f-... just sex.' He gazes at me like a huge toddler, injured and bewildered. 'My mum's completely pissed off with me because they came in and searched the house – everything – the garage, the shed, the loft – the lot.'

'Do you know what they were looking for?'

'Kelly's iPhone. She always had it with her but it wasn't

– you know – on the beach and they haven't found it in the shop or her flat.'

'So they think you've got it.'

'I think I was the prime suspect,' he says, 'until —'

'Until Farid came into the picture.'

I consider him. I've always thought of him as harmless, like one of those big, bounding dogs which might knock you over accidentally but would never bite you, but now I can't take my eyes off those enormous hands. Kelly was a strong, fit young woman; someone had to push her pretty hard to send her over the sea wall. And then that someone lifted her head and bashed it repeatedly on the stones. Big hands. And what comes into my mind now is the last time I saw Kelly. She stood in the shop doorway, watching Matt stride away with his big bag hoisted onto his shoulder. 'Nice lad,' I said, and she said, 'That's all you know.' At the time, I took it just as Kelly's usual sourness; I wonder now what she meant.

I tear myself away from all this. It's never constructive to speculate on the homicidal possibilities of one's pupils, although I have taught several of whom I could have said, *That boy will be hanged.* We turn to the matter in hand, which is *Hamlet*. Matt is seriously adrift here. He can't understand why Hamlet piddles around instead of just getting on with dealing with his wicked uncle, and I suspect he would like the whole thing translated into Key Stage 3 vocabulary. 'The pretending to be mad stuff,' he asks, bewildered, 'what's that about? How does that help?'

'Well, that's an interesting question, Matt,' I say, encouragingly. 'You've hit on one of the key questions.'

'But you're not going to tell me the answer, are you?' he says. 'You're going to ask me what I think.' He groans and rubs his face again.

'*The time is out of joint. O cursed spite*
That ever I was born to set it right,' I quote. 'Hamlet knows

88

what he's expected to do but he knows he's not the right person to do it. He finds all kinds of reasons to hesitate, and he's got no one to confide in: his mother is married to his father's murderer; his college friends are working for the murderer, too, and his girlfriend conspires in a plot to trap him. It's enough to send anyone genuinely round the bend.'

'So he's not pretending?'

'It's a grey area,' I say.

'I hate those.'

'I know,' I say.

We struggle on. When I think any more complexity will finish him off, I go against all my principles and give him a list of prescribed quotes. *Drop these into any essay and you're bound to pick up a few marks.*

He brightens up. 'Magic,' he says.

When he has gone, I put the kettle on and go upstairs to check on Freda. The miniature scene has shifted now from the aftermath of an orgy or domestic tragedy to the morning after a bombing raid. The dolls' house is empty, the bodies are laid out in a row and the furniture is spread around, recovering from Freda's ministrations with the damp sponge. I notice how much of it is broken – missing chair legs, wobbly tables, torn seat covers. Freda has gathered the maimed pieces in one place.

'I'm only putting the nice things back,' she says firmly.

Well, she doesn't get that from me, that sort of ruthlessness. Give me the maimed and damaged – animal, vegetable or mineral – and I will take it under my tattered old wing.

'We could try and mend the others,' I say.

Freda scoops up the broken pieces and dumps them into my hands. 'There you go,' she says, and turns back to cleaning the little front door with her greying sponge.

I go back downstairs and by the time I have made the tea, I realise that, for the first time, Dora is late for her lesson.

When she does arrive, she is not herself at all. She is not in her school uniform, it being half term, but neither is she carrying her sturdy briefcase. She offers me no plastic-foldered essay and doesn't really apologise for the absence of the essay or for being late. She seems to be in a daze – so much so, that when I offer her tea, she actually accepts, and drinks it. We have a go at the end of *The Tempest*. I'm particularly interested in Prospero's unforgiving forgiveness of his brother, but I can't say that Dora is. Several times, as I am talking to her, her eyes slide away from mine to look out at the sea, which is rapidly being consumed in the evening murk. She says nothing, really, just answering my questions with a hopeless shake of her head. I manage twenty minutes of this before I say, 'Look, Dora, I know your father is making things hard for you and Farid, but —'

I get no further. She shakes her head violently and gets to her feet. 'It's not…' she says. 'You don't… I can't…' and she rushes out of the room. I follow her to the front door, where she turns and says, 'I'm sorry. Sorry.' Then she runs out into the dark.

I stand and watch her as she passes under the nearest lamppost, then go inside. 'Bloody hell,' I mutter, and consider, quite seriously, whether the exam boards would accept special consideration cases for either Matt or Dora. It is a long time since I taught in a school but I doubt that there is much truck with *emotional distress* under Michael Gove's malign dispensation. I google, and discover that the death of a close relative can earn you up to an extra 5 per cent. Where does having your girlfriend murdered rank on the scale, I wonder? Especially if you're not really sure that she was your girlfriend? Are you entitled to anything if it was *just sex*? As for Dora, an enforced sundering from a boy you've known for only a few weeks would hardly count. Adolescent heartbreak lives in its own bleak world; we who are old forget its terrible intensity.

Telling myself, unconvincingly, that youth is intense but resilient, and that it is, after all, still only February, I clear away the tea mugs and go upstairs to Freda.

Here order reigns. Furniture has been allotted rationally to rooms (though the cat in its basket is, oddly, in the bathroom) and the people are sitting at the kitchen table or reclining in the sitting room. I am delighted to see that Freda is blind to class barriers, so the shirt-sleeved retainer sits on a sofa, while the vicar is in the kitchen. There is only one disturbing feature to this tranquil scene. The mother figure is lying in the garden, clearly the victim of a savage sexual assault. Her dress has been ripped from her torso and one of her arms is missing.

'What happened to her, Freda?' I ask.

'She had an accident,' she says, unconcerned, occupied with the tiny cups and saucers on the kitchen table.

'What sort of accident?' I ask.

'I don't know, Granny,' she says. Then she turns to look at me. 'I didn't do the accident,' she explains patiently. 'It was a long-ago accident.'

'So that's how you found her?'

'I'm afraid so.' She adopts a suitably mournful expression. 'It's quite sad, isn't it?'

'It is.' I pick the little figure up. It is oddly disturbing. The Salem witch trials come to mind – the evidence of mutilated 'poppets' got several people hanged, I think. But there is no witchcraft here, of course, just clumsy fingers. I saved the dolls' house for Ellie and didn't give it to her until she was old enough to enjoy it properly, but Annie got at it, of course, at an age when destruction is more fun than construction. She was probably trying to undress the little woman, I assume, and the arm was collateral damage. The fact that it was the mother figure that she maimed was surely incidental. There was no malice intended, was there?

Later, when I am cooking supper, the doorbell rings and I find Dora on the doorstep once again. She is white and ghostly in the lamplight.

'They've taken him,' she says. 'They've taken him, and I don't know what to do.'

Chapter Ten

DISGRACE

Tuesday 18th February 2014

Dora

There was nothing wrong with the revision schedule, as such, Dora Karalis thought, as she looked at it lying on her desk under her bedroom window. A lot of care and thought had gone into that schedule, and it looked great with its different colours for different subjects – blue for Greek, red for French, green for English. The mock exams would start as soon as they went back after half term and she had calculated nine hours work a day for six days – three hours per subject per day, eighteen hours per subject in total. She had been on several websites which gave advice about avoiding exam stress and she had followed their advice scrupulously: none of her work sessions was more than two hours long, she had sensible breaks scheduled for taking some exercise, eating and rewarding herself with treats. Those were important, all the websites agreed. Only the treats she had imagined were not the chocolate bars and exotic smoothies that she knew some of the other girls had planned. Her treats were to be calls to Farid, and now, without those, she couldn't even get started. She looked at her watch. It was ten-fifteen on the morning of the second day of her schedule and she was already nine and a half hours behind. She had managed three quarters of an hour the previous day, but she couldn't remember anything she had read and after her father had gone off to London for a church meeting she had crawled into bed and spent most of the day there. She looked again at her schedule. She could rewrite it, reallocating the sessions she had missed yesterday. The websites told you not to do that; a *distraction tactic* they called that, along with tidying your room, reorganising your books, taking the dog for a walk and making cups of coffee other than at the allocated times. Well, her schedule didn't include Sunday. She had given herself the day off on Sunday, as the websites advised, but she would work then, if she felt like it.

If she felt like it. She folded her arms over the mocking schedule with its neat boxes and bright colours, and laid her head on them. It was over a week now since her father had broken her heart. She knew that sounded melodramatic but it was the only way she could describe it – as though the heart had literally gone out of her, as if her body and mind were going on working mechanically but there was no blood pumping through her. She couldn't believe that her father – who did love her, she knew – could have done this to her. She kept thinking about how she had defended Prospero to Gina – the only time she had ever argued with Gina, she thought. She had said that Prospero put difficulties between Miranda and Ferdinand out of love, to make sure that Ferdinand didn't win her too easily. A bit of her still hoped that her father might be doing the same, that if she and Farid could keep loving each other even though they were kept apart, then he might, eventually, change his mind. But she couldn't get him to talk about it. *Let us just put it aside, Dora,* is all he would say when she tried to talk. *It was a mistake of youth. Now we forget it.* And he had been kind and gentle to her, as though she was convalescing from a serious illness. She couldn't hate him.

She sat up. She could hate Kelly Field, though, who had

told him about Farid before she had a chance to introduce them and make her father see what a good person Farid was. She could hate Kelly and she could be glad that she was dead – glad, actually, that someone else hated her enough to kill her.

She picked up her schedule. She would do this: it was her test, like Ferdinand being made to carry logs. If she worked hard and did well in her exams and made her father proud, then it could still be all right. If only she could just speak once to Farid, just to tell him that she had walked away with her father because she had to, because it would have disgraced all three of them if she had struggled and made a fuss in the street, that she loved him and would always love him, that she needed him to say that he loved her. Her father had taken her phone. He had asked her to promise not to see Farid and she had promised because she knew she couldn't see him without being spotted by someone, but when he asked her if she would promise not to ring Farid, she knew it was a promise she couldn't keep, so she had let him take the phone. She was almost sure she knew where it was, though. It would be on top of the wardrobe in her father's room, in the place where he kept birthday and Christmas presents. From when she was very small, presents had been kept up there, because she couldn't reach them. It never seemed to have occurred to him that it wasn't inaccessible to her any more. The day after he took the phone, she heard it ringing from somewhere in his room; since then it hadn't rung again. He had turned it off, she assumed, or it had run out of charge. Or Farid had stopped ringing. It would be so easy to go in and find it and just give Farid one call, but it would be the end of her and the person she was. It would be ignoble, she thought, and she wouldn't deserve Farid.

She looked at her schedule again: French. She took down from the shelf her copy of Maupassant's short stories. They suited her mood with their sad, bitter little twists. She thought he was an unkind writer but then the world was unkind, wasn't it? She started, pencil in hand, underlining words and phrases, occasionally rubbing out her old pencil notes and rewriting them, but she had been at it only a few minutes when the doorbell rang. Her father had gone down to the church. Most likely he had forgotten his door key again, she told herself, but she almost slid down the stairs because it might – just might – be Farid.

The young police detective was on the doorstep, the one who had questioned her about her copy of *The World's Wife*, but he had someone with him this time, a woman in a smart coat and high-heeled boots, who waved an ID card at her.

'DI Paula Powell,' she said, 'and this is —'

'DC Aaron Green,' he said. 'Theodora and I have met before.'

He smiled at her; she didn't smile back.

'May we come in?' DI Powell asked. Dora's knees felt so weak that she thought she might just fall down on the spot. Something bad had happened. To Farid.

'What's happened?' she asked.

'We'd just like to ask you a few questions.'

The woman spoke quite quietly, but she was giving her a narrow-eyed look that she didn't like. Dora looked at Aaron Green.

'What about?' she asked.

'About Farid Khalil,' DI Powell answered for him, and took a step into the doorway.

Dora stood back, distracted for a moment by the realisation that she hadn't even known what Farid's surname was. DI Powell strode past her and stopped at the sitting room door. 'We'll go in here, shall we?' she said, and walked in.

Dora tried a token protest. 'My father's not here,' she said. 'I want him to —'

'You're eighteen, Theodora,' DI Powell broke in. 'We can question you without your father present.'

'And it's just a few questions,' Aaron Green put in. 'No one's accusing you of anything, Dora. You do like to be called Dora, don't you?'

'I don't care,' she said.

They sat down, DI Powell in her father's chair by the fire, she on the sofa, where Aaron Green joined her. She had watched enough TV crime dramas to know that you were supposed to offer tea or coffee at this point, but she didn't. Her knees had stopped shaking and she was ready to fight for Farid. If they were trying to deport him – to pin some crime on him – because she had heard that was what they did – so that they would have an excuse, then they would get no help from her.

'I'll come straight to the point, Dora,' DI Powell said. 'We'd like to know about your relationship with Farid Khalil.'

'I don't know what you're talking about.' The answer came automatically and she wasn't sure why. They couldn't make anything of their relationship. She was eighteen and, anyway, she and Farid had never had sex. That was what *a relationship* meant, wasn't it? They had never done anything except sit on the bus together and talk.

'Come on. He's your boyfriend, isn't he?'

'No.' Which was, strictly speaking, true, Dora thought, at the moment.

'Yes, he is, Dora. You've been seeing each other. Kelly Field told your father about your relationship, and Farid threatened her, isn't that right?'

'People are lying. None of that is true.'

'We have spoken to your father, Dora. Is he a liar?'

'She lied to him,' she flashed back. 'She deceived him.'

'*She* meaning Kelly Field?'

Dora could feel her face growing hot. That was stupid, to

say *she*. 'Farid is not my boyfriend,' she said. 'We just talked sometimes on the bus to school. It was no big deal.'

'But your father thought it was, didn't he?'

She allowed herself a minimal shrug but said nothing.

'Where does Farid live, Dora?' Aaron Green asked. 'He lives somewhere in Dover, doesn't he?'

'Somewhere. I don't know.'

'You don't know his address?'

'No.'

'But he lives somewhere in Dover?'

'I suppose.'

'So what's he doing in St Martin's?'

She looked at him. 'He likes to cycle,' she said. 'Sometimes he borrows a bike and cycles along by the sea.'

'But that's not when you see him, is it? When he's cycling? We're talking about the bus.'

'Sometimes he takes the bus back again.'

'Why?'

'It's a long way.'

'Where did he borrow the bike from?' DI Powell asked.

She shrugged again. 'I don't know.'

'Did he travel with you on the bus the morning that Kelly Field died?'

'No.'

'Did you see him here in St Martin's that morning?'

'No.'

'One morning is much like another, isn't it? How can you be so sure?'

'Because I wasn't seeing him then. That was after my father –

'After your father stopped you from seeing him because Kelly Field told him what was going on and he threatened to make her sorry.'

Stupid. Another mistake. 'He didn't threaten her,' she said, 'and, anyway, if you think that's a reason for Farid to kill her, why couldn't I have done it?'

'Did you kill Kelly?'

'Maybe.'

Aaron Green said, 'You can't mess the police about, Dora. It'll get you into trouble.'

DI Powell said, 'We shall be asking your father about your movements that morning, and we shall need to take a look at your phone, your mobile. Can you fetch it?'

'I haven't got one.'

'Really? I find that hard to believe. Well, we can check that, with your father, too – he's down at the church, isn't he? If we find that you do have one, you could be charged with obstructing us in our inquiries, so I'll ask you again. Do you have a mobile phone?'

'No,' Dora said, looking her in the eye. 'I don't.'

DI Powell stood up. 'Well, we'll see,' she said. 'And we'll see what Farid says about your relationship.' She looked at her watch. 'We'll be having him in for questioning as soon as we've tracked him down.'

As soon as Dora had closed the door on them, she raced upstairs. She had no scruples now about looking for her phone. She needed to delete Farid's messages before the police got to her father and came back.

She couldn't feel anything as she groped along the top of the wardrobe as far as she could reach, but when she dragged a chair over and stood on it, she could see the phone, in a corner at the back. Snatching it, she replaced the chair, scuffing with her foot at the marks on the carpet made by the dragging. Then she locked herself in the bathroom and switched the phone on. It was not out of charge; her father had turned it off soon enough for that. As it came to life it buzzed and twittered with messages. Ten times Farid had tried to call her. And then there were the text messages. She scrolled rapidly through them. He thought she was ignoring him; it didn't seem to have occurred to him that her father would have taken the phone away. Now she was going to have to destroy them all. Precious as they were, she was too agitated now to grieve over them; she started pressing *delete*. Then there was the sound of the front door opening, her father's return. At the same time, she remembered that she had heard that you could retrieve deleted text messages if you knew what you were doing. She would have to destroy the sim card, but before she opened up the back of her phone, she scrolled to Farid's number and committed it to memory. Then she took the tiny card out. The sensible thing would be to flush it down the toilet but she couldn't bring herself to do it. It was her lifeline; without it, Farid would never be able to contact her again. She went to the airing cupboard. In there was her hot water bottle with its scruffy, padded Winnie the Pooh cover. She got it out, considered putting the card into the bottle itself but knew it would be too wet, then thought about the cover and the hole in the seam of one of Pooh's ears. She pushed the card deep into the ear and bundled bottle and cover to the back of the cupboard.

She put the phone itself in her pocket and emerged from the bathroom to meet her father on the landing.

'Are you all right, Dora?' he asked, and she realised that her face was red and sweaty.

'Stomach ache,' she said. 'You know…'

'Ah, yes.'

He was still embarrassed by references to her periods; it was mean to make use of that but this was no time for scruples. She slid past him into her room and closed the door. She waited until she heard him go back downstairs, then slipped along the landing and returned the phone to its hiding place. It wouldn't make much difference, really; when the police found the sim card was gone she would have to say she had destroyed it, and if they arrested her, well, so be it.

She went downstairs and heated up some soup for their lunch and, after avoiding the subject for a while, they eventually acknowledged that they had each had a visit from the police.

'What did you tell them?' he asked.

'There is nothing to tell,' she said. 'What did you tell them?'

He cut himself another slice of bread. 'I said nothing against the boy,' he said. 'I know nothing against him except that he saw my daughter in secret. That doesn't make him a murderer.'

'Of course he's not a murderer, Pappas. How could I love a murderer? He is the gentlest, kindest – he wants to be a doctor, to heal people! He —'

He held up a hand. 'We won't speak of it, Dora,' he said. 'Finish your soup. You're not eating enough and you need your strength.'

She swallowed a couple of spoonfuls and then sat rolling her bread into soggy pellets.

'Did they ask about my phone?' she asked.

'They did,' he said, and went on drinking his soup.

'And?' she asked.

'And what, Dora?'

'What did you say, Pappas?'

Still apparently absorbed in the business of drinking his soup, he said, 'Well, they asked me if you have a mobile phone and I gave them a truthful answer.'

'So you're going to give them the phone?'

'I gave them a truthful answer. You do not have a mobile phone at present, do you? So that is what I told them.'

She stared at him. 'You told them I have no phone?'

He wiped a piece of bread round his empty bowl. 'I

imagine that you have messages from that young man on your phone, and I would not wish them to become public property. My daughter's indiscretions are her own affair and they can have no relevance to this police inquiry.'

'So you do believe Farid isn't a murderer?'

For the first time in their conversation, he looked directly at her. 'I believe in you, *Dora mou*. I believe you would know if a boy was a murderer. I think we will leave the phone where it is and say nothing.' He got up from the table. 'I have a baptism this afternoon,' he said, 'and you have your English coaching. You have been distracted lately. I hope you have done your homework.'

'I'm just going to finish it now, Pappas.'

'Good girl.' He dropped a kiss on the top of her head and left the room.

She cleared the lunch things and waited for the sound of the front door closing. She watched from her father's bedroom window, checking that he wasn't going to turn back for something forgotten, then went downstairs, picked up the phone in the hall and dialled Farid's number. This way the sim card could stay where it was, at least, and Farid's messages need not be public property. But they would take Farid's phone, of course, and find her messages, unless he got rid of it. She had to warn him.

He answered warily. 'Yes?'

She couldn't speak; her mouth was so dry she couldn't prise her lips open.

'Dora?' he asked. Had he heard her breathing?

Then she spoke, the words tumbling out as though she needed to say everything at the same time. 'The police want, you – they think you killed Kelly – or they're pretending they think that – they'll try to send you back home and I tried not to tell them about us but they know and they're looking for you – my father took my phone – I couldn't get your messages but now I did and I hid my sim card – you have to get rid of your phone – they'll see our messages about Kelly and they'll use them to get you.' She stopped. 'I love you,' she said.

She thought she could hear him smiling as he said, 'You could win a prize for speed speaking, Dora. Don't worry. I'm not worried. I've done nothing wrong and no one is going to be able to say that I have. If the police are looking for me, I'll go to see them and we'll sort it out. Even if the Border Agency is rubbish, I still believe in British justice. Where are you phoning from?'

'My house. The house phone.'

'Ring me later, if you can. I'll tell you how I've got on. And don't worry.'

'But your phone —'

'I love you,' he said, and hung up.

She stood, holding the receiver until it started to wail its complaint at being off the hook. Then she put on her coat, ran upstairs for her key and left the house. A surge of restless energy carried her down to the seafront, where she hurtled down the steps and started running along the wet sand, head first into the ferocious, rain-filled wind. She ran until her chest burned too much to carry on, and then stopped and leaned against a breakwater, gasping and heaving. She wanted to run on, because stopping made space in her head for terror, but she couldn't. Her legs were shaking and it still hurt to breathe. She turned and walked back, glad of the wind driving behind her. She looked at her watch. It was after three. At four she had a coaching session with Gina and she had no essay to take to her. She had lied to her father; there had never been a chance of her finishing an essay this afternoon, even without Farid's call. She had managed one paragraph yesterday before giving up and going back to bed. What was the point, after all? It was just stupid, wasn't it, to be worrying about a 400-year-old play when the real drama was here, in her own life?

Back at home, she turned the TV on and sat, without taking her coat off, watching children's programmes until she realised that it was after four, and she trailed, unwillingly, back to the seafront, to Gina's house, where Gina talked and her words slid like warm oil off the surface of Dora's mind.

As she walked back into the house, the phone was ringing. She picked it up without any particular expectation and heard Farid's voice, ragged and rasping.

'Dora. Thank God. I've been trying —'

'I was at my English class. Is it the police? What's happened, Farid?'

'No, not the police. At least, I don't think – I don't know.'

She heard him draw a long, shaky breath.

'I'm in detention, Dora.'

'So it is the police.'

'No. Immigration. The Border Agency. I went to the police station. They were pretty aggressive but they couldn't keep me – they've got no evidence. So they took my phone – sorry – and let me go. But the Border Agency guys were waiting for me outside. The police must have told them I would be there. They say I'm a murder suspect, so that changes my status as an asylum seeker. They've got me in the IRC.'

'Where's that?'

'The Immigrant Removal Centre. You know, it's the big place like a castle, up on the hill.'

'But that's a prison. They can't put you in a prison. You haven't done anything —"

'Well, they can. I think they can do pretty much what they like. I think – I've been thinking about this while I've been trying to get through to you – I think they can't send me back to Syria – not yet – because I have an asylum application pending. But I think the police are using this to keep me in detention. They can't keep me themselves because they haven't got a case against me, but they can keep me here and make sure I don't sneak away and join the illegals in London or somewhere.'

'You need a lawyer, Farid. Surely you're entitled to a lawyer? On TV —'

'I have a lawyer for my asylum case but I don't think he's any good. Everyone says the asylum lawyers are the worst. It's the lowest-paid work and nobody wants it. There are just a few good ones who do it from good motives, but mine isn't one of them. So here's the thing. I'm allowed this one call but I don't know if or when I'll be allowed another one. So I have to rely on you, Dora. You have to find me a good lawyer.'

'I…' She felt stupid and helpless. She had no idea how to find a lawyer, let alone judge if they were any good. 'I'll try, Farid,' she whispered. 'I'll do anything I —'

'There are two people who might help. There's Ernest at the drop-in place at St Saviour's Church. He may know of someone good. The other person – and you know her, so it might be easier – is Gina. She knows a lot of people; she's the kind of person who gets things done. I think she may be the person to ask.'

Chapter Eleven

THE OLD DEVILS

Wednesday 19th February 2014

When Dora came back to see me yesterday with her wretched news, I knew absolutely what I had to do. Farid needs the best human rights lawyer I can find. I can't tell myself that if he's done nothing wrong, nothing bad will happen to him. I know that's not true. He is in genuine danger of being stitched up. And I know just the man to sort this out. I know him very well, actually; I used to be married to him.

Andrew Gray, my former husband, is quite distinguished in the human rights field these days. When he was married to me, he was no more than a wannabe, really, but in the past fifteen years he has done some quite flashy things – cases at The Hague and everything. And, if I ask him, he will do this for me, I am sure, because he will want to impress me. It frustrates him, you see, that I, who know him so well, am the one person who doubts his motives and fails to be impressed by him.

So, last night, my way was clear. I intended to ring him first thing in the morning, put the case to him and give Dora the good news that Farid was in expert hands. This was, I knew, the right thing to do. It is now ten-thirty, however, and I have not picked up the phone. This morning, I see things differently. This morning, I am a worse person than I was yesterday. This morning, my fifteen-year grudge against Andrew has me in its thrall and I am motivated by self-centred pride. This morning, I cannot bear to give Andrew the satisfaction of riding to the rescue and meriting my admiration. This morning, I move to plan B.

What I tell myself is that Farid is not, actually, in imminent danger. Of course, he would like to get out of the IRC, and I would like to get him out, but a better approach presents itself. I will find out who killed Kelly Field, I will present Paula with the evidence and Farid will have to be released. Then, I tell myself, then I will contact Andrew and ask him to help Farid with his asylum application: a nice, low-level job, nothing dramatic. I shall be quite happy with that. I hope you understand that I'm not proud of any of this and what it says about me. The only thing I can say in mitigation is that this course of action does present dangers for me: Paula Powell has threatened me with the full majesty of the law if I interfere in this case, so I am taking a risk. I'm not all bad, you see.

I can't start thinking about my plan until Freda goes home. Her mother will be picking her up later this morning, but in the meantime I am fully occupied, first with pancakes for breakfast, then with tracking down her belongings, scattered liberally about the house, and then with the issue of a present to take home to her little brother. This last demand came as a blow, since it looked as though I would be forced to make the trek into Dungate to find something suitable. I feel guilty about minding the inconvenience of the village shop's being closed – it's like minding the inconvenience of being in a tailback on the motorway because of a fatal accident – but I am beginning to think that we may have to organise a community shop as well as a community library. How very *Archers*.

Without much hope of success, I suggest that we make

some chocolate crispies for Nico, but Freda has a better idea; she will draw him a picture of the sea, she says. And so we wrap ourselves up and go and stand by the sea wall to study the scene. Freda has insisted on bringing her sketchbook and her new pastel crayons with her, to draw the picture *in situ*, but the wind blows the paper about, the fine mist smudges the pastels and she can't draw with her gloves on, so she declares that she will draw it *from my mind* and we go back inside.

My offers of creative criticism are rejected so I occupy myself with trawling the house for Freda's abandoned paraphernalia. I find her pyjama bottoms and a hair scrunchie in Caliban's basket, where he has made a sort of nest of them and is lying in it with a distinctly sheepish expression on his face. I look into his eyes, trying to fathom his motivation. Is he jealous of Freda because she owns things? Does he love her and want the smell of her close to him? Would he take my clothes to bed with him if I left them lying around on the floor? I have no idea. Dogs ought to be simpler to fathom than people, but Caliban is a complete mystery to me. A friend of mine, who studied philosophy at university, wrote an answer in her Finals paper to the question, *If I think my cat is a person, what kind of mistake am I making?* Really, we should all study philosophy, I think, because we all ought to consider these things.

When Freda calls me to show her finished work, I am as bewildered by her as I have been by Caliban. She has done a rather good, slightly post-impressionist picture of sand, sea and sky but the sea and sky are in vibrant shades of blue and the gold of the sand is echoed in the large golden sun that presides over all. This, then, is what comes from Freda's mind – not the picture she has been seeing for the past three days – a bleak study in relentless, dirty greys and browns – but the *schema* of the seaside, the picture-postcard, half-a-dozen-days-a-year-if-you're-lucky model of the English seaside that remains lodged in our heads and refuses to be dislodged by any amount of empirical evidence to undermine it. The notion of the *schema* is one I like. It explains a lot about the way we experience everything from books and paintings to war and motherhood. Before I share with you my thoughts on *schemata*, I'm afraid I have to go on a brief diversion about plurals, though; in my former life I taught linguistics, you see, and these obsessions die hard. If this bores you, feel free to skip the next paragraph.

Schema is a Greek word, and though I have come across references to *schemas*, really the plural should be formed in the Greek way – *schemata*. It's the same pattern as *stigmata* – one scar is a *stigma*, many scars are *stigmata*. A lot of these Greek (and Latin) plurals are regarded as optional these days, but I like them. Whatever happened to *syllabi*, for example? When I started my teaching career, that was the plural of *syllabus*; now they're *syllabuses*, making me think of a party of double-deckers in a frisky mood. That's all right, though. Language changes; English has always adapted foreign words and anglicised them. They become so English that an 's' ending for the plural is completely natural. The problem, though, with losing sight of these plurals is that if a word doesn't have an 's' on the end, some of us don't recognise that it's plural at all. Take *panini*, for example (the Italian sandwiches). They are plural already. They don't need an 's' on the end. Will someone tell the catering trade this? If you want to know whether an 'Italian' deli is really Italian, see whether they put 's' on their panini. One sandwich is a *panino*, by the way. But it is the Latin plural 'a' ending that is the greatest casualty. We seem to get on all right with *data* (one item of information is a *datum*, several are *data*). *Data* feel plural – there are clearly lots of facts – so we say *The data suggest/demonstrate/support* and so on. So why can't we deal with *media*? Aren't media obviously plural, too? TV is a medium, radio is a medium, the press is a medium; together they form the media. And yet I hear all sorts of people say, *the media is*. What do they mean? What do they imagine this singular *media* is? I am mystified. In the interests of full disclosure, I should admit that even Shakespeare could get these things wrong. Latin and Greek he could cope with but he came unstuck with Hebrew. Prospero, in *the Tempest*, tells Miranda that when she was an infant she was *a cherubim*, but we all know that the cherubim and seraphim are plural, don't we? She was just a cherub. Though, thinking about it, I wonder if Will knew this quite well but went with *cherubim* anyway because it fitted the iambic pentameter so well. Pedantry can't always win out.

Well, now I've got that off my chest, back to the *schema*. I'm talking to you about this not just *vis-à-vis* Freda's picture, but because I think it has relevance to murder inquiries and it may help me with my current project. *Schema* is a term from cognitive psychology. A schema is a mental structure, a preconceived idea. A stereotype, if you like. Together, our schemata form a framework for our understanding of the world and we fit new ideas into this framework. What psychologists have found is that people are more likely to notice things that fit into a pre-existing schema, and confronted with a contradiction to a schema they will be likely to reinterpret it as an exception or distort it to fit. Schemata are remarkably tenacious: we depend on them for making sense of our experiences and we resist evidence that challenges them. Thus, in Freda's mental world, the sun's taking a winter break and leaving the beach to the wind and the rain has done nothing to shift her seaside schema. Her yellow sun even has a smiley face. Well, good for her, I suppose.

I've been thinking a lot about our schema for asylum seekers and refugees because I think this is one that has actually changed quite radically. You can't know, of course, what other people's schemata are like exactly, and I suppose my earliest asylum-seeker schema was influenced by *The Railway Children*. Do you remember the Russian who collapses on the railway station and is rescued by the children and their mother, who talks with him in French? Add this to Karl Marx and other bearded émigrés working in the British Museum Reading Room, and that's a schema I still have tucked away. Other schemata have nudged it out of the way, though, as the ripples from one conflict after another have washed the persecuted and homeless onto our less and less welcoming shores. I remember the Ugandan Asians, thrown out by Idi Amin: I remember the solemn-eyed, tongue-tied brown children who started arriving at my primary school. They would gather in a huddle in the playground, talking unintelligibly to each other, while we ignored them, swirling and yelling around them in our raucous London way, and then, at some point, when we weren't noticing, they stopped being separate and became part of the general mayhem. Successful integration, you would have to call it, but those solemn, bewildered faces form another asylum schema for me.

Then, our twenty-first-century schemata are different again. I'm not sure how conscious I was of choosing my metaphor when I said that the ripples from global conflicts were washing refugees up on our shores, but watery images dominate our discourse about asylum seekers these days: they come in waves, they threaten to swamp us, we fear being overwhelmed. And then there is the literal wateriness, the horror of men, women and children set afloat in leaky boats by the traffickers and dragged ashore half-drowned if they are very lucky. So we sit in our living rooms and watch all this on television and the schemata jostle with each other in our overheated brains because while fear has started to dominate, fostered by the relentless rhetoric of the right-wing papers and the craven politicians who trail in their wake, fear that we shall drown under the waves of would-be immigrants rolling onto our shores, at the same time, we haven't – yet – altogether lost our humanity, so another schema battles for space – the schema presented by the beleaguered Italians, pulling their fellow humans out of the sea week after week and offering them, once they are on land, what I – faith-free though I am – can only call Christian kindness. It's a schema we like, don't we? We would like to think that we would do the same. If it weren't for the numbers.

Ah, the numbers. It is the numbers that dehumanise, wouldn't you say? They both take away our humanity and – with alarming ease – they make us see desperate people as less that human. Which takes me to my third schema: the hideous makeshift camps – the jungles – in Calais, in which destitute refugees eke out an existence somehow and from which, night after night, young men – and women – even pregnant ones – desperate to the point of insanity, try to get onto lorries coming through the tunnel to us. The metaphors here are not watery ones, they are about infestation: the men *swarm* out of the camps, they *crawl* into lorries or *cling on* to their outsides. What can we do about such infestation except, like good householders, repel it with any means available to us? How can we be so foolish as to attract it with the lure of a weekly pittance to live on – surely the equivalent of putting out dollops of jam to invite an army of ants into your kitchen? With this schema, there comes no counter-schema like that offered by the benevolent Italians. The French people seem untroubled by the inhumanity of the Calais jungles, by the beatings and harassment by the police. Why aren't they out on the streets protesting at this blot on a civilised country? They take to the streets at the drop of a hat, the French – they regard it as a god-given right. Why are they silent about this?

Well, there we are. None of this is new to you, I know. I don't pretend that my analysis is clever or original – or even right, necessarily – but I thought the language aspect might be enlightening. And I have one more thing to say which just might make a difference to our asylum-seeker schemata: just 2 per cent of the world's asylum seekers are in the UK. People seek asylum, very largely, in a neighbouring country and since our neighbours are blessed with the same security and stability as we are, we are really not a target source of refuge, whatever anyone may tell us about the magnetic draw of the princely £36.95 a week we provide to those seeking asylum here.

Enough. I must peel potatoes and make sausages and mash for us all for lunch. Freda has ordered this as it is Nico's favourite, and I am touched by her affection for her little brother. It shows a nice nature, I think.

Ellie and Nico arrive in good time and I call Freda in from the garden, where she has been talking to Sam and Joe through a hole in the fence. We eat lunch early. I have a lot to think about and would like to despatch them fairly smartly but it would not do to let this show, so I offer second helpings, I dish up apple crumble and ice cream for pudding and I encourage Freda to discourse on the delights of her seaside break. She does this pretty well, though children have a gift for lighting on the small and insignificant, with hardly a passing nod to the main events. Come to think of it, quite a lot of adults do that, too; there is no legislating for what will grab the imagination. So Freda talks about pancakes, the creaky floorboard in her bedroom, Ariel's refusal to sleep on her bed and *Harry Potter and the Goblet of Fire*. 'And Granny's not a witch,' she adds sadly, 'even she's got a broomstick.' Then she brightens. 'But Sam and Joe's mummy has gone away,' she says, and opens her arms with a dramatic flounce. 'Simply vanished!'

I am taken by surprise. What makes Freda think that Alice

has vanished? Her departure was a bit sudden, it's true, and Simon was a bit cagey about it, but I didn't think Freda had noticed anything odd. She was talking to the boys earlier, though; maybe they said something about Alice vanishing. I look at Ellie. 'A row,' I mouth silently, but Freda has no inhibitions.

'They shouted,' she says, 'her and Sam's dad, and now they don't know where she is.' She picks up her spoon and returns to her pudding. 'Joe was crying,' she says through a mouthful of crumble.

Ellie seems inclined to linger by the woodburner and it takes a couple of prompts by me about getting home before dark to get them on their way. Once they are gone, I make myself a cup of tea and sit down with a notepad. Freda has alarmed me about Alice. If Simon can't tell the boys where Alice is, that is worrying. Alice is devoted to her boys; what could possibly make her go out of contact completely? Even if she wants to punish Simon, why wouldn't she ring and reassure the boys? But the Alice issue I am putting on the back burner for the moment. I have only so much brain space and I have more urgent obligations.

Kelly Field, I write at the top of the page. *Murdered Feb 13th 2014*. And underneath that I write, *Means, Motive, Opportunity*. Means is simple: Kelly was pushed off the sea wall and then had her head bashed on the pebbles. This last detail was revealed to me unguardedly by Paula Powell; it is not in the public domain. It tells me that whoever pushed her really wanted her to die, was prepared to take the risk of going down onto the beach (not so much of a risk, really, since the weather was vile and it was still semi-dark) and was angry or ruthless enough to kill at close quarters. My amateur sleuthing experience tells me that it would be misguided to rule out a female perpetrator just because a lot of physical force was involved, so the means hardly helps in narrowing the field of suspects.

Which takes us on to motive. Paula, of course, thinks she has found her motive, but any reader of crime novels knows that the person who says *You'll be sorry for this* never turns out to be the killer. So, setting aside Farid, who else? Well, I still have my suspicions of Matt and those big hands of his. I'm not sure what his relationship with Kelly was like but there was something quite aggressive about both of them that time I saw them together. I don't remember exactly what was said, but I do remember that she yelled at him that he *fucking better* come round tomorrow, and that when I commented that he was a nice lad (what made me say that?) she said, *That's all you know*. Hardly love's young dream, were they?

However, the main clue to motive, I still believe, is the book. And not just the book but the page it was open at, with the Medusa poem highlighted. The female monster who turns men to stone – who unmans them, you might say. Are we talking about someone who suffered sexual humiliation by Kelly? Or just someone who resents women in general and whatever female assertiveness he feels our book group stands for? In either case, it has to be someone with connections to the book group and we went through the husbands and boyfriends the other night and sort of ruled them all out. However, it is worth giving them another thought. I write down:

Matt O'Dowd	*(Kelly)*
Don Dering	*(Lorna)*
Peter Harper	*(Lesley)*
Simon Gates	*(Alice)*

And then, because I am determined to be scrupulously impartial, I add:

Farid Khalil	*(Dora)*

I start with the first four names, though. Matt is already a suspect in my mind, and I remember how he looked at Kelly's copy of *The World's Wife* and called it *one of those women-getting-their-own-back books*. I put an asterisk against his name. Then there is Don Dering. I must be dispassionate here and not discount him just because I'm fond of Lorna and I couldn't bear it to be him. However, I have met him a few times and if he is a secret woman-hater then he hides it very well. He gives every impression of being both fond and proud of Lorna, and she has the serene composure of a woman who has a good man at home. And if we're thinking of a particular grudge against Kelly, I really can't put him and Kelly into the same mental frame. He is a rather good-looking man of the fair, unobtrusive kind, with a Scottish accent modified by years of life in the South so that it just gives a gently ironic edge to his remarks. He has two passions (besides Lorna, I assume) and these are his job as an ecologist, trying to protect the local wildlife from the effects of cliff erosion, and playing the cello. So, you see, he is a gentle, serious, cultured man and, even taking into account the unpredictability of sexual attraction, I can't see how he could have been drawn to Kelly, who was neither good-looking nor serious nor cultured. I may be deceiving myself here, but I'm not giving him anything more than a question mark. Peter Harper, Lesley's husband, really can be ruled out. The fact that he was 'away' when Kelly was killed, can't, of course, be taken on trust: if the killing was premeditated, then that could have been a blind. However, his gammy leg really does rule him out, I think. I don't altogether accept Lesley's defence that he wouldn't have been able to climb through people's windows to steal their library books, because there are other, more cunning ways of doing it, I imagine, but the picture of him jumping out to push Kelly over the wall and then hobbling down the slippery steps with his stick, lowering himself painfully onto the pebbles to finish her off and then starting the long, effortful ascent seems just crazy. If he had wanted to kill her, wouldn't he have chosen a more convenient way?

So this takes me to Simon Gates, and he is certainly worth an asterisk. That man is a bully: his children are scared of him and I happen to know, because I'm the kind of person people tell things to, that his first wife divorced him on the grounds of cruelty. Also he drinks in the pub with the old codgers and, no doubt, shares their attitudes. Horrid Harry, our neighbour, is one of the codgers and Simon is pretty thick with him – given to blokey chats over the fence. Simon doesn't like the book group and it is just possible, I suppose, that he could have got himself involved with Kelly. Kelly was plain, dim and sour-tempered, while Alice Gates is pretty, bright and nice, so it seems improbable, but there's no understanding men. I put an asterisk against Simon's name.

I had, in my mind, ruled out the old codgers because, although their stupid remarks irritate the hell out of me, I couldn't think of them as ruthless killers. There are three of them, including Harry – the other two going by the inventive names of Chalky and Taff – and they are all in their seventies and not spry for their age, so they are unlikely candidates all round. There is George, though, I realise suddenly, as I visualise the corner where they hang out of an evening. George Mead is the landlord of the pub, the man who labelled us *The Broomstick Brigade*. He is a thick-set man, in his fifties, I suppose, with the ruined complexion of a drinker and a head of extraordinarily inauthentic black hair. I don't know if he ever had a wife but he doesn't have one now. The black hair suggests that he's a vain man; could he have been seduced and then dumped by Kelly? Then another thought comes to me – one that is enough to produce a sort of nervous fizz in my brain. Lily died while she was cleaning the pub windows. Didn't Jack say that George was there when he ran round to the back of the building after he heard the crash of the ladder falling? I write down *George Mead* and put a box round it. I haven't lost sight of what Eva told us the other night: *It was clear to me that Jack does not think that Lily's death was an accident.* Paula pooh-poohed the serial killer scenario on the grounds, partly, that anyone who hated the book group would pick me off first, as the most eminently infuriating member of the group, but it is a question of opportunity, isn't it? I'm actually quite hard to get rid of because I generally have a dog with me – a mild-natured dog, in actual fact, but with a distinctly threatening demeanour. It is possible that someone killed both Lily and Kelly simply because they had the opportunity.

Opportunity. Well, the killer obviously had to know about Kelly's morning swim habit, but that doesn't narrow the field much because nothing much goes unnoticed in our cosy hamlet. Matt obviously knew about it, and so did Simon Gates, presumably, since she jogged past our houses every morning, and he could well have told George and the codgers about it. On the other hand, Don Dering and Peter Harper are less likely to have known. They both live inland and though their wives knew about it, as everyone in the book group did, they aren't gossipy types. And Farid knew about it, I'm pretty sure. He must have seen her sometimes when he returned my bike early in the morning. I'm not going to think about that yet.

Knowing that Kelly would be there wasn't enough, of course; you would need somewhere to wait and take her by surprise. This bit of thinking can't be done from my armchair. I drag myself away from the seductive embrace of the woodburner, pull on my anorak and push open the front door into the gusty, darkening afternoon. I walk along to the end cottage – Jack Terry's – and walk a little way up the passageway that runs beside it. This, I am sure, is the route Kelly used to take. It's the way I always walked to the shop, the obvious route. I turn and walk back onto the pavement and across the road to the sea wall. I stop there, more or less exactly where Kelly must have gone over the wall, and I see a problem. Running out of the passageway and heading for the steps at the other end of the terrace, wouldn't it have been natural to cross the road at slant, in the direction of the steps, especially at that hour of the morning when there would have been no traffic on the road? In that case, she wouldn't have stood opposite the end of the passageway at all. Come to think of it, she wouldn't have stood anywhere. She was jogging, wasn't she? And pushing a moving target over that wall would have required strength, speed and surprise. Someone would have needed to hide and then take a rush at her. A male someone almost certainly. But she wouldn't have ended up where she did; she would have been nearer the steps. And Caliban and I would have heard something. I have to rethink this.

Did someone waylay her as she came out of the passageway? Someone she knew, who greeted her and then gave her a shove? I try to imagine it. From a standing start and facing her it would have been very difficult to push her over, wouldn't it? She was strong from all that swimming; wouldn't she have pushed back? Surely she must have been pushed from behind, but why would she have been standing there? I stand and look out to sea myself and a memory edges in. When the children were small, and Andrew was still around, we rented a cottage on the Sussex coast for a fortnight one summer. It was virtually on the beach. You opened a gate at the end of the garden and stepped straight onto the pebbles. It was great for swimming because you could get into swimming costumes in the house and then run down onto the beach. Except no one ever, I think, just ran out and straight down into the sea. You always stopped and took in the sea for a moment, assessed its roughness and the state of the tide and looked for other swimmers. Wouldn't Kelly have done that, too, before turning and running to the steps?

I know where the most likely hiding place would be for a waiting killer. There is a side gate into Jack's garden from the passageway and I don't think it is ever locked. I don't think Jack and Lily locked anything; friends and band members seemed to let themselves in and out at will. You could lurk there, listen for Kelly running by, rush across the road and surprise her with a hard shove. And, I have to admit, a woman could have done it.

In theory, at any rate, though when I consider the members of the book group – who have to be considered first because of the book connection – they seem most unlikely candidates. Eva can certainly be ruled out as too frail, and Lesley and Lorna, though fit and healthy, are women in their fifties and no match for a strong young woman, even with the advantage of surprise. Which leaves, Dora, who had a motive of sorts but is tiny, and Alice, who seems, suddenly, alarmingly possible. She would certainly have been aware of Kelly's morning routine and could have watched her out of one of those angled front windows any time. And she would have known about the open gate from the passageway. If Kelly had threatened her marriage, could she have done it? She is quite a steely young woman, and now she has disappeared. Keeping out of the way while the police blunder off in another direction? I go indoors, add her name to my list of suspects and put a box round it. Then I make another pot of tea and think some more.

The books. Those are what Paula and her crew seem to have forgotten about now they have found a stellar suspect in a dodgy asylum seeker who was heard to threaten the victim just days before she was killed. What possible reason would Farid have had for leaving a copy of *The World's Wife* beside her body? His grudge against her was specific – she had informed on him and Dora – so the turning-men-to-stone theme was irrelevant for him. And where would he have got the book from, since Dora's book was still safely in her briefcase? Well, I know what Paula's answer will be to that: she will say that it was my book. Borrowing my bike, popping in for cups of tea, generally making himself at home, she will say, he had opportunities galore to pinch my book. You will notice that my musings have moved from the conditional to the indicative; I am considering what Paula *will* say. You are right. I am going to have to ring Paula and get her to look at this. Has she even taken the surviving copies of the book to be examined? I didn't go in to the library while Freda was with me, so I don't know. I pick up the phone. It is Lesley who answers.

'Lesley,' I say, after the usual preliminaries, 'have the police taken the copies of *The World's Wife* away?'

'No,' she says, 'but Lorna has put a DO NOT TOUCH notice on the box.'

'Right,' I say. 'I'm going to make a phone call. If I get arrested, will you make sure Caliban and Ariel are all right?'

She laughs. 'Who's going to arrest you, Gina?'

'Detective Inspector Powell. She has warned me off interfering in her case.'

'Then don't interfere.'

'It's not so easy. Young lives depend on me and I am beset by guilt.'

There is a brief silence. 'Have you been doing a bit of daytime tippling?' she asks. 'The dark winter afternoons getting to you?'

'Sober as a judge. Soberer than many, I imagine. They've put Farid Khalil in the IRC.'

'Dora's secret boyfriend?'

'Yes. They took him in for questioning about Kelly, and then spirited him off to the IRC. I think they're determined to pin her death on him.'

'It's a terrible place, the IRC. I used to go in there sometimes for work.'

'Lesley,' I say. 'That's brilliant.'

'Brilliant how, exactly?' she asks.

'I need to get to see Farid and I don't know how to do it. But you know the ropes.'

'I'm not a social worker any more, Gina. I don't —'

'Yes, you do. Come for coffee tomorrow and we can talk. If DI Powell hasn't taken me into custody. In which case you'll find a hungry cat and dog and the key in the hanging basket by the front door.'

I ring off and, without giving myself time for second thoughts, I pick up Paula's card from beside the phone and dial. She is about as unfriendly as I expect her to be. She recognises my voice immediately and says, 'What do you want, Gina?'

I had intended to be emollient, to win her by a combination of reason and tact to see the error of her ways and come round to my way of thinking, but I hear myself say, instead, 'The books, Paula. Why aren't forensics onto them? Why are they sitting in the library office getting contaminated?'

'Gina, have you actually got any information for me or have you just rung to harass me, because I have to tell you –'

'Yes, I have got information for you. You are way off track. You think you can pin the murder on Farid Khalil because he's an asylum seeker and defenceless, but you won't find the real killer unless you find out whose book it was that was left on the beach.'

'Well, we don't actually think the book is of much importance, Gina, but we know whose book it was, anyway. It was yours, wasn't it? Khalil had several opportunities to take it from your house. Or did you give it to him?'

What did I tell you?

'And the other books?' I ask. 'How did he get hold of

those? Eva Majoros's, Lesley Harper's, Alice Gates's? We don't even know whose books we've got in the box, do we? We don't know what kind of game has been going on. I don't understand why you haven't taken all our fingerprints and checked them out. We're all willing to have our prints taken if it will help to find the actual killer rather than a convenient scapegoat.'

'What did I say to you, Gina?' she asks. 'Didn't I warn you about involving yourself in this investigation? You are treading on such thin ice, you really —'

'You threatened to prosecute me for tampering with evidence because I brought the book in off the beach. Now you're saying the book isn't important. You can't have it both bloody ways, Paula.'

There is a short silence. 'Oh yes I can,' she says.

Chapter Twelve

THE BLIND ASSASSIN

Wednesday 19th February and Thursday 20th February 2014

Eva

Eva Majoros drove sedately into the designated parking space in front of the library and came to a halt. She gave the handbrake an extra tug for safety's sake and climbed carefully out of her car. She locked the car and walked circumspectly across the few icy yards to the library doors, taking short steps in her high-heeled, fur-trimmed boots. They were unwise footwear for these conditions, she knew, and her bossier friends – Gina and Lesley, in particular – would tell her off if they could see her, but they were really only small heels and if she had to start plodding about in clumpy flats then she might as well just give up – *throw in the towel, give up the ghost, call it a day* – she liked those English expressions.

Safely at the door, she turned and flashed her key at her car to be certain that she really had locked it, then put away the car key and drew out the library keys from their designated pocket in her handbag. This – just these few moments – were what she didn't like about doing this evening duty at the library. Otherwise, she quite enjoyed it. It was just on Wednesdays that they opened in the evening and she and Gina were happy to manage these evenings between them;

people with families were not so keen. She turned the key in the lock, forcing it through the point where it always stuck, and then, as the door swung inwards, she groped to her left, found the light switch, and flicked it down. As light flooded the room, she let out a breath. Done. All well. She turned the notice on the door to *Open* and closed it behind her.

Walking through to the issues desk, she considered taking off her coat but decided it was not warm enough yet. She went into the office, where she took off her hat, examined herself in the small mirror on the wall and tidied her hair. She looked round the room, noticed that the box of copies of *The World's Wife* was still there, considered looking inside to see if any more books had turned up, decided to heed Lorna's DO NOT TOUCH message on the lid, switched off the light and went out.

She looked at the clock on the wall – a traditional school clock with Roman numerals. It was just seven o'clock. Seven-thirty to eight-thirty was the time most people came – half a dozen of them at most, probably. She checked the pile of reserved books and saw that a couple of them were for Wednesday evening regulars. Then she turned her attention to the returned books trolley. She organised the books into Dewey Decimal order and proceeded round the room, returning them to their places. This was always a pleasure. She liked to think about people reading the books and she liked the orderliness of putting them in their allotted places. There was nowhere as comforting as a library if you were a person who liked order.

When she got to the far end of the room, she decided she would have to go to the lavatory. *Cold weather and old age*, she thought irritably. *A fatal combination.* It would be better to go now, before anyone arrived, but it was such a performance. Berating herself in Hungarian, she took the bunch of library keys out of her bag, unlocked the door at the back of the room, waited for the security light to come on and crossed the corner of the school playground to unlock a side door of the school and use the staff lavatory. Then, locking doors carefully behind her, she returned to the library.

It was still empty but there was something in the atmosphere – a hint of cold, fresh air – that made her pause and listen. Nothing. She took up her trolley from where she had left it and proceeded on her way round the room. It was when she got back to the desk that she saw that the office door was open and light spilling out of it. Had she not turned it off? They were as careful as they could be about the lighting and heating; as it was the electricity bill ate up most of their small grant. She felt certain that she had turned the light off but she was getting frighteningly forgetful – a stupid old woman. '*Buta öregasszony*,' she muttered as she trotted to the office door and pushed it open.

She was never able to describe properly what happened after that. She caught just the briefest glimpse of scattered books, and then 'Like a whirlwind' was all she could say. 'Not even like a person. Just a force. And down I went. Pouff!' But it was a person, of course, she knew that. She caught a whiff of something familiar and human, heard him run out and the library door slam behind him, felt the blast of cold air from outside as she lay with her head under the desk, feeling no pain as yet, only the roughness of the cheap carpet on her cheek.

The pain came as soon as she tried to move. It was a deep wrenching pain in her arm that made her gasp and brought on an alarming loosening of her bowels. 'Not that,' she prayed. 'Dear God, not that.'

It was, surprisingly, Jack Terry who found her and he was, as she told the police officer later, very kind. He phoned for an ambulance, took his jacket off and put it over her because she was shivering, turned the notice on the door to *Closed* and dispatched a couple of people, who tried to come in all the same, with 'Piss off. There's been an accident here.' Then he sat down on the floor beside her, lifted her head in its awkward position under the desk so that she could take a few sips of water and talked to her, quietly, until the ambulance arrived. He told her he had come in looking for one of the graphic novels he liked. He wasn't much of a reader, he said, and he didn't have a library ticket of his own, but Lily used to get one out for him on her ticket sometimes, and he'd hoped he could get one this evening because he wasn't sleeping much and it would help to pass the time. 'Better than the bottle,' he said. 'Been doing too much of that. Lily'd be furious.'

When the ambulance arrived, being loaded onto a stretcher was briefly agonising but then one of the ambulance people – a nice young woman – gave her an injection, which eased the pain but made it harder to answer questions. Questions. So many questions. How? When? Why? What? She could tell them nothing; her mind seemed to float free. And then, finally, there was oblivion and waking up with a dry mouth and a great weight on her right arm. And that woman police officer with more questions.

'What did you see in the room?' she persisted. 'When you opened the door, what did you see?'

She was so tired. Opening her mouth to say yet again that she had seen nothing, she said instead, 'The books. The books were out of the box.'

She saw the colour flood into the young woman's face. 'What books would those have been?' she asked.

'Our book,' she mumbled. *'World's Wife.'*

As she started to slide back into sleep, she thought she heard the young woman say something. She wasn't sure, but she thought she said, 'Oh, fuck!'

When she woke again, a cold morning light was seeping into the room and she lay, piecing together her recollections of the previous evening, remembering the vicious pain and afraid to move for fear of rousing a nagging ache into fury again. A nurse appeared, surveyed her, took her temperature, said, 'Good', asked if she needed a bed pan and disappeared. Later, they raised her into a sitting position, brought her a cup of tea – with milk in it, which she hated – and she gradually felt strong enough to assess her injuries. Her right arm was in plaster and she could feel a dressing of some sort on her forehead. Apart from that, she seemed to be able to move her legs all right and thought she was probably in one piece. She must look terrible, though. She looked down with distaste at the hospital gown she was wearing. If she was going to be staying here she would need her own night things – and a mirror and a comb and some makeup.

She looked round the room. There were four beds, one of them unoccupied and the other two containing supine, sleeping forms, so there was no one to see her except the nurses, and they, no doubt, had seen worse. Still, she must get hold of Lesley and ask her to bring things from her house before any visitors arrived. She turned her head cautiously to look at her bedside table. Had anyone picked up her handbag last night? It had been on the desk, hadn't it? And the keys to the library were in it. Had anyone locked up? She didn't want to lose that handbag, a good crocodile bag, bought years ago but she had looked after it well. To have all this trouble and lose the handbag would really be too much. Then she remembered there had been that policewoman here yesterday. So the police must have been to the library and they would surely have made it secure. She lay back on her pillows and tried to relax, but there was still the nightgown problem.

As it turned out, Lesley arrived in the late morning,

unbidden. She came in with a bag, breathing rather hard. She was overweight, of course, Eva thought. She herself was rigorous about her diet and, at eighty, she weighed no more than she had done as a girl. She had tried to talk to Lesley about her weight but Lesley had simply laughed at her. 'I'm a social worker, Eva,' she had said. 'We have to find our comfort where we can. For women in the caring professions it's an occupational hazard. Sex would be better comfort but you can't have sex in a ten-minute coffee break – well, not easily. You can eat two chocolate bars, though. I know. I've done it.'

Still, she was a comforting sight this morning, tipping the contents of a bag out onto the bed and saying, 'I mustn't stay long. It's not visiting time yet, but I told them I was your social worker. How are you feeling? I won't ask you what happened unless you want to tell me. Leave it till later if you like. How's the pain? You look a bit pale but I've brought your war paint so that should help.'

She had brought two of Eva's silk nightdresses, two pairs of knickers, her makeup bag, a toilet bag into which she had put her perfume spray as well as essentials, the book from beside her bed and a library book. 'Lorna brought it round this morning,' she said. 'It was she who told me what had happened to you. The police had let her know. So the library's closed while they crawl about looking for clues to your attacker but Lorna and Gina are determined to keep the book group going, so she's got our next book. *Notes on a Scandal* – Zoë Heller – it was shortlisted for the Booker about ten years ago. Have you read it?'

'I saw the film. With Judi Dench. I see everything with Judi Dench.'

'The book's better, I think. It'll keep you occupied, anyway.' She looked at the book she had brought from Eva's bedroom. 'Dorothy Sayers?' she asked. 'Haven't you read them all?'

'I have translated them all,' Eva said. 'But I like to reread. With a good book you can always find something new.' She took the books. 'I need my glasses,' she said, 'and I don't know what they've done with my handbag.'

When Lesley found the bag in the bedside cupboard, Eva brightened immediately. 'That is excellent,' she said. 'I have my glasses, my phone and my diary, and you have brought me the other necessities of life. Thank you.'

'No problem. I'll scoot off now. Gina's coming to see you this afternoon.'

'Ah,' Eva said.

She and Lesley exchanged a look. 'I'm sorry,' Lesley said, 'but I just had coffee with her and I couldn't not tell her, could I?'

When Lesley had left, Eva said to the sleeping room, 'Gina has many good qualities, but she is perhaps not the best person at a sickbed.'

She lay back and closed her eyes.

When Gina arrived in the early afternoon, she was carrying a bunch of snowdrops and a jam jar. 'From my garden,' she said. 'I found them nestling there, blushing unseen, so I thought you might like them. They smell of snow. The jam jar is standing in for a vase.'

She sat down beside the bed and Eva was distressed, as she always was, by her appearance: the hair, so wild and unkempt; the clothes, so liberally scattered with dog hairs; the boots so suitable for the weather and so uncompromisingly flat. She was really quite an attractive woman with a good figure under that terrible anorak. What had possessed her to give up as she had, to surrender? She talked so much and still revealed so little. She was a puzzle.

She realised suddenly that as she was surveying Gina, she was being scrutinised in return. 'You're a wonder, Eva,'

Gina said. 'You look positively glamorous. You've even put makeup on.'

'Hardly glamorous,' Eva protested, 'not with this.' She touched a finger to the dressing on her head.

'Oh, I don't know. It gives you a rather rakish air. You look gallant.'

She glanced round the room. One of the inhabitants of the other beds was still sleeping and the other was occupied with a cluster of noisy visitors. She leant forward. 'You know what this means, don't you?' she said. 'It looks as though you might have been right.'

'Right?'

'About a serial killer. Don't you think you were intended to be the next victim?'

Eva looked at her. She was not a stupid woman but could she not see that this was not something she wanted to contemplate? It was all very well as a theory when you were sitting sharing a bottle of wine with friends, but, in reality, no. She could still feel it, the rush past her, the sheer physical force – and a smell, vaguely familiar and disturbing. All of that was enough without adding in murderous intent as well.

'Oh, I don't know,' she said, brushing Gina away with a little flap of her hand, 'I think I just disturbed something with the books.'

'How disturbed something?'

Eva sighed. Did she really have to tell it again? 'In the office. I went in because the light was on, and the books – the copies of *The World's Wife* – were out of the box and on the floor. And then he rushed past me, I suppose, and I fell.'

'You don't think he hit you? What about that bump on your head?'

'I really don't know.'

'Well, it goes to show that the books are key to all this,

doesn't it? I told Paula so but she wouldn't listen. How many books did you see?'

'I don't know. It was just a moment. They keep asking me.' She closed her eyes; she was already exhausted and Gina had been in the room for no more than three minutes.

'Was it a lot or just a few?'

'A few – I think. Now, no more. No more.'

'All right. All right. Sorry.'

There was a silence; Eva kept her eyes closed.

'All the same,' Gina said, 'I do think they ought to have a policeman guarding this ward. I mean, you'll probably start to remember more – about what he looked like, won't you, and –'

'No, my dear. I won't. And I don't want to talk about it any more. Thank you for the snowdrops.'

Would she take this as her dismissal, Eva wondered, squinting from beneath her lowered lids to assess her body language. She saw her stir in her chair and glance towards the door, which seemed hopeful, but then there were the sounds of someone coming in, someone who brought the cold of the outside world in just as her intruder had the previous evening. She kept her eyes closed.

There was a touch on her shoulder that she identified as a nurse's touch. 'Eva,' a voice said, 'there's a policeman here to see you.'

'It won't take a minute, Mrs Majoros,' a young male voice said. 'I just need your fingerprints.'

She opened her eyes. A uniformed policeman was unpacking things from a case and Gina was being steered away to the foot of the bed by the nurse.

'Special treatment for you,' the young man said. 'We usually call people in to the station for this but in the circumstances...'

She opened her eyes but remained passive, allowing her

fingers to be placed on the inky pad, pressing down, having the ink inadequately swabbed from her fingertips with a chemical wipe.

Gina, she saw, was avidly attentive. 'This is to do with last night, is it?' Gina asked.

The young man looked evasive. 'It's for purposes of elimination,' he said. 'Just routine.'

'Well, will you be taking anyone else's?'

'I really couldn't say.'

He left. Eva closed her eyes. She heard Gina hesitating and then heard her leave. She counted to a hundred and opened her eyes. When she felt strong enough, she reached out for the copy of *Notes on a Scandal* which Lesley had left on her bed. She looked at the front cover, which carried pictures from the film, and then turned the book over to look at the blurb on the back. Judi Dench had been perfect as Barbara, she thought, because she did normality so well. It took a while before she let you see how mad she was. But the other woman – a woman like that having an affair with a boy, an uncouth boy, not even beautiful – it was impossible to believe in her, she had found. Perhaps the book would explain her, she thought, when she felt strong enough to start it.

Chapter Thirteen

THE ENGLISH PATIENT

Thursday 20ᵗʰ February 2014

This has not been a good day. I have behaved badly. I have reverted to the self I hoped to leave behind when I fled from Marlbury. I shed my life there like a wrinkled, scabby old skin, and I intended to emerge pure and free. I suppose it was sin that I hoped to purge myself of, though I didn't think so at the time. I was confident that I already scored rather low on the deadly sins league table. I have never been slothful; if anything, I have irritated people with my bustling energy. In the greed area – gluttony and avarice – I think I do pretty well; I don't have cravings, either for food or for anything else, really. Lust? Well, back in the day, perhaps, but not for quite a long time now. Which leaves envy, pride and anger. Envy I disclaim – I'm too proud to be envious of anyone else – but pride and anger were woven into the old skin I planned to leave behind, and I thought I could shed them with it. Free of work and family, I would surely have nothing to make me angry, and the old clothes, the salon-deprived hair and the cliff-top hovel would be quite enough to signify the death of pride, wouldn't they?

Well, it seems not. It seems that anger and pride, unlike beauty, are more than skin-deep, and they drove me, this morning, to bully Lesley into arranging a visit to Farid, and this afternoon, under the pretext of making a compassionate hospital visit, to bully an eighty-year-old woman with a broken arm and a head injury. Anger and pride. Despite fifteen years and a post-divorce affair which gave me some considerable delight, I am still angry enough with Andrew for his desertion to refuse to do the sensible, humane, altruistic thing and ask him to help Farid. And the pride is in there, too, of course. The hair and the clothes and the hovel are just a blind; I still think I'm twenty times smarter than everyone else and believe that I can cut through the tangle of this case with my laser brain while the police are still tying their shoelaces.

And so, even by my lax standards, I behaved badly. I could see from the moment I walked into the ward that Eva didn't want me there, but did I deposit my snowdrops and melt away? No. I stayed. I stayed and I questioned and I probed and I nagged, and it was only the advent of PC Plod that winkled me out of there. And now I am back home in the late afternoon gloom with my spirit liberally draped in chagrin, but with my mind still rampant with questions.

The first of these is *Where is Alice?* If the police want her fingerprints and can't find her, will they start looking for her and should I tell them about her row with Simon? The other major question is whether Paula is getting the partners' fingerprints as well, because they are still the real suspects in my mind. Of course she needs to know whose books she has actually got in that library box, but she needs to know who else has handled them, doesn't she? She'll have Farid's, of course, and I assume she'll have got Matt's when they were going over Kelly's flat. In my mind, I've ruled out Peter Harper and Don Dering, but there's still Simon, who really needs looking at, it seems to me. And that takes us back to the question of what has happened to Alice. I would like to ring Paula and ask her but I feel that a more roundabout approach might be better, so I ring Lorna.

'So they've taken the books away, finally,' I say.

'They have,' she agrees.

'And how many books were there in the box, actually?' I ask.

'Just the four, Gina. Mine, Dora's, Kelly's and Lily's. Did you think they might have bred somehow in here?'

'Well, books have disappeared so they could always reappear, couldn't they?'

'Maybe,' she says.

There is something a bit off about Lorna's tone this afternoon, a bit withholding. I begin to wonder if she has heard about my mistreatment of Eva. Could she have done?

'I went to see Eva,' I say.

'You did,' she says, and then, after a pause, 'I spoke to her on the phone.'

Ah.

'I think I may have been a bit bouncy for her,' I say

'Yes.' She is sounding very Scottish – a bit Presbyterian, if you know what I mean. 'Yes, I'm glad you realise that.'

I decide to move on.

'Have you been asked to give your fingerprints?' I ask.

'I have. And you?'

'They've got mine already – because I handled the book on the beach.'

'Oh, yes. Well, I'm going in with Lesley tomorrow morning. Dora's going separately; her father wants to take her.'

'Right.' I let a pause rest in the air and then I say, 'I was wondering if you'd like me to come with you – you and Lesley. I mean, I know the ropes and so on – and I know where the police station is in Dover. It might help, don't you think?'

I can hear the conviction leaking out of my question even as I utter it. Lorna is impeccably polite but very firm.

'Lesley and I are two grown women, you know,' she says. 'We really don't need our hands held. And Lesley knows very well where the police station is, of course, having been a social worker in Dover. So, no need, Gina. No need.'

I say nothing, which surprises her, I think – as it does me, in fact. For a moment we both breathe into our phones. Then, 'Was there a particular reason why you wanted to go to the police station with us? Apart, you know, from the drama?' she asks.

Rumbled.

'I was hoping I might bump into DI Powell,' I say. 'There are a couple of things I want to ask her and I thought it might be easier if —'

She interrupts. 'I don't think relying on bumping into someone is ever a good strategy really, is it? If you need to see her, better to make an appointment, don't you think?'

She sounds like a kind teacher advising a wayward fifteen-year-old.

'Yes,' I say. 'OK.'

I don't ring right away, however, I stall. I pick up the copy of *Notes on a Scandal* that Lorna has left for me and I flick through it, remembering how much I hated it when I read it before. Not that it's a bad book; it's a very clever book, but I found the insanity of Sheba's obsession with the unsavoury teenage boy acutely painful and the inevitable trainwreck of her humiliation unbearable. I'm not sure I can bring myself to read it again. Certainly, I won't while I'm in my current state of agitation.

I find a few more diversionary activities: I clear the draining board and put stuff away in cupboards, something I rarely do these days, preferring to bypass cupboards and use things straight from the draining board – sometimes straight from the washing-up bowl. I throw away some flowers, which Freda brought with her and which expired some time ago. I decide to wash the cat's and the dog's blankets and I even make a start on picking some burrs out of Ariel's coat until she scratches me quite nastily and bolts through the cat flap. Caliban, thinking he might be next in line for grooming, has slunk upstairs and is cowering under my bed. Enough. I pick up the phone.

When I get through to the police station, I get stalled by someone who says that DI Powell is not available. He doesn't say that she is out of the building, however, so I take a chance and ask if he will give her my name and say I have some information about the Kelly Field case. This may be completely counter-productive but I'm banking on Paula's believing that I know things I'm not telling her. I wait a long time, listening to the burble coming from some multiply-occupied room, but eventually the receiver is picked up. 'I'm putting you through,' he says.

'What do you want, Gina?'

And good afternoon to you, too, Paula. I'm well, thank you. How are you?

I consider saying this but instead I opt for matching my tone to hers.

'Alice Gates,' I say. 'You'll be wanting her fingerprints.'

'Among others. What has this to do —'

'But you can't find her, can you?'

'We haven't located —'

'She's disappeared, Paula. She disappeared on Monday night. She has been missing for three days. She had a screaming row with her husband on Monday night and no one has seen her since. She has two small sons and they don't know where she is. She's a good mother. She wouldn't have walked out on them. She wouldn't have gone anywhere without telling them where she was going.'

'She has not been reported as a missing person. Her husband says she is in London.'

'Does he say he has heard from her?'

'No, but —'

'But you believe him?'

'We have no reason not to.'

'Except that she is a member of a group that seems to be under attack. Two dead, one missing and now one assaulted. When are you going to start taking this seriously?'

'We are taking the death of Kelly Field very seriously. That's the only confirmed crime we have to deal with, and we are dealing with it. We are also looking into the circumstances of Eva Majoros's fall. What I can absolutely do without is people like you muddying the water. This is wasting police time and —'

'If Alice Gates is in London, you should be able to get her on her mobile, shouldn't you?'

'We —'

'But you haven't, have you? Let me guess. It's switched off, isn't it?'

'There are all sorts of reasons why someone switches off a mobile. Or she may have forgotten to take her charger with her.'

'Do you believe that?'

There is a silence. Finally, she says, 'Well, you tell me there was a row, maybe she's switched it off so her husband can't call her. She's waiting for things to cool down.'

'Three days is a long time for cooling down when you've got small children wondering where you are.'

'Her husband doesn't think there's a problem. I can't institute a misper inquiry if she's not missing.'

'You're not listening to me, Paula. I'm saying it's very possible that he's not reporting her missing because he knows exactly where she is – where he's put her. What you need to be doing is digging up his back garden.'

'Oh, for God's sake, Gina. Listen to yourself. This is fantasy stuff.'

'Have you looked into his background? He's a violent man. His first wife divorced him because he put her in hospital with two broken ribs. Alice told me. And he's a drinking crony of the men in the pub who hate us and think we're witches. And he was the person who drove Harry Timmins in to the station so he could tell you his cock-and-bull story about Farid Khalil. It's a load of bollocks but it conveniently lets everyone else off the hook. Do your bloody job, Paula. You're not stupid. David always thought very highly of you. But you're being stupid about this because you don't want to admit that I might be right. So, forget about me, just do your job.'

I don't know what I expect her to say but what I get is silence, quite a long silence, and then she breaks the connection. I sit in the kitchen for some time with the curtains open, expecting some sort of activity in the road outside. Something must happen, surely, after my outburst, when I said things, to be honest, that I didn't know I thought until I heard them coming out of my mouth. Do I really believe that Simon has killed Alice and buried her in the garden? I don't know. I listen for the sounds of sirens. I imagine police rapping on Simon's door and I imagine them at my door, making good Paula's threats of arrest. I sit for a long time and nothing happens at all. Will they dig up Simon's garden in the morning? Probably not. For a moment I have a pang of longing to talk to David, a pang so painful it takes my breath away. I pick up my phone. I did throw my old one into the sea, and my stored numbers with it, but I still know David's number off by heart. Before I can think about it, I dial it. The number, I am told, is discontinued.

I take Caliban across the road for a pee, I check that the woodburner is damped down and I make a tray of soup and bread, which I take upstairs and place on the table under my bedroom window. It is only eight o'clock but

I shall eat this, have a long bath and go to bed with *The Diary of a Provincial Lady*, my reliable comfort read when all else fails. I sit at the window, with my curtains open, dunking bread into my soup and watching the shimmer of the moon on the sea. The cloud must have lifted, I think. Maybe tomorrow will be a dry day. As I get up to clear my tray, I hear the sound of a door opening below and I see, in the light that spills from his door, Simon Gates coming out of his house. I turn off my light so I can see better in the darkness outside and I can just make out his figure in the pale moonlight. He stands by the sea wall, apparently looking out to sea, and I see a small flare of light – a cigarette being lit, maybe. Then he turns and walks past my house to the top of the steps to the beach. Again he stops to look out, then he starts to descend the steps and disappears. I sit in the dark, watching and waiting for him to come back. As the minutes pass, I wonder if it's possible that he is contemplating drowning himself, overcome by guilt. It wouldn't take long in this icy sea. But the boys are in the house, aren't they? He wouldn't just walk out on them like that. Then maybe they're not in the house. Maybe he has sent them to grandparents. Maybe this was planned. On the other hand, maybe he is just being a responsible parent and not smoking in the house. Perhaps it's just as mundane as that. An odd kind of responsibility if you had just killed the children's mother. But what – apart from my overheated imagination – says that is what he has done? The burning certainty that swept me along when I was talking to Paula is beginning to die away, and as I see Simon reappear from the beach and cross the road quietly to his front door, I suspect that what is happening here is more of a mundane muddle than I would like to admit. I close the curtains.

I feel, suddenly, so exhausted that even a bath seems

too much effort. 'Leave it alone,' I say out loud. 'Ring Andrew. See Farid. Leave the rest to Paula. Anger and pride. Let it go.'

Chapter Fourteen

POSSESSION

Friday 21st February

I sleep well, perhaps because my conscience is now clear, and wake early, brimming with good intentions. I pad downstairs in my dressing gown and slippers, light the woodburner and put the kettle on. Then I find my address book and look up Andrew's number. I should, I suppose, ring him at work but I'm hoping a call at home will take him unawares. Besides, I'm not sure what sort of reception I might get from anyone in his chambers. I have made scenes there in the past and fear I might get the *I'm not sure if he's available* treatment. Better to get him at home, surrounded by the domestic delights of his lovely wife, Lavender, and their charming children, where he can congratulate himself on his escape from me and feel prepared to throw me some crumbs of comfort. Besides, I have found that before breakfast is a very good time to take a man off his guard.

Lavender answers the phone, and I can hear the echoing space of the high-ceilinged Georgian manor house behind her greeting.

'Hello, Lavender,' I say. 'It's Gina. How are you?'

'Oh, hello, Gina. I'm fine – no, Arthur, don't. It's Hubert's, don't —'

'And the boys?'

'Fine, too, thank you.'

Lavender is a sweet woman. The girls and I have always called her The Fragrant Lavender, or TFL. She is twenty years younger than Andrew, not terribly bright, very posh, and wifely in an old-fashioned sort of way. It is as though Andrew drew up a list of all my failings and sketched a blueprint for the perfect wife based on their opposites. She and I get on perfectly well, actually, although I am always beset by residual guilt at having handed over to her a husband so badly rehearsed in the role. This morning, however, I detect a slight edge to her voice, light and sweet though it is.

'Is this too early?' I ask 'I hadn't realised —'

I look out of the window. It is still dark, really. I look at the clock on the cooker. Seven-thirty-two.

'Oh no,' she says. 'Nothing's too early for the boys.' She breaks off and I hear her say, 'In just a minute, Hubert. You can see I'm on the phone.' She comes back. 'What can I do for you, Gina?' she asks.

'I wanted a word with Andrew, actually, if he's —'

'He's not here,' she says, and there is definitely an edge to her voice now. 'In fact, I hoped it might be him calling. He's in Argentina. On a case which seems to be taking an unbelievably long time. And our au pair has gone home because her mother's ill, and it's half term so Arthur's not at school, and, frankly —'

'Oh, poor you,' I say, restraining myself from pointing out that it must be the middle of the night in Argentina and so an unlikely time for a call. 'When will Andrew be back?'

'He hasn't said.'

'No,' I say. 'I don't suppose he has.'

This was a possibility I had not reckoned with. I don't know why; Andrew's work as a lawyer is always taking him off somewhere, and Argentina would be a lot more fun than Kent in February. So, what to do now? My resolutions last night were to phone Andrew and see Farid. Lesley has promised to work on getting to Farid but I don't expect that to move fast. What else to do?

I make tea and drink it, and by the time that is done, it is light enough to take Caliban for his walk, so I prepare myself against the elements and off we go. As we step out of the house, we encounter Simon and his boys leaving their house. The boys are both carrying mini-sized backpacks and Simon has a larger one.

'Going somewhere nice?' I ask

'Hope so,' is all Simon says, and they head off to the bus stop.

Dover, I guess, is their destination. There is really nowhere else worth mounting an expedition to on that bus route.

'Enjoy!' I call cheerily, and then, as I'm tramping the pebbles with Caliban, the question of what to do next begins to clarify itself beautifully in my mind. I know I resolved to leave the Alice question alone and focus on helping Farid, but I've been thwarted by Andrew's absence and the slow-grinding processes of the Border Agency, and really Alice's continued absence is worrying and what are friends for if they're not ready to look for you when you disappear? What occurs to me is that Simon and the boys are clearly out for the day and I am pretty sure I can get into their house. It would be easier, of course, if we had done the neighbourly thing and swapped spare door keys in case of emergencies. Alice did suggest it, in fact, but I stalled, 'forgetting' to get a spare cut until the moment passed. I don't remember why, exactly, I was unwilling to part with a key but I suspect that I just didn't like the idea that Simon would be able to get into my house.

So, I shall have to break in, but I don't think that will be difficult. I am not an expert housebreaker, you understand, but I am a connoisseur of human behaviour. I am prepared to bet that a man managing two small boys single-handed and aiming to catch an early morning bus will not have thought to take the key out of the back door.

By the time I get home, I have a fully worked-out plan. I chuck some biscuits into Caliban's bowl and, without bothering about my own breakfast, I go out into the garden, pull some leeks, wrap them in yesterday's paper and carry them, with a kitchen chair, down the side of Jack Terry's house and along the alley that runs behind our houses. At Alice's and Simon's garden gate, I position my chair, climb onto it and lean over to unbolt the gate. I am proud of myself for remembering to bring the chair; my working model for this enterprise is an occasion when I had to break into my own house, having left my key in a jacket pocket. On that occasion, I borrowed a chair from Alice to unlock my gate; now I'm returning the compliment. There are advantages to living in a row of identical houses, I realise.

The chair was a bright idea, and so were the leeks. Harry, you see, will be bound to have spotted me, since his main occupation is snooping and I made quite a lot of noise with the bolt on the gate, which was stiff and awkward. The leeks are my excuse for being here. I do give Alice some of my veg from time to time and, though I'm quite sure Simon won't want to be bothered with them, they will just about do as cover. If challenged, I shall need a bit of a circumstantial story, but you wouldn't expect to leave a bundle of leeks on a front doorstep, would you?

I force myself not to look up at Harry's window and I stroll, all innocence, to the back door, where Harry will no longer be able to see me. If he has seen me come into the garden and watches for me to leave, I may be called on to explain why it took me so long (ten or fifteen minutes to scan the house for clues?) to leave a bundle of leeks at the back door. I shall say that I was talking to the cat. This is not an altogether improbable story; he does quite like me, insofar as cats like anyone, and he has come over the fence to greet me. He is a timid creature, terrorised by the boundless energy of the boys – and, I wouldn't be surprised, the odd kick from Simon – but I feed him when they are on holiday and he does like to commune quietly over a bowl of Whiskas.

The next part of my plan depends on my arm being long enough to reach through the cat flap and take the key out the lock. I get down on the ground and push my arm through almost to the shoulder. The cat is entranced. I grope around for the key, but can't find it. Has Simon prudently removed it after all? I stand up and squint through the window beside the door. I think I can see the key and realise that I have been groping in the wrong place. I get down on the ground again. I am getting wet and filthy but these are my dog-walking clothes. I grope again. The cat purrs and rubs himself against me helpfully. I touch the key, get a hold on it and tug. It remains stubbornly in place. I yank hard and it flies out and clatters to the tiles inside. I mutter curses; the cat backs off. I look again through the window pane, think I see the key, feel around at ground level and find my hand, suddenly, groping in a mess of something cold and slimy. I pull it out and gaze in horror at my sticky, brown fingers. I sniff them tentatively and get a blast of fishy decay. Cat food that has been around for some time. Why hasn't he eaten it? Is he afraid to be in the house without Alice? I offer him my fingers to lick but he refuses them. I wipe them on a clump of grass and get down on the ground again to resume groping.

I do, eventually, locate the key, unlock the door as quietly as I can, and step inside. The smell of burnt toast is there again, as it was the day Alice went missing. If Simon can't even manage the toaster then single parent life must be tough. The kitchen is pretty chaotic and if the rest of the house is the same it's not going to make my search easy. I know the sort of thing I am looking for. Some years ago, a student of mine went missing and I was in her college room when the police came to search it. Like me now, they were looking for signs of violence, and also for signs that she had made a planned exit. It was much the same time of year – March, I think – so they were looking for her outdoor coat and boots, as well as handbag, suitcase or travel bag, keys, toiletries, mobile phone and so on. There is a little plaque beside the back door, with three hooks on it and labelled *Keys* in something like poker work. No keys hang there. Simon will obviously have taken his. Does/did Alice keep hers there, too, or in her handbag? I decide that upstairs may be a better hunting ground.

Accompanied by the cat, I head for the front bedroom and am disoriented to find bunk beds and a chaos of toys and clothes in there. Wondering how Alice and Simon manage to share the little back room, I look in and see that pretty uncomfortably is the answer. The bed takes up almost the entire room. It is unmade and the doors of the fitted cupboards are hanging open. I approach the bed tentatively, lift a pillow and see a pair of pink pyjamas under it. Not Simon's, I take it. I scan the rack of Alice's clothes but I don't know what I'm looking for. I survey the jumble of shoes; there are no boots there. And now I picture Alice's usual outdoor wear, I see her in smart black leather boots and a longish grey coat. The coat I shall look for downstairs; up here I'm after handbag and toiletries. Travel bags, in this tiny house, must be kept in the loft. I scan the room for a handbag, and as I do so I experience the conventional shiver down the spine. There is a mobile phone on the little shelf beside the bed, on the side where I found the pink pyjamas. I pick it up. It is, I see at once, quite a fancy effort, and I haven't the time now to work out how to get into it. The cat conversation alibi is already beginning to wear thin. I shall need to take it away with me. It just might be Simon's but why would he go out for the day without it?

And, besides, it seems to belong with the pink pyjamas. I put it in my pocket. If it turns out that it is Simon's, I shall be in deep shit, but there it goes. If this is Alice's phone, I'm too scared about what it means to worry about anything else.

When I go into the bathroom, I start to feel shaky. There are four toothbrushes in the rack and Alice's comb and makeup sit on the shelf. Why haven't the police been in and seen this? I want to rage, except that what I know, chillingly, is that time is not of the essence here. Simon won't have abducted Alice and be holding her tied up somewhere, will he? If she disappeared on Monday night, more than three days ago, without her phone or her toothbrush, then she is dead, isn't she?

I go downstairs and take another look round. In the kitchen I see Alice's anorak still hanging on the back of the door; in the living room, I see a copy of *May We Be Forgiven* lying on the floor; by the front door, I see her leather boots, lined up neatly below the coat pegs. The long, grey coat, though, is not there. But you could wrap a body in a long coat, couldn't you?

All of a sudden, I can't wait to get out of the house. I turn and blunder through the kitchen, sending the cat skittering away. I go out of the back door, lock it from the outside, then go shoulder-deep into the cat flap again to shove the key back into place. I position my offering of leeks outside the door, go out through the back gate, bolt it and carry my chair back home. The clock on my oven tells me that I have been away for nearly half an hour.

I lay the mobile phone on the kitchen table, strip off my filthy trousers and put them in the washing machine, wash my hands, make a cup of coffee and settle down with it to work out how to use the phone. It is not actually all that difficult here in the safety of my own kitchen. I manage to wake it up and then find the message icon. It is Alice's phone;

the last two messages are about a social arrangement for the boys – an arrangement they have missed, apparently. Dated yesterday, the last message reads, *Hi Alice. What happened to you? Was expecting the boys this am. Have I got it wrong? Jenny x* Yes, Jenny, you have got it wrong, I'm afraid, wronger than you can imagine.

What do I do now? I shall have to ring Paula, shan't I? If Simon has killed Alice, then he killed Kelly, too, didn't he? And attacked Eva. And possibly killed Lily, if Jack's right. And surely I have to be next, don't I? When he finds the phone gone, he will know I have it, won't he? And, anyway, as Paula so cogently put it, I am the most completely bloody infuriating person in the group.

I really should eat some breakfast first, though, because I feel pretty shaky and coffee is probably too strong in the circumstances. I make a piece of toast, but as I start to butter it, the burnt toast and cat food smell of Alice's kitchen revisits me and I think I'm going to throw up. I drink a glass of water and take some deep breaths. Caliban gets the toast.

There is nothing for it but to ring Paula, and I can't feel any worse than I do already, so I reach for the phone and, as I lay a hand on it, it shrills into action, making me fumble and drop it.

When I retrieve it, a voice says, 'Are you all right, Gina?'

For a moment, I don't know who it is, because I am, stupidly, expecting it to be Paula. 'Yes,' I say cautiously.

'It's Lesley here,' she says. 'Is something the matter?'

'No – no, I'm fine. I just… dropped the phone.'

'OK. Well, I've got good news. It's fixed.'

'Fixed?'

'Yes.'

'Sorry, Lesley. What's fixed?'

'The appointment.'

What is she talking about?

'With Farid,' she says.

How could I have forgotten? I pull myself together and try to sound brisk and competent.

'That's terrific, Lesley,' I say. 'I've got the diary right here. If you can give me date and time, I'll —'

'This afternoon,' she says. 'Two-thirty.'

'Oh,' I say, 'I don't think – I mean, I'm not really —'

I expected a long wait – time enough, perhaps, to talk to Andrew. With this morning's discoveries, I'm just not ready for this.

'Gina!' she says, and her voice is unexpectedly sharp. 'Yesterday it was a priority – you had to see Farid urgently. I've had two quite difficult conversations with the IRC, pushing them for an appointment as soon as possible. Have you got something more important to do this afternoon? Because if you don't go this afternoon, I can't guarantee that you'll get another appointment. I'm certainly not doing any more negotiating. You're on your own.'

I have a horrible feeling that I'm going to cry.

'Sorry, Lesley,' I say, and I hate the pathetic wobble in my voice. 'I've had a bit of a shock, um… and I'm not quite —' Should I tell her about Alice? Something tells me not to. 'This afternoon will be fine,' I say. 'Thank you for organising it. Sorry if it was difficult.'

She relents. 'It wasn't that difficult,' she says. 'They just do their best to make it difficult.' Then she asks, 'Would you like me to come with you? I'm going into Dover later this morning. Lorna and I are going to get fingerprinted. We were planning to do a bit of shopping and have some lunch afterwards. I could meet you at the IRC at two-fifteen, and give you a lift home afterwards.'

'Oh, no,' I say. 'Don't worry. There's no need. I —' Then I stop. 'Actually, that would be great,' I say. 'I mean, because you know the ropes and so on…'

'I'll see you there, then. Do you know how to get there?'

'I'll find it.'

'OK, then.'

'OK.'

'Oh, you'll need to have your passport with you.'

'Jesus, Lesley. They're not going to try and deport me, too, are they?'

'For identification. To prove you are who I've said you are. They'll have done a background check on you. Mainly, they want to make sure you're not a journalist, I imagine. I would normally say bring your driving licence but I assume you haven't got one of those?'

'No.'

'But you do have a passport?'

'Somewhere. If I can find it.'

'Find it.'

'Yes.'

I sit down at the kitchen table and rest my head on my folded arms. The urge to cry has passed but I feel incredibly tired. Ariel the cat, who rarely takes an interest in my feelings, jumps onto the table and nuzzles at my hair. I guess she is alarmed at my apparent collapse because she fears I may not be strong enough to feed her.

'It's all right, cat,' I mumble. 'I'm not dead yet.'

Chapter Fifteen

RITES OF PASSAGE

Friday 21ˢᵗ February 2014

Lesley

'Lesley Harper,' she said, for the second time. 'I phoned yesterday to make an appointment to see Farid Khalil. I was making an appointment on behalf of a fr-colleague, Mrs Virginia Gray – or Sidwell.'

There was a silence at the other end. Then the voice, thin and nasal, said, 'Well, which is it? Gray or Sidwell?'

'I explained yesterday – and I'm pretty sure it was you I spoke to – *Gray* is her married name but she is divorced and, informally, she now uses her maiden name. She hasn't changed it officially, so any documentation will be under *Gray*. There is nothing sinister about having the two names.'

She heard – and was intended to hear – a sigh. There was a rustling of papers.

'I can't find your name anywhere here. Harper, you said?'

'Yes, but the appointment isn't for me. I explained that yesterday, too.'

'There's no need to take that tone, Mrs Harper. We're dealing with these calls all the time. There's nothing special about you.'

'Of course not,' she said, injecting as much pleasantness into her voice as she could manage. 'I realise that you are very busy.'

'Anyway, why doesn't your colleague ring for herself?'

'As I said, I'm a social worker. I've had dealings with the IRC before. She wasn't sure what to do. And you're not the most user-friendly of institutions, are you? You're used to the place, but just looking at it scares most people.'

'What do you want? You want us to have Open Days, do you, with tea and cakes?'

'Great idea.'

He sighed again. 'Khalil, was it, you wanted to see?'

'Well not me – Mrs Gray.'

'Yeah, yeah.'

The rustling of papers had stopped and she detected, as she heard him say, 'O – kay... Khalil... Farid' that he was now looking at a computer screen.

'Yup,' he said. 'Hold on.'

She listened intently. He seemed to have moved away from the screen and was talking to someone. She thought she heard him say, 'Gray, probably.'

Nothing happened for a long time. She could hear movement, though – footsteps, odd bangs, the occasional word. She watched the kitchen clock. She would give it five minutes exactly. If he hadn't got back to her by then she would decide he was just playing a power game with her, hang up and tell Gina she'd have to sort things out for herself. After four minutes and twenty seconds, he returned.

'You still there?' he asked.

'Is it still Friday?' she answered.

'Oh, a joker,' he said. 'That's all we need.'

She waited, saying nothing.

'This afternoon,' he said.

'I'm sorry?'

154

'This afternoon, your friend can come in. Khalil is seeing his lawyer at two, so he'll be in the visitors' centre already. Tell her two-thirty and she can have twenty minutes.'

'But don't you need to check —'

'She's been CRB checked, your Mrs Gray. She'll do. Tell her to bring her driving licence with her.'

'She doesn't drive, actually. Will a passport do?'

He gave a laugh that came out as a sort of strangled shout. 'British passport, is it?'

'I assume so.'

'Well, tell her not to wave it about then. They'll rip her apart for one of those up here.'

Resisting the temptation to say, *A joker. That's all we need,* she said, on impulse, 'I'm CRB checked myself. Does that mean I could go in and see him, too?'

She thought she could hear him sucking his teeth. 'No more than two at a time,' he said, 'so don't bring your friends.' Then the line went dead. *And you have a nice day, too,* she muttered into the handset before reaching for the biscuit tin and dialling Gina's number.

When she put the phone down three minutes later, she allowed herself a muffled growl of frustration before putting the kettle on and diving back into the biscuit tin. Dunking a choc chip cookie into her coffee, she considered Gina. Was she drinking? She had thought she might be a couple of days ago when she called with her talk of being arrested and needing Lesley to look after the dog, and now, this morning, she had sounded so out of it. Not slurred, though. Wobbly, as though she might have been crying, but not slurred. Preoccupied, but more than that – emotionally preoccupied, somehow. Bereaved, actually. In her work life, Lesley had seen people in the first shock of sudden bereavement and she thought she recognised that disconnected tone, the effort needed to focus on the here and now. But if Gina had just had bad news, why hadn't she said? If something had happened to one of the daughters, or the grandchildren, then Gina would need her friends and Lesley, whose warm heart had not been chilled by years of working for Social Services, wanted to take her into her ample embrace.

She was glad, she thought, as she got up to cut a couple of slices of bread and put them in the toaster, that she had thought to ask about going in with Gina to see Farid. She had thought of it, really, because you never knew with Gina how she would behave and she was afraid that the congenital obstructiveness of the staff at the IRC would arouse an equal obstructiveness in Gina. She had seen her role as exercising restraint, but now she thought she might be needed just to see Gina through. She spread her toast liberally with butter and opened a new jar of what looked like excellent gooseberry jam. It was going to be a trying morning, she reasoned, and better tackled on a full stomach. And they might not eat lunch till late.

Picking up Lorna half an hour later, she was amused to see how smart she was looking, in a cashmere coat, silk scarf and black patent shoes with heels. They had both had the same instinct to dress up for this visit to the police station. Lorna's clothes, like her own, said, *I am not, of course, a criminal or even a suspect. I am a public-spirited member of the community doing her bit for law and order.* As though criminals couldn't own cashmere coats.

'I'm afraid I've complicated things a bit for the journey home,' she said as they took the coast road towards Dover. 'Gina's got an appointment to see the Syrian lad.'

'Which Syrian lad?' Lorna asked.

'Dora's boyfriend. The one the police suspect.'

'The police have a suspect?'

'Yes. Didn't you know? They took him in for questioning and then the Border Agency picked him up and he's in the

IRC. I'm surprised Gina didn't tell you. She was straight on the phone to me. She's incensed about it.'

Lorna looked out of the window. 'She did ring me yesterday,' she said. 'She wanted to know what had happened to the copies of *The World's Wife*. She's obsessing about them. But we didn't talk long. I was cross with her.'

Lesley glanced at her. 'Really?'

'Yes. She'd gone bouncing in to see Eva. You know she's got this theory that we're being picked off one by one by a serial killer, so she was grilling Eva about what happened at the library and completely wore her out. So thoughtless. And I told her so.'

'She means well,' Lesley said. How many times had she said that about people who were a pain in the neck? 'She's gung-ho to defend this lad, Farid, and I got her the appointment at the IRC. But the thing is, she sounded really rough when I spoke to her this morning and I wasn't sure that she would cope, so I've offered to go with her, which means I won't be ready to leave till about three. Can you fill the time with shopping or would you rather get the bus back?'

'I shall go to the library,' Lorna said, 'and see what they've got new in. I shall be quite happy.'

Having negotiated the constricted streets of Dover's clogged town centre, Lesley drove boldly into the car park behind the police station. She was not sure whether people coming in to be fingerprinted were entitled to use it but she had always parked there when coming for work purposes and she was prepared to brazen it out if challenged. She felt bold this morning, she realised, more like her old work self, the woman who could cope with anything – the distressing, the deviant and the dangerous – and come up smiling. Being made redundant had knocked that out of her a bit but this morning, striding ahead with Lorna trotting anxiously behind her, she felt like her old self. She also felt oversized, but Lorna did that. So slight, so neat, so self-contained, she could make anyone feel that they took up too much space.

The desk sergeant recognised her, which was gratifying, but did not help to speed up the process. They waited, making desultory conversation, in an area that resembled a tired doctors' waiting room. Lesley would have liked to talk to Lorna about her concerns over Gina, but neither of them, she judged, was sufficiently relaxed to have that conversation, so they talked a bit about *Notes on a Scandal*, which Lorna had read before and Lesley had just started, and were, eventually, summoned in to have their prints taken. The young woman who took their prints was perfectly polite and took trouble to get the ink off their fingers afterwards, but Lesley could see that Lorna hated it and she didn't like it much herself.

Outside, they found it was raining, dashed to the car in their best coats and high heels and drove to the Marks and Spencers car park, ready for some consoling shopping. Inside, though, they soon became disconsolate. February, they agreed, was the worst possible time for buying clothes. The racks were packed randomly with sale items – the bad colours, unwise patterns and odd shapes of the unbuyable and persistently unbought, and Lesley, though she knew that now was a good time to find the odd size eighteen at a knock-down price, was too proud to go outsize shopping with Lorna so sleek beside her.

'An early lunch?' she proposed, and after buying a few token items in the food hall to justify their parking, they went round the corner to a restaurant Lesley knew, which offered a substantial set lunch menu. Settled here, each with a glass of white wine, Lesley ate her way through pâté and roast chicken while Lorna nibbled at a salade niçoise. Between pâté and chicken, Lesley asked, 'So how did you leave things with Gina yesterday?'

'How do you mean?'

'You said you were cross with her.'

'Oh, it was nothing major. We didn't have a row. I was just a bit short with her.'

'Only she sounded really upset this morning. As though she'd had a bad shock.'

'Well that won't be me. Gina's too tough to be upset by me being a bit cool.'

'I think she's more vulnerable than she seems.'

'Oh, certainly. Though don't let her hear you say it. But I really don't think I can have upset her that much. Did you ask her what was wrong?'

'No. I was quite cross, too, actually. I'd gone to a lot of trouble to set up this appointment at the IRC because she'd badgered me, and then she seemed to want to back out.'

'That doesn't sound like Gina.'

'No, it doesn't. That's why I'm worried.'

'I wonder if Alice knows what's wrong.'

'I haven't seen Alice all week. I wondered if they'd gone away for half term.'

'No. I've seen Simon and the boys. They've been into the library. But not Alice.'

At this point their main courses arrived.

'Perhaps we can get her to talk on the way home,' Lesley said. She picked up her fork. 'We'll try a two-pronged attack.'

She had been to the IRC three or four times but the first view of it shocked her every time. It was the most brutal building she had ever seen up close, far more intimidating than any prison she had visited. Standing vast and isolated on the heights, it crouched like a gigantic, malevolent toad above the town. It had been built as a fortress, she knew, during the Napoleonic wars, to keep out the French. Now, with its modern festooning of vicious barbed wire, it was designed to turn alien invaders round and send them back where they came from. It was secretive, hostile and a law unto itself. For the second time that day, she drove into the privileged parking area and, as she expected, her arrival brought an armed prison guard sprinting across from the visitors' centre.

The guard, who was female but only marginally, banged on her window and, when she wound it down, said, 'This is a restricted area.'

'I'm a visitor,' Lesley said, 'and that's the visitors' centre.'

'Are you with the other one?' the guard asked.

'I don't know. What other one?'

'Name of Sidwell.'

'Then, yes.'

'Name?'

'Sorry?'

'Your name?'

'Harper. Lesley Harper.'

The woman took a tablet from the breast pocket of her uniform jacket and moved her thumb over it.

'Harper? All right. Driving licence.' She held out a hand.

Lesley cursed herself for not having it ready and needing to fumble in her bag for it under this woman's hostile eye. She took a deep breath and refused to be hurried, found the driving licence and handed it over.

The woman examined it as though she would like to bite it to test its authenticity. Eventually she handed it back, turned away without a word and set off back to the visitors' centre. Lesley got out of the car, smoothed down her coat, put her shoulders back and walked briskly after her. When the guard reached the door to the centre, she turned and stood waiting with her arms folded over her bulky bust.

'You've been here before, haven't you?' she demanded.

'Yes.'

'Take my advice and keep a grip on your friend. Any trouble and you're both out. No second chances.'

'Has she caused trouble?'

'Not yet. She's only just arrived. But I can smell the troublemakers.'

'Right.'

She followed the woman into the waiting area, signed herself in, when instructed, and might have missed Gina if she had not been the only other person in the room. She had clearly made an effort for the occasion. Her hair was tamed and tied back with a scarf and she was wearing a dark blue coat, slightly creased as though it had been lying in a trunk somewhere, but better than her all-seasons anorak. Her black trousers seemed to be free of dog and cat hairs and she was wearing respectable black boots. Her eyes, however, were wild.

'The bloody woman shouted at my taxi,' she said by way of greeting.

'Hello, Gina,' Lesley answered, and sat down beside her. 'Take it easy,' she muttered quietly, while making a performance of taking off her gloves. 'She's looking for any excuse to throw us out. Play it cool.'

She was startled to see tears in Gina's eyes as she said, 'I can't bear it, Lesley. I can't bear him being here.'

'I know,' Lesley said in her best professional voice. 'But we're going to get him out of here, aren't we?'

She looked round the room. Waiting rooms, she supposed, were bound to be grim. When did you ever sit and wait for anything good? This one showed no sign of any effort to cheer it up – not even a wilting pot plant. There was a desk for the guard on duty at one side and regulation grey plastic chairs were ranged round the other three walls. There were no magazines or children's toys.

Soon afterwards, a door opened and a short, balding man

in a shabby suit came into the room. He glanced at them and then came across. 'You are Mrs Sidwell?' he asked Lesley.

'No, that's me' Gina said.

'I am solicitor for Khalil.'

'Oh, yes.' Gina jumped up and offered her hand. 'I'm so pleased to meet you. What do you think about Farid's case? He's done nothing wrong, you know, and the police will realise that. And then they have to let him stay and finish his studies, don't they?'

The solicitor ignored her proffered hand and avoided her eye. 'Not good case,' he said. 'He has trouble with Police.' He shrugged. 'Must go back, I think.' He turned away and headed for the guard's desk, where he signed out and then turned to look at them. 'But do my best,' he said without any detectable conviction, and walked out.

Gina turned to Lesley, eyes blazing. 'He can't even speak English,' she said. 'How the hell –'

A second guard came into the room. 'Come on, then,' he said, and held the door open. He led them into a small, overheated room, which was furnished with three chairs upholstered in that institutional fabric that Lesley had always labelled *vomit tweed*, and a low, flimsy table. A young man was pacing the room. Lesley had not seen him before but, as Gina approached him, she had the opportunity to examine him. He was very young, and his face still had the softness of youth in spite of the obvious signs of stress, the pallor, the purple stains under the eyes, the tightness around the mouth.

He came towards them, unsmiling. Gina stepped towards him, arms lifted as though to hug him, but stopped and put her hands in her coat pockets, as if to stop herself from touching him.

'How are you doing?' she asked.

'I think my lawyer is no good,' he said, and glanced at

Lesley, hoping perhaps, she thought, that she was the super lawyer who would get him out.

'This is my friend, Lesley,' Gina said. 'She's a social worker.'

Lesley saw the hope die in his eyes, but saw, too, the triumph of good manners. He shook her hand. 'Thank you for taking the trouble to come,' he said.

They sat down in a little semi-circle on the vomit-coloured chairs. The guard settled himself on a plastic chair by the door and kept his eyes fixed on them.

'We could see your lawyer was no good,' Gina said. 'Just judging from his suit and his inability to use the definite article.'

For the first time, the young man's face relaxed into the beginnings of a smile. 'I'm glad you said that. In here, I think I'm losing my judgement about what is correct English. We speak a language of our own here. Even I do. If I speak like an Englishman, no one understands me. So we have our own English: only the present tense, no articles, simple words. No idioms but plenty of swear words – in twenty languages. You would find it interesting.'

'I would,' Gina said. She unbuttoned her coat and sat back in her chair. 'I ought to come up with a research project to analyse what happens to the language under these conditions. I might be able to get in here under academic cover.'

Farid's face turned hard. 'You really wouldn't want to do that,' he said. 'It's ...' he glanced to where the guard sat watching them '... it's not that interesting.'

Lesley watched Gina glance at the guard, too, then nod in understanding. 'Anyway,' she said brightly, 'I'm getting you a new lawyer. I know him well – top of the tree. No problem with his English. And no problem with the money. He'll do it for me.'

If she was disappointed by Farid's reaction she did not

show it, but Lesley felt disappointment herself. Gina had not told her this – a free top lawyer up her sleeve. It sounded too good to be true. Perhaps that was what Farid thought, too. 'Thank you,' he said, but the words were no more than polite, the tone flat.

'We shall have to be patient,' Gina sailed on. 'The man I have in mind is in Argentina at the moment, but I've spoken to his wife and the moment he gets back I'll... Well, I may be able to get his mobile number... I can see...' She trailed off, deterred finally by the blankness on his face.

'How is Dora?' he asked.

Since Gina seemed not to be ready to answer, Lesley stepped in. 'I think she's doing all right,' she said. 'It's the half-term holiday, you know. She's revising for her exams. I met her when she was taking a break – out for a walk. She seems very organised.'

For the first time, he smiled properly – a young, wide, delighted smile. 'She is,' he said. 'She will do well.' He looked from one to the other of them. 'Did she give you any message for me?'

Lesley watched Gina as she put her hands to her head in an extravagant gesture of exasperation. 'I didn't think!' she moaned. 'I didn't hear till this morning that I'd got this appointment and I didn't think. I'm so sorry, Farid.'

'It doesn't matter,' he said.

It did, though, and Gina moaned again. 'I should have thought. Bugger it!'

At that moment a buzzer rang, loud and imperious, in the corridor outside. The guard got up, went outside, locked the door and, they could hear, set off at a run down the corridor.

'Let's hope that's not a fire alarm,' Gina said, 'since he's locked us in.'

Farid stood up and paced about as he had been doing when they arrived. 'I have to tell you how terrible it is

164

here,' he said. 'I couldn't while he was here but —' He came back to his seat and spoke rapidly. 'It is too crowded. Six men sleep in my room. There is no space. We can do nothing except lie on our beds. And the others – they can be disgusting. Spitting on the floor. Defecating in the showers. The food you can hardly eat even if you are hungry, and medical services are a joke, really. There is a doctor but he doesn't believe anyone is ill. You go to him and he says you are lying to make your case better to stay. And so much violence. Everyone is so stressed, so afraid. We don't know how long we will be here or what will happen. Fights break out all the time for nothing. And the guards let them happen.'

Gina put a hand on his arm. 'We will get you out of here, Farid. I'll get in touch with this lawyer. I'll get his mobile number from his wife.'

Farid turned and looked her full in the face. 'Don't bother with that, Gina,' he said. 'You are kind, but I don't need the lawyer. I'm going to go home.'

Lesley watched the colour come and go in Gina's face. 'But your studies, Farid. Your career. And you won't be safe. You can't —'

'I can,' he said. 'And I should have done it before, only my mother didn't want it. Syria is my home. I should be there and I should be looking after my mother and my sister. And I want to be where I have a right to be. I am not wanted here and I'm tired of that. I want my home.'

He got up again and resumed his pacing. Gina watched him for a while and then got up and walked over to him. 'Actually, Farid, you're not thinking straight. I'm not surprised. It must be hard to do in this place. But I don't think going home is an option for you. You're a suspect in a murder inquiry. That's why they've put you in here – so they've got you pinned down. They're not going to let you go.'

He turned to her. 'Well,' he said, 'maybe the top lawyer can prove I'm innocent and then I can go home.'

In the car, on the way home, Lorna sat in the front passenger seat while Gina sat in the back in a bleak silence. Lorna filled the silence with chat about the reorganisation of the library, and both she and Lesley were startled when, in a brief conversational lull, Gina said, abruptly, '*Immigrant Removal Centre* is so in your face, isn't it? So unlike our usual British obfuscation about unpleasant things. They really want to be sure that immigrants know exactly what it's for. I thought at first that *IRC* stood for *Immigrant Return Centre*, which is unpleasant in its intentions, but *Return* at least implies that it might be voluntary. *Removal* is quite unequivocal. We only remove things that are dangerous or offensive, don't we? *Removal* is for tumours, rotten teeth, diseased organs, undesirable female hair, pests, threats to your computer, household waste —'

'*Disposal*,' Lesley said.

'What?'

'It's *waste disposal*, isn't it? Not *waste removal*.'

'I suppose it is.' She sounded briefly deflated, but recovered. 'Just give it time,' she said, 'and it'll be *Immigrant Disposal*, and then our immigrants will really know where they stand.'

Lesley was aware of Lorna turning round in her seat to speak to Gina. 'How about furniture removal?' Lorna asked her. 'You don't want rid of your furniture, do you, when you see it put into a removal van? You hope very much to retrieve it the other end.'

This was daring talk, Lesley felt, challenging Gina when she was in this mood. She waited. There was a silence in the back of the car. Then Gina said, as if she was praising a worthy student, 'That's a good point, Lorna. I wonder why *removal* is the word for furniture. Because you don't want it actually removed, do you? You want it moved – transported from one place to another. *Removal* is actually a misnomer. How interesting. I wonder if the first removal firms specialised in working for bailiffs – taking away furniture that hadn't been paid for. I shall research it.'

Lorna turned back to face the front. 'We're benefiting from its being half term,' she said. 'We'd be tangled up in the school run otherwise.'

'Mind you,' Gina said, 'the image of removal vans is scary, isn't it? If you were an immigrant and you'd seen *Removals* on the sides of pantechnicons, you'd picture yourself being packed into one of those to be sent home, wouldn't you? And some of them have been through that already, getting here. So it's a crap name however you look at it.'

Lorna said – and Lesley again admired her courage – 'You don't actually think we should simply open ourselves up to all comers, do you, Gina?'

'Well, of course I don't,' Gina snapped. Then she groaned. 'Oh God,' she said, 'I really do hate a situation that even I don't have an answer to.'

Lorna laughed. 'You mean if you can't find a solution, how can mere politicians be expected to do it?'

'Exactly,' Gina said. And she was not laughing.

Chapter Sixteen

HOW LATE IT WAS, HOW LATE

Saturday 22nd February 2014

When the doorbell rings, I have no idea who it can be. I reach for my phone and see that it is eight-fifteen. Caliban and I sleep late these days, without Kelly to wake us. I haven't been sleeping much at all, actually, but after hours of reading and listening to The World Service, I generally drop off in the early hours and wake late and groggy.

Caliban is enraged by the bell and charges downstairs, barking ferociously. I haul myself out of bed and pull on my dressing gown. At the front door, I shout, 'Who is it?' over Caliban's racket, and hear a familiar voice say, 'Call off the dog, will you?'

I open the door, holding Caliban by his collar. Paula is looking first-thing-in-the-morning perky and ready for anything. 'I just wanted a word,' she says.

We go into the kitchen, where I put the kettle on and shove Caliban out into the garden. He barks a bit more in protest against being denied his walk, and then, I see as I look out of the window, he snuffles morosely among the vegetable beds, looking for things to pee on. It's a good thing nothing is growing at the moment, or he could wreak his revenge.

I make us some coffee and offer Paula some toast, which she accepts. I don't know whether it's because I'm still slow-witted from sleep, or because I'm in my dressing gown, or because eating toast with someone is a companionable thing, but when Paula says, 'You went to see Farid yesterday?' I don't bite her head off.

'I did,' is all I say, and then fill my mouth with toast.

'How is he?' she asks.

I take time over my mouthful and consider my answer. 'Not good,' I say. 'Have you ever been into that place?'

She shakes her head.

'It's vile. It's defeated him. He wants to give up on his asylum claim and go home.'

'Really?'

'He has his pride. Imagine it. Would you want to stay in a country that is so obviously desperate to get rid of you?'

I expect her to say that his wanting to be sent home is further evidence of his guilt, but she says nothing.

'Of course,' I say, 'I pointed out that he can't be sent home while he's a murder suspect.'

She makes a business of stirring her coffee, although there's no sugar in it. 'He does actually have quite a lot going for him,' she says.

To my credit, I don't barge in to point out that that's what I've been telling her all along. I wait.

'He's got really good references from his university lecturers,' she says, 'personal as well as academic. Doesn't necessarily rule him out, but there's no suggestion that he's got a temper. And then there's Dora and her father.' She looks up. 'Would there be another slice of toast?' she asks.

I get up to put more bread in the toaster. I'm pretty sure this is a ploy so she can say what she has to say to my back.

'Talking to them is like going into a bit of a time warp,' she says, 'but I think I believe them. I think I believe that all Dora and Farid did was talk to each other on the school bus, and if all Kelly did was to put a stop to that, then it doesn't make sense that the guy his lecturers describe would have been driven to murder over it.'

I plop a slice of toast on her plate and she looks at me. 'No surprise to you, I know,' she says.

'The only surprise is you admitting it,' I say.

'So,' she says, buttering her toast, 'I think we're getting to a point where we're ready to say that he's no longer a suspect.'

She's not looking at me so I don't look at her. 'You've got evidence against someone else?' I ask as casually as I can, licking a finger and mopping up crumbs from my plate.

'Possibly,' she says.

'Anyone I know?'

She doesn't answer.

'It's Simon Gates, isn't it? You know what's happened to Alice.'

She does look at me now, with something of her old malice. 'For a bright woman you can be a fool, Gina. Nothing's happened to Alice.'

'How do you know?'

'We know. And you do, too, if you think about it.'

I don't know what she means but I'm not going to get sidetracked.

'So not Simon?'

'No.'

'Who, then?'

'Did you know that Matthew O'Dowd was prosecuted for GBH last year?'

'No? What happened?'

'He was prosecuted for an assault on his then girlfriend – not Kelly. The case came to court but, at the last minute, the girl decided not to give evidence and the case collapsed.'

Of course, I'm not really surprised; I think again about his big hands. But still it doesn't feel right. 'It's pretty circumstantial, though, isn't it? As evidence that he killed Kelly?' I say.

'The thing is the nature of his assault on the girl,' she says.

'What did he do?'

'He pushed her off the sea wall.'

I experience a buzzing in my head – the sort of mental panic I can remember getting sometimes in Maths exams. I can see Matt giving a girl a shove in an adolescent rage, but not as a woman-hating serial attacker, stalking his victims one after the other and planning all the stuff with the books. And, as Paula argued, if he hates the book group and all it stands for, why hasn't he gone for me? He comes to my house all the time and Caliban would be no protection against him. Caliban likes him – it's some kind of male bonding thing. Matt would have no trouble dealing with him.

'What do you think his motive would have been?' I ask. 'For killing Kelly, I mean.'

She shrugs. 'With some men it doesn't take much. He assaulted the other girl because he was drunk and she didn't like it. It could have been anything.'

'But the others, Paula. Lily, Alice, Eva. What about them? And the books?'

'The books.' She cuts a square of toast into smaller squares. 'The forensic evidence from the books isn't clear-cut. Our working hypothesis is that he marked up Kelly's book and left it on the beach to advertise his reason for killing her – that she was a sort of monster. And then he realised that her book could lead us to him, so he pinched as many of the other books as he could to muddy the waters, and returned one of them to the library, claiming it was Kelly's. It would have been easy for him to pick up yours, at least. And he probably got into Alice's house the same way you did yesterday.' She swallows the last of her tea and stands up.

I feel myself turn scarlet.

'We had a call from Simon Gates,' she says. 'Someone got into his house and took Alice's phone. And, would you believe it, you were seen in the Gates's garden.'

She is looking hard at me and I start to sweat. 'So, are you here to arrest me for breaking and entering?' I ask. 'Is that what this is really about? Because I think I was justified. When a young woman has a furious row with her husband and then disappears, and the police decide to believe her husband's story and not do anything about it, I think a neighbour has a duty to—'

'Not for the moment,' she says, and picks up her bag. 'I'm not planning to arrest you right now, but you need to give that phone back to Simon Gates and I want your help. You can stop defending Farid and you can stop, for God's sake, worrying about Alice, but —'

'Why? Why not worry about Alice?' I'm on my feet, too, not ready to let her go without an answer.

'You're not a driver, Gina,' she says, 'that's your problem. Think about it.' She takes her coat down from the hook behind the door.

'You say help you,' I say as she puts the coat on and walks down the hall. 'What sort of help?'

'You know Matt,' she says. 'Once you stop fixating on your serial killer theory, you may come up with something useful. Anything you think of, call me.' She turns at the door. 'Just don't pursue anything yourself. I can still arrest you if I choose.'

I stand at the door, watching her as she walks to her car.

'Why, Paula?' I call.

'Why, what?'

'Why did you come to tell me this?'

She half turns, still walking away. 'We were stuck so I called David,' she says. 'He told me to trust you, so I'm trying.' She gets to her car and turns. 'Tell me I'm not making a mistake.'

I don't actually answer because I'm not sure I can. Instead, I find myself making an odd gesture that is both histrionic and ambiguous. I put my hand on my heart. Then I go indoors.

There is a lot to think about and Caliban is scratching at the back door, so I put some clothes on and take him down to the beach. The tide is out, exposing acres of wet, grey sand but, perversely, instead of revelling in the freedom, Caliban trudges along morosely at my heels. I dismiss this, at first, as mere sulking, but then I wonder if he might not be well. Could he have eaten something malign out in the garden? I bend down to look at him more closely and am hit immediately and violently in the backs of my legs. I fall, half on top of Caliban, and think, as I go, *So this is it. This is my turn.* I close my eyes, put my arms over my head and curl up into a ball, waiting for the next blow, but all I can hear is an odd panting noise close to my head and a voice shouting vaguely in the distance. I move an arm, open an eye and find a dog's face very close to mine. It is not Caliban's. This face is black and the mouth is open as though it is laughing at me. I can hear what the voice is saying now. 'Get away, Chaka,' it says. 'Lie down.' Then the dog is yanked away and I uncurl and haul myself to my feet. The owner of the voice is young, female and fulsomely apologetic.

'I'm really, really sorry,' she says. 'He's only young and he doesn't mean any harm. He's my brother's dog and I'm looking after him while he's away. But I don't seem to be able...' she tails off. 'Will you be all right?'

I tell her I will, though I am not so fulsomely forgiving in return. I am wet and filthy and a minute ago I thought I was about to die. Also, something about her tone tells me that she thinks I am old, and that is annoying. I put Caliban on his lead and turn for home.

Back indoors, I strip off my clothes and consign them to the washing machine, then go upstairs for a shower, taking some time to get the sand out of my hair. Reclothed and warm, I return to the kitchen for a cup of coffee and hear an odd, regular rattle coming from the washing machine. *Something in my pocket* I think, and consider what it might be. My phone. My bloody phone is in the wash. I stop the machine, wait, fuming, for the regulation two minutes before I can open it, and then retrieve the phone.

The screen is expectedly blank and nothing happens when I try switching it on. I have a vague idea that I have heard that putting a wet phone in a bowl of dry rice can work, the rice absorbing the moisture, so I find a plastic food tub, put the phone into it, pour on rice, fix on the lid and leave it in the unsure and uncertain hope of its resurrection. Then I tip away my cold coffee, pour myself a slug of cooking brandy and consider the consequences of being phoneless. I have no landline so I am cast adrift here, out of contact with the world. Normally, I would quite welcome this, but just at the moment things are too uncertain. Paula may want me, or any of the book group. I have a sudden, urgent sense that there will be an emergency for which I will be needed and found wanting. It occurs to me that, given an emergency of my own, I could summon help using Alice's phone, but I can't be any help to anyone else. And no one can phone me a warning.

Calmed by my brandy, I think about Paula and her suspicions about Matt. I am glad, of course, that Farid is being ruled out but I am still sure that Kelly wasn't the only victim and the business with the books doesn't seem like Matt at all. Matt doesn't believe in books, really. He can't link what books contain with his own life. That's his problem. That's why I've been asking myself for weeks why it is English A level that he's trying to get. Then there's Alice. Paula obviously thinks that she's got sure-fire evidence that Alice is all right, but I think she may be being conned by Simon. Alice's phone worries me and Simon is still top of my suspect list.

I lean back and close my eyes and let the brandy do its work. *Phones,* I think. *There was something else about a phone. Not mine, not Alice's.* I open my eyes and look up. *Kelly's.* I remember now Matt telling me the police had turned his house upside down, looking for Kelly's phone. Of course they were. My phone is just a pathetic little thing: you can make calls and send texts on it, you can take photos and set alarms, but that's it. It is not a smartphone in any sense. Kelly's was, though. I can see it now, lying beside the till in the shop. It was an iPhone or something of the sort – all-singing and all-dancing. She would have sent emails on it, wouldn't she? And if it is missing then her killer took it. Why? Because there was stuff on it that would incriminate him. Whoever it was had some sort of relationship with Kelly that would be revealed. That could have been Matt, of course. The police didn't find the phone at Matt's house, but he could easily have chucked it into the sea. Except there was always the danger of its being washed up and found, and I'm pretty sure it's not the sim card that gets ruined by the water. Much safer to hide it in a safe place. Why didn't I think of that before I searched the Gates's house? I was looking for signs of Alice, but I should have been searching Simon's things. I think, with a tingling of terror, that, in spite of my half-pledge to Paula, I may have to go back in there.

After a start like this, there is no hope for a day, really. This one dribbles along. I do odd jobs and I try to read but *Notes on a Scandal* unsettles me. Sheba's wanton self-destruction gets under my skin. I start to fret about the phone calls I can't make. I should phone my daughter Annie. She only ever rings me when something is wrong, and I suspected it was dissatisfaction with her boyfriend that was the problem last time she called. When I asked after him, she said, 'He's fine – when I see him,' and then changed the subject. Jon is a junior doctor and no doubt is short of time to lavish on

Annie, but I'm not the person to complain to. Privately – and I am slightly ashamed to admit this – I think Jon is too good for Annie. I love my daughter, but she is self-centred and inconsiderate and I live in fear that she will throw away a good man in a fit of pique. I wonder if my mother felt the same about Andrew. Thinking about Andrew makes me fret again. I must ring Lavender and see if he is back from Argentina or get his mobile number. I have been so stupid about Farid. Now it seems absolutely imperative to me to get Andrew on his case. Andrew's overweening confidence and certainty, which usually annoy the hell out of me, are, I see now, exactly what Farid needs. I can picture Andrew sweeping in, bending Border Agency clerks to his will, settling the asylum claim in days and dispatching Farid back to his student life with a light heart. I could almost love this Andrew of my fantasies.

I should really take the bus into Dover and buy myself a new phone. Phones like mine cost hardly anything, after all. Instead, though, I keep opening up my box of rice and trying to give the kiss of life to my phone, which remains stubbornly dead. The day drags on. At about three o'clock I eat some lunch, and then answer some emails. After that, I abandon one of my cardinal rules and sit down to watch daytime television. Almost instantly, it seems to me, I fall asleep.

I am woken by a ringing at the door, which may have been going on for some time since it got itself incorporated into a dream I was having. I am completely at sea. I register the black windows, the babbling television, the ringing doorbell and – an afterthought – the silent dog. Caliban, I realise, knows who this is and trusts them. *Is it Dora or Matt,* I wonder, as I stumble towards the door. *Should I be teaching now?* I pull the door open and the person on the doorstep pushes urgently past me into the house.

'Alice?' I ask.

'Hi Gina,' she says.

'Wh-?' I say, and then 'H-how?' and finally, 'You're alive.'

'Of course I'm alive,' she says, but she doesn't laugh at me. She looks white and tense and a bit feverish. 'What did you think?'

'I thought Simon had —'

'Killed me? Not this time. He did hit me, though, and I always promised myself he wouldn't do that more than once.' She walks through to the sitting room. 'I walked out,' she said. 'And I've been making arrangements.'

'You left your phone.'

'I know. I didn't want the police to track me in case they told Simon where I was. I drew a wad of cash at the first service station so I wouldn't need to use my credit card.'

'Service station?' I say stupidly. 'You took Simon's car?'

'It's not Simon's car, he just thinks it is. It's our car and I paid for most of it.' She stops and looks at me. 'Didn't you notice that the car had disappeared?' she asks.

'*The trouble with you is, you're not a driver.*' That was what Paula meant. And I saw Simon go off on the bus with the boys. When did I ever see Simon get on the bus? So much for me as the sleuth *extraordinaire*.

'I don't tend to notice cars,' I say lamely.

'I would have thought you'd have heard Simon roaring about it,' she says. 'He'll definitely have missed the car more than he's missed me.'

'Do you want a drink?' I ask.

'No. I've got to get going, but I've got a massive favour to ask you.' She is perched on the arm of a chair, as if ready to take off at any moment. 'I'm taking the boys,' she says. 'I've rented a place near my parents and I'm signed on for supply teaching. There's plenty at this time of year and I'll get something permanent later. I've come to take the boys tonight. I don't want to confront Simon. There'll be a fight,

177

he's quite likely to hit me again and even if he doesn't the boys will be scared.'

'How can you not confront him?'

'That's where the favour comes in. I need you to distract him.'

'Oh, no, Alice —' I have a farcical picture of myself donning a plunging neckline and sashaying round to Simon's to seduce him on the sitting room sofa while Alice creeps upstairs to steal away her boys.

'I need you to get him round here,' she says. 'Some domestic emergency. Play the helpless little woman. Make him feel competent and manly. The boys are in bed. I've been watching outside for their light to go off. I'll go and wait in the alley. You get Simon round here. I'll slip in and pick up the boys. The car's parked up in the shadows beyond the lamppost. Get me ten minutes, Gina. That's all I ask.'

Nobody, I think, has ever asked me to do something so terrifying before. 'When he finds them gone,' I protest weakly, 'he'll be beside himself. How will he know you've got them?'

'I've got a note for him. I'll leave it on one of the boys' beds.'

'And he'll realise what I've done and come roaring round here and kill me. Or hit me, anyway.'

'He won't. He cares too much about his reputation and his job. Besides, you've got Caliban. Si's scared stiff of him, didn't you know that?'

'Caliban hates him.'

'Well then.'

'What sort of domestic emergency? I can't just create one of those.'

She looks round the room. 'Have you had anything trip the trip switch since you've been here?'

'Yes, there's a lamp upstairs. I don't use it any more

because it was annoying. But I know how to deal with that. You just –'

'Act stupid!' she says.

'But Simon will think –'

'For ten minutes. For ten minutes he'll think you're an idiot. And then he'll realise you've outsmarted him.' She gets up off her perch and comes towards me. 'Please, Gina,' she says.

'How will I know it's safe to let him go back home?'

'I'll give a toot as I drive away.'

'Do you want your phone?'

'I'll pick it up when I get the boys. I can't hide from Simon forever. We'll need to sort things out properly. He'll need to see the boys – they'll need to see him. He's a good father. It's the reason I stayed with him longer than I should have. But if I leave them with him, he'll never let me see them.'

'The phone's not at your house. It's here.'

For the first time, she's the one who is nonplussed. 'What?' she asks.

'Long story,' I say. 'I'll fetch it.'

I bring her the phone. We hug and wish each other good luck. I feel sick.

When she has gone, I go upstairs and get the dodgy lamp from the cupboard in the spare room to which it has been consigned. There is something the matter with its switch mechanism. I tried changing the plug but it still tripped the trip switch nine times out of ten. I carry it into the bedroom, put it on the dressing table, plug it in and switch on. The house is obligingly plunged into immediate darkness. I curse myself for being an idiot. I should have prepared before I did this – found a torch and my keys. Then I think that, actually, this is better. It looks more authentic if I am unprepared.

I grope my way downstairs, stumble over Ariel, who doesn't grasp the concept of not seeing in the dark, fumble along the hall to the front door, put it on the latch and go round to ring on Simon's door. When he opens it, glass in hand – his reward for getting the boys to bed, I assume – the light pouring out from his house seems startlingly bright. When he sees me, he makes a move as though he would like to shut the door on me. I jump in to stop him.

'Simon,' I say, 'I'm terribly sorry but I'm in need of help.' My heart is running so hard and so fast that I sound quite convincingly panicked. 'I'm in total darkness,' I say. 'I thought it might be a power cut, but obviously…' I gesture at the bright warmth of his hallway. 'So I've got no idea what to do.'

He stares at me. This is the last thing he expected and he doesn't know how to react. I have to play up my role. I abandon any lingering pride. 'This hasn't happened since I moved here, and before – you know – my husband used to deal with this sort of thing.' I give a helpless little shrug. 'Call myself a feminist,' I say, though I can hardly get the words out through my gritted teeth, 'but when it comes to this sort of thing it's a man I need.'

I follow up my shrug with a self-deprecating little smile, but he is not charmed. His face is set hard and doesn't move.

'I've got the boys,' he says. 'I can't leave them.'

'No, of course,' I say but I make no move to go; I just stand there, looking helpless, defying him to shut the door in my face.

'Have you got a torch?' he asks.

'Somewhere, I think, but I can't remember where I've put it. Have you got one? If I could borrow it, then maybe I could manage till the morning, only it's so cold and the heating will have gone off, I suppose, and —' I resist an insane urge to twist a curl of hair winsomely round one finger but I do gaze up trustingly into his face.

He avoids my eye. 'I can tell you what to do,' he says. 'You know where your fuse box is?'

'Fuse box,' I say vaguely. 'What would that look like?'

He sighs. It is an eloquent sigh, compounded of impatience, incredulity and triumph. 'I'll go and check on the boys,' he says. 'If they're asleep I can leave them for a bit. It probably won't take five minutes.'

'Probably not,' I say wistfully, 'when you know what you're doing.'

He doesn't ask me in out of the cold while he goes upstairs. I step back and peer down to the alleyway to see if I can spot Alice. There is just a glimpse of a white face and I raise a thumb in encouragement. Simon returns with a powerful torch and we proceed to my house, where Caliban breaks into frenzied barking and ominous growling – dogs are excellent judges of character, I think – and I'm afraid Simon may slip from my grasp as he backs away, so after some fruitless shouting, I grab Caliban's collar and drag him out to rage in the garden.

It takes a little while to negotiate my way in the dark, and by the time I get back, Simon has already found the fuse box – on the wall in the hall – and is opening it up. Panic grabs me. I had banked on distracting him, leading him to places where I 'thought' the fuse box might be. I pictured a good bit of time running the torch round the cupboard under the stairs. Too late. He has only been in the house for two minutes maximum and in another thirty seconds he'll have located the trip switch and that will be it. And Alice can barely have entered her house by now. Ten minutes suddenly seems an unfeasibly long time for keeping anyone anywhere, let alone keeping a man who hates me and has sleeping children to get back to. I start to babble.

'You found it!' I cry. 'I should have known where it was, really, shouldn't I? Only it's above my head, of course. One of the penalties for being small. You have no idea what the world looks like from down here.'

The cover of the fuse box sticks, I know, so he is tugging

at it, but it soon gives in, and there are the switches, exposed in the bright glare of his torch.

'Gosh,' I say. 'Is that what they look like?'

He summons me closer with a silent, beckoning finger. It is a gesture both patronising and threatening. It makes me want to bite him, but I advance obediently. 'The Trip Switch,' he says, with heavy emphasis, putting a finger on it. 'It should be down but it is up. I push it down and —'

'Let there be light!' I exclaim as brightness floods the hall and strange clicks and whirrs indicate machines around the house coming back to life.

'Thank you *so* much,' I gush. 'I would never have worked out what to do. You really saved me. I'm so sorry to disturb your evening, and just when you'd got the boys off to bed —' He slams the fuse box closed and says. 'The place probably needs rewiring. You certainly need a new fuse box. I doubt this one even conforms to HS regulations.'

'HS?' I ask, sounding as dim as I can manage. This is promising. I reckon I need to fill another five or six minutes and he is actually helping me out.

'Heath and safety?' he says, with the upward inflection that implies, *Doesn't everyone know that?*

'You mean it's dangerous?' I ask, wide-eyed.

'You've got everything on the one circuit,' he says.

'Now you're losing me,' I say. 'Can you explain?'

He opens his mouth and then changes his mind. 'Get someone in,' he says. He turns towards the door.

'Let me at least offer you a drink,' I cry, hopelessly aware that I have only cooking brandy, which is far less appealing than the nice glass of whisky I have taken him away from.

'I need to get back to the boys,' he says.

Damn.

He is moving down the hall.

'The thing is, Simon,' I say, the panic rising to my throat and audible, I'm sure, in my voice, 'I must have done something to make this happen, mustn't I? So how can I make sure it doesn't happen again?'

'If it happens again, you'll know what to do, won't you?'

'Well, yes, but it's so scary with electrics, isn't it? I mean if something isn't working properly – and what you were saying about health and safety – I could have a fire, couldn't I?'

Am I overdoing this? He is a man with a low opinion of women but, even so, can this convince him?

It seems it can. He is standing by the door now, poised to leave, but he asks, as to a half-wit, 'Well did you switch something on just before the power went off?'

This I can manage. This I can spin out. 'Well,' I say, 'the thing is, I'd fallen asleep, and I woke up and realised it was dark and cold, so I switched several things on.' I pause, as if in painful thought. 'The lamp by the sofa – I turned that on. And then, because I was cold, I put the electric fire on. I wonder if it could have been that because I don't use it much these days. I've got this wonderful woodburner, you see, so I don't need the fire. But it had burnt down while I was asleep and I just needed some quick warmth, but the electric fire did give out quite a nasty burning smell. I thought it was just that smell you get when a fire hasn't been used for a while – it's the dust burning off, isn't it? But maybe it was something more serious.'

'Don't use the fire,' he says. 'If you're worried, stick with the woodburner.' The subtext is clear: *Just don't bother me any more.*

He turns the door handle.

'The toaster!' I cry desperately.

'What about it?'

'That's what I switched on just before the lights went out. I was going to make cheese on toast for supper. Though, come to think of it, I did turn the grill on, too. I like to toast the bread lightly before I put the cheese on and finish it under the grill. It's so much better that way, isn't it – so the toast is crisp? So I couldn't say which one it was that did it, but I suppose if I go back and try again I'll find out, won't I?'

'Oh, for Christ's sake!'

He pushes past me quite roughly and barges into the kitchen. He looks around and then picks up the toaster.

'Where's the bread?' he demands.

Rumbled.

'The what?' I ask, stalling.

'The bread. You said you were making toast.'

'Oh! Yes. I hadn't cut it yet. I always put the toaster on first, to heat up.'

Does this make any sense? Does anyone actually do that?

'It takes a while to heat up,' I add feebly.

'Well, that's probably what did it. I'm surprised it hasn't happened before. You're not supposed to do that. It'll heat up too fast.'

'Oh, I see,' I say mournfully. 'No one's ever told me that. My fault then.'

I am exhausted. However many minutes it has been of feigned idiocy have worn me out.

He pushes past me again and stomps off down the hall, calling, 'Get that fuse box changed' as he disappears.

I am pursuing him with no idea how to delay him further when I hear a faint double toot from a car some way down the road. I have to stop and lean against the wall to stop my knees from buckling in relief. My front door slams closed and then I hear his open and close. How long will it be until he is back?

Not long at all is the answer. I just have time to double lock the front door and put the chain on and to bring Caliban in from the garden, locking the back door and removing the key, before my front door is under siege. He must have gone straight up to check on the boys and found empty beds and Alice's note. Mixed with my terror at the furious pounding on my door and the stream of invective that accompanies it is a first pang of conscience. Was this actually the right thing to do? I picture him running upstairs and the moment of panic as he saw the empty beds, before he found the note. I do understand that Alice didn't want a row but I'm not sure this was the right way to go about it. A screaming row would have been bad for the boys, obviously, but isn't this scary for them, too?

Well, it's done now and all I can do is to lie on the sofa with a cushion over my head while Caliban barks his heart out. Eventually, it stops, and Simon retreats with a last cry of 'Fucking bitch!' Or is it *witch*?

I spend the rest of the evening lying on the sofa. I can't eat anything and, though the television is on, I really don't take anything in. And I have the sound down low because I am gripped by the fear that Simon will try to burn the house down. I picture a paraffin-soaked rag through my letterbox, followed by a lighted match. My rational self tells me that he won't do this because he knows that he must have been seen and heard creating the rumpus at my front door and would therefore be the prime suspect, but when it gets to bedtime, I can't go upstairs to sleep in a room I could be trapped in. I fetch a blanket and pass a night of sleepless terror on the sofa, while Caliban sleeps on my feet.

Chapter Seventeen

THE GHOST ROAD

Sunday 23rd February 2014

Lily

Emma Terry had been in the house for almost two hours before she finally lost her rag with her brother, and she thought that was pretty good going. She had arrived soon after nine and, finding Jack asleep on the sofa, had made a start on clearing up the kitchen. Glad that she had thought to bring rubber gloves, she started by throwing stuff out: bread covered in a flourishing coat of blue mould, cheese likewise, and a bottle of milk, solidly sour, lodged in the fridge beside a fresh bottle. The fresh bottle was encouraging: he had probably been eating cereal, then. Cereal and pizzas, it looked like, from the toppling pile of boxes that leaned beside the back door, smeared with congealed tomato sauce. She carried the pile, in two armfuls, out to the bin in the garden. *Did grief really prevent you from walking to the rubbish bin*, she thought irritably. It was a traitorous thought. She had promised herself to try to understand Jack's complete giving up on the world. As their mother kept saying, Lily had been his world so why wouldn't he give up on a world without her? And Emma herself had never experienced any loss that came near to his, so who was she to judge? It was barely more than two weeks since Lily's accident. She had to be patient with him.

By the time she had swabbed, scoured and mopped the little kitchen to her satisfaction, it was ten o'clock. She looked in on Jack again to see if he wanted a coffee. He was awake, but humped himself away from her, muttering into the sofa back. She opened the curtains and let the probing, grey light illumine the room's squalor. Beer cans littered the floor; a nearly empty bottle of whiskey stood beside the sofa with an overturned glass beside it in a dark brown pool. A pile of unopened mail lay on a chair. She picked it up and saw that it consisted mainly of cards – condolences, heartfelt no doubt, because everyone loved Lily, and abandoned unread.

'I'm going to start on Lily's clothes, Jack,' she said to his unresponsive back. 'I'll clear everything out and then you can tell me if there's anything you want to keep.'

And then, she thought, maybe he would start sleeping in his bed again, instead of down here in all this mess.

Upstairs, the bedroom was not tidy exactly – Lily and Jack were never tidy – but the untidiness felt alive, unlike the dreary mess downstairs. There was the expectant feel of a room that had been suddenly abandoned. Emma wasn't a fanciful woman – not a dreamer like Jack or a reader like Lily – but even she felt that the room was waiting for Lily to come back. A couple of the vivid bandanas she liked to wear were draped over the mirror as if waiting for her to try them on, makeup lay scattered over the dressing table and a pair of red pumps lay at an angle as though she had just kicked them off and would slip them back on at any moment. Of course Jack couldn't sleep in here. She had offered before to come and collect Lily's stuff but he had turned her down. He'd agreed only grudgingly this time and she was not sure still if he would actually let her take it all away.

She went over to the bed. On the floor by the bed lay a

book, open and face down, where Lily had dropped it, she supposed, before going to sleep on the last night of her life. She looked under the pillows. Lily's pyjamas lay under one of them – black with a deep pink heart on the front. A faint scent of patchouli hung about them, as it always used to hang about Lily. She added them to an IKEA bag in the corner of the room, which seemed to be doing duty as a laundry bag, and carried the bag downstairs to put a wash on. There was very little of Jack's stuff there. She wondered if he had changed his clothes at all since the day of Lily's funeral, when she and her mum had come over and more or less put his clothes on for him.

Going back upstairs, she took with her two suitcases she had brought from home, and a bin bag. Lily, she knew, bought most of the clothes she didn't make herself from Second Hand Rose in Dungate, which sold 'vintage' or, as they liked to say, 'pre-loved' clothes. Emma planned to see whether they would like to take them back to be loved all over again. Her mum had a friend who did amateur operatics and might like some of the costumes Lily had made for her singing gigs.

Working methodically, she went through the wardrobe, separating the clothes into second-hand and homemade and putting them into the two cases. Anything that was too ragged she put in the bin bag, along with underwear, to go to the fabric recycling. There was a radio beside the bed and she turned it on and up to loud, drowning out, as best she could, thoughts of Lily as she worked. You couldn't drown her out that easily, though, not Lily. It was her contradictions, she guessed, that had gone to Jack's heart. They were there in her looks – dark and sexily gipsyish, but innocent somehow, with her skinny body still like a teenage girl's. Then on stage, she strutted her stuff like a pro, but off stage she was all nerves and shyness. She could be infectiously high-spirited, the sparkling centre of everyone's attention, and then you'd catch her face drooping as though she'd got the sorrows of the world on her shoulders. And she was so sweet, so thoughtful, so loving, and at the same time so stubborn in wanting her own way and so ugly sometimes if she didn't get it. *A true original* someone had said at the funeral, and so she was. Jack was a good-looking guy and plenty of women would be after him now, but Lily wasn't an act you could follow on stage or off.

She lugged the cases downstairs one at a time and then went back for the bin bag. She left them in the hall and went in to Jack. She gave him a shake.

'Come on, Jacko,' she said. 'Come and look in these cases and see if there's anything you want to keep.'

He rolled over. 'What cases?' He looked terrible – red-eyed, stubbly and sick.

'Lily's things,' she said, doing her best to sound no-nonsense and kind at the same time.

'What things?'

She sat down on the sofa by his feet. 'Lily's clothes,' she said. 'We agreed I was going to come and pack them up today. I'm taking them to good homes.'

'You're not taking them fucking anywhere.' He was up off the sofa, almost knocking her to the ground. Out in the hall, he picked up the cases and started up the narrow stairs with them, scraping the wall as he went. Emma remembered Lily painting that wall. *Smoked paprika, that's the colour*, she had giggled. *Delicious!*

Emma stood at the bottom of the stairs and yelled. 'What are you going to do with them, Jack? Hang them up again? Or leave them out in a heap on the floor and turn upstairs into a tip like you have down here? Either way, you won't sleep up there, will you, not with Lily's things there? What are you going to do? Sleep on the sofa forever? Not wash?

Not change your clothes? Live on pizzas and invite the rats in to share them? Not work? Not pay the rent? Let the band down? Can you imagine what Lily would think if she could see you? She sorted you out, Jack. The least you can do for her memory is stay sorted.'

He stood still, head bowed, and she waited for an explosion. They'd always had furious fights, she and Jack, since they were kids. Then he let go of one of the cases, just opened his hand and let it fall, so that it somersaulted down the stairs and landed at Emma's feet. Then he turned and brought the other case down , throwing it against the front door. 'OK,' he said. 'Take them. I don't want to see any of it. Do what you like.'

She put her arms round him. 'You smell terrible,' she said. 'Go and have a shower and put some clean clothes on. I'll clear up in there,' she jerked her head towards the living room, 'and make us a cup of coffee.'

He was a long time upstairs, so long that at one point she panicked and went and banged on the bathroom door to ask if he was all right. She thought of him cutting his wrists, which was ridiculous because everyone used electric razors these days, didn't they? But she cursed herself for not clearing Lily's stuff out of the bathroom. They would all be there still, her bottles and oils and creams. Stupid to leave them.

By the time he came down, she had blitzed the living room and was making coffee. 'You look better,' she said, although truth to tell he didn't much. He was cleaner, certainly. He had washed his hair and shaved but that only emphasised how pale he was, how sharp the bones in his face, how red-rimmed his eyes, how dark the circles under them. They sat with their coffee in the sitting room and Emma produced a Twix which she had brought with her, and handed him a stick.

'I was thinking about Lily's books,' she said. 'You won't read them, will you?

They both looked across at the four short shelves that housed Lily's collection of paperbacks.

'They're not doing any harm, are they?' he said.

'They'll make you sad if they stay there.'

He jerked back with a rough crow of laughter that sent his coffee slopping over his hand. 'We can't have that, can we?' he said. 'Can't have me being sad. Get rid of every trace of Lily and bingo! Everything'll be fine!'

She felt herself flush. 'I didn't mean that,' she said. 'I know how hard this is for you.'

He put his mug down on the floor and got up. 'Actually, you don't,' he said. 'You've got no idea. You can't begin to imagine it. All those songs I've sung about losing the one you love and I didn't come close to knowing what it's like.'

He walked out of the room and came back wearing a jacket. 'I'm going to meet the guys down at the pub,' he said. 'Do what you like with the stuff.'

When he had gone, she finished her coffee and ate Jack's stick of Twix. Then she went over and looked at the books. She was no reader herself, except for magazines, and the titles didn't mean much to her. One or two of them she thought were probably famous, and they all looked in decent condition. She went and rummaged around in the cupboard under the sink for some plastic carriers and started loading the books into them. When she got to the bottom shelf she stopped. The books there were different, hard backs, more like school books, she thought, from when Lily was doing A levels, and probably not the sort of thing that a charity shop would want. She sat back on her heels and considered. What she needed was someone who could tell her whether it was worth lugging these books into Dungate to the Oxfam shop, or whether they would turn them away. Alice, two doors down, ought to be able to tell her; she was a teacher. Emma was not all that keen on teachers. She had been a practically minded child for whom ordinary life was full of interest and what she learnt in school didn't seem to connect to that. Teachers got disappointed with her and school had seemed one long nag. Still, she had met Alice a few times and she seemed nice. She got up and went out.

Ringing and knocking brought no one to the door, however. She stood, shivering, on the doorstep, listening to a dog barking from next door, and it occurred to her that next door was that woman who organised the book group Lily had been so keen on. She was a bit weird, and she reminded Emma of some of her teachers, but it was worth a try.

She rang the bell and the volume of the dog's barking increased. She heard footsteps inside and then a voice called, 'Who is it?'. The unfriendliness of the tone took her aback but she said, trying to keep a note of apology out of her voice, 'I'm Emma Terry. I'm Jack's sister.'

The door opened a crack. The woman wasn't old – no older than her mum, at any rate – but she opened the door like old people do, as though only an armed robber could possibly be on the doorstep. When she saw Emma, however, she opened the door wider and held onto the dog's collar. 'Come in,' she said. 'I'm Gina.'

From then on, it was quite straightforward, if a bit embarrassing. She agreed to come round, took a look at the shelf of books and said, 'Ah, bless her. She'd have done well if she'd carried on with her A levels, you know.' Then she had knelt down and gone through the books and looked at them and her face had settled into a frown. Looking up at Emma, she said, 'I'm afraid some of these aren't, technically speaking, yours to give away. Lily seems to have had them on "permanent loan".' She made a little speech marks gesture with her fingers. Then, when she saw that Emma didn't understand, she said, 'Lily nicked them, I'm afraid. They've got school labels or library labels in them.'

'Oh, bollocks,' Emma said. 'Sorry – but what am I supposed to do with them?'

And Gina took pity on her. She said she would take them and see if the county library and the school wanted them back. 'Leave it to me,' she said, as she bundled the books quickly into two bags. 'I expect you've got enough on your plate. How do you think Jack's doing?'

'He's angry,' Emma said.

Gina picked up her bags. 'Wouldn't you be?' she said.

Chapter Eighteen

THE SENSE OF AN ENDING

Sunday 23ʳᵈ February 2014

I think I probably doze a bit in the hour before daybreak, as you often do after a sleepless night. I come to, stiff and miserable, and my stomach immediately curdles in apprehension. I look at Caliban, who has been unsettled by my apparent collapse and is eager for the reassurance of our routine morning walk. I know that I am too frightened to leave the house, though. Even with the dog beside me, I can't face encountering Simon. 'Sorry, Cal,' I say. 'You'll have to wait a bit.'

I make a cup of tea and sit down with it, dunking digestives into it in the hope that they will quieten my gastric churning, and berating myself for short-sighted stupidity. How could I not see that this would happen? It was all very well for Alice to tell me that Simon would be frightened off by Caliban, but I'm still living next door to a man who hates me, aren't I? And who still might be Kelly's killer, even though it turns out that Alice is safe. If he doesn't move house, I shall have to, and that is ridiculous.

I say quite a lot of this out loud and Caliban listens attentively, thinking, I suppose, that I might drop some clues about my intentions vis-à-vis our morning stroll. 'All right,' I say, 'but mind you stay close by.' I wrap myself in outdoor gear and go out to the garden to squint up at Simon's bedroom

194

window. The curtains are closed and my hope is that he took to the whiskey bottle last night and is now sleeping it off. We walk out into the purplish grey silence of a February dawn and walk alone and unmolested along the soggy sand. I almost enjoy it.

Steadied by this successful foray into the outside world, I shower, wash my hair and change into decent clothes. Then I make some toast and take a look at my phone in its bed of rice. It remains resolutely dead. I consider a trip into Dover for a new one. The buses are few and far between on a Sunday, though. Tomorrow will be soon enough.

So, how to spend the day? Domesticity seems to be the answer, so I change the bed and do some hoovering, which I haven't done since I cleaned up for Freda's arrival. Then I trawl the fridge and fish out ingredients for a chicken casserole, which I shall cook slowly in a low oven so that its aroma fills the house and comforts my ragged senses. Chopping and stirring with the radio on, I begin to feel almost tranquil, until a ring at the door startles me into terror all over again.

I take my time, washing my hands and taking my apron off before I go to the door. I call out, 'Who is it?' in a ridiculously old-lady fashion and it turns out to be Jack Terry's sister, whom I have met once or twice and who seems quite harmless. I open the door and let her in, hanging onto Caliban, who is as primed for danger as I am. It seems she wants help with Lily's books, and she is looking quite frazzled so I go with her to have a look at them. The house smells powerfully of bleach and air-freshener and feels startlingly alien. Is this young woman consciously eradicating even the scent of Lily? Lily moved in a musky aura of aromatic oils, and she extended that to scented candles and joss sticks around the house. How does Jack feel about this new, aseptic environment? And where is he, for that matter?

I don't ask and I don't comment. Emma is doing her best and I am running out of neighbours to antagonise so I turn my attention to the books. Lily's little bookcase has been cleared except for the bottom shelf, so I get down on the floor to see what is there. They are mostly hardback classics – her A level texts, I assume: *The Canterbury Tales*, *Troilus and Cressida*, *Sense and Sensibility*, Toni Morrison's *Beloved* and a selection of Keats' poems among them. Lily was at the grammar school and I am surprised that she would have had to buy her own texts. When I pull a couple out and look at them, though, I see that she didn't. The school labels are still stuck into the front of them. When Lily dropped out of school she took a few trophies with her. And I'm not sure anyone else could have used them anyway. Lily was into heavy annotation – comments scrawled in any available space and lavish highlighting. There are also some History textbooks and Eric Bentley's *The Life of the Drama* and David Edgar's *How Plays Work*. These last two are paperbacks with the plasticised covers of library books and I see that they have county library labels in them. *Oh, Lily*. Pulling out the next book, Clare Tomalin's biography of Jane Austen, I feel something tucked behind it, between the book and the wall. I pull it out and I know immediately exactly what it is. I glance round at Emma Terry, who is half watching me but not really paying attention. I slip the thing between two books and sit back on my heels, thinking, with a rising panic, about what this means and what I should do.

I probably would have offered to take the books and restore them to their owners anyway, but as it is they make a convenient cover for spiriting away my find. I ask for a couple of carrier bags and I carry it all away. Back at home, I drop the bags, get my gloves from my coat pocket, put them on and dig out my alarming find from one of the bags. I lay it on the kitchen table and look at it. I will not, I decide, investigate it further. This time, I won't get into trouble with Paula. I shall ring her immediately and hand it over.

Except I don't have a working phone. I look once more into the box of rice but the thing is obviously never going to speak again. I think about phones I might beg the use of and immediately rule out all my neighbours. Simon is out of the question, obviously; Harry, I wouldn't ask a favour from except in direst need; and I can hardly go back and ask to use Emma's phone, can I? I could cycle round to Lorna's or Lesley's but I am reluctant. It's Sunday lunchtime and they will be spending a cosy day with their husbands – even doing family lunch, perhaps. I don't want to turn up like a sorry petitioner on their doorsteps, single and helpless. Pride again. So there is nothing for it but to make the trip into Dover and hand this thing over to Paula myself. I run down the road to the bus stop to consult the timetable, find that the next bus is at two o'clock and scoot back, heart pounding as I pass Simon's door.

Back home, gloved again, I slide the thing into a plastic freezer bag and then sit down to eat some of the chicken casserole, which would have been better with another half an hour's cooking. Then I brush my hair, put on some lipstick, dress myself in my decent coat and boots and depart for the bus stop. I notice, as I pass, that there are no lights on in Simon's house, although it is the sort of day when you are likely to have a light or two on all the time. I worry briefly that he may have gone in pursuit of Alice and the boys but remember that he doesn't have a car. Where is he then?

The bus is ten minutes late, leaving me anxious and exposed on the deserted road, and when it comes it is virtually empty. An old man is dozing at the front and a young woman is struggling to control two small children at the back. I settle myself midway and devote myself to thought. I have a pretty good idea now of what my find means, and Paula will know for sure once she has had a look at it. I don't need to work it all out but old habits die hard.

As I am walking towards the police station, it occurs to me for the first time that Paula might not be there. It is Sunday, after all, and Paula is convinced that she is not looking for a serial killer so she won't necessarily be working round the clock. I try to imagine Paula's Sundays. The gym, I think, and maybe a trip to the supermarket. Perhaps a pub lunch with friends? Or with family? Is she the sort to go to her mum's for Sunday lunch? Does she have nieces and nephews she dotes on? I really don't know. I have never thought of her as anything other than a police officer, but she must have another life, mustn't she? Or perhaps not.

At the station, I ask the desk sergeant if I can speak to her and he says she is not available. That doesn't tell me whether she is in the building or not and he won't be pressed to elaborate.

'Look,' I say, brandishing my evidence bag, 'this is important evidence in the Kelly Field murder case. DI Powell needs to see it right away and I need to explain to her how and where I found it. Otherwise she won't understand the significance of —'

He raises a hand to stop me, and then prises the bag from my fingers. 'I'll pass this on, Mrs...' he checks my name in his log '... Sidwell, and DI Powell will be in touch if she needs any further information. If I can just take your phone number?'

He stops, pen poised.

'I don't have a phone,' I say.

He puts down his pen. 'No phone at all?'

'Not of any kind. I only have a mobile and I put that in the washing machine. Not on purpose, you understand, but because it was in a pocket and I got attacked by a dog.'

I have, I can see, lost any credibility I ever had with him.

'Address?' he says. 'Or haven't you got one of those either?'

Meekly, I give him my address, but I am not convinced that he is going to make passing the bag on to Paula any sort of priority.

'It really is important that DI Powell gets that asap,' I say, 'and I think I ought to leave a note with it, explaining where I found it.'

He makes a *be my guest* gesture but he doesn't offer me the wherewithal to write the note, so I find an old shopping list in my bag and pick up his pen. I cross out *dog biscuits, milk, washing powder, potatoes* and *printer ink* and, on the back of the paper, I write:

> *Found this among*
> *Lily Terry's books.*
> *Have not investigated it.*
> *Over to you*
> *Gina*

I go to put it into the bag but the sergeant stops me.

'Don't want to contaminate the evidence, do we?' he says. 'Not if it's so important.'

He condescends to find a paper clip and attaches note to bag.

That's it then,' he says.

Back outside, I head for the mobile phone shop I have seen. I know what these places are like and what the expectations of their staff are, so I rehearse my manifesto before I go inside.

'No bells and whistles,' I say. 'Something I can phone people with and they can phone me on. I like to send texts, and if I can set an alarm on it and take the occasional photo, that's a bonus, but absolutely nothing else required.'

I am a huge disappointment, of course, to the skinny

young man in an over-large suit who is on lonely duty in an empty shop on this grim Sunday afternoon. I can see that he longs to tempt me to consider something more exciting. His eye lingers on a display of smart silver phones and he starts to explain how very simple they are to use and what a great offer they have on them at the moment, but he sees the steely glint in my eye and takes me reluctantly to a neglected corner of his emporium, where he flaps a disdainful hand at a huddle of little phones in unsmart colours. I choose a green one and say I will have it.

And I expect that that will be pretty much that. I have had the forethought to bring my dead phone with me and assume that it will be a matter of moments to substitute the living for the dead. I could not be more wrong. I am not just purchasing this phone, I am entering into a solemn and binding agreement, an agreement hedged about with no little ceremony and a good deal of signing. I could be adopting this phone, so complex is the procedure. We start with payment options. I say briskly that I don't want to pay as I go, since this inevitably involves running out of call time just when you most need it, and I want the cheapest monthly tariff as I don't talk to people much and if I want long conversations I go to people's houses and talk to them. I think cutting to the chase like this is helpful, but I can see it is sending him into a panic. He is like an actor who finds that someone has cut several speeches in a scene so he doesn't know where he is in the script. There is nothing for it but to let him take me through all the options, dilating on their pros and cons, until it is my cue to say I will take the cheapest monthly tariff and we can move on. I recklessly give out my bank details and sign a sheaf of documents in places marked with a cross. Then I get out my debit card in preparation for paying and departing for the three-thirty bus home.

But we are not done yet. Now, the laundered sim card

must be replaced with a new one, and a Byzantine series of operations performed in order to transfer my number to the new phone. Now the new card must be registered. Now the real interrogation starts.

I am asked searching questions about my provenance (mother's maiden name) and history (I am asked the name of my first pet; this is to be *memorable information* to support a password which I expect never to use). My salesman types the information I give him into his computer and gazes solemnly at his screen. He then moves away to make a phone call, *for confirmation,* comes back and does more typing. The prospect of the three-thirty bus fades and vanishes. Finally, he says that all seems to be in order and I prepare to sign again in multiple spaces. He stops me in my tracks. 'Before we do that, he says, 'there is the question of the disposal of the old phone,' and he launches into a lecture on *Defunct Mobile Phones, Safe Disposal of.*

I make a huge effort to remain pleasant. 'Feel free to do whatever you like with it,' I say. 'Really.' And I reach for the forms to sign. He snatches them from me. I cannot sign those, he tells me, until I have signed over the old phone. He produces a new sheaf of papers and starts to ask me my details all over again for this new form.

I break. I simply snap. The grief, the frustration, the fear, the lack of sleep of the last two weeks, combined, it seems to me, with the disappointment, disillusionment, anger and guilt of a lifetime, rise up uncontrollably in me and I dump the lot on the hapless head of this spotty boy. I stand up. I snatch up the forms, signed and unsigned, and I rip them in pieces. 'I have bought houses in less time than it's taking to buy this sodding phone,' I yell, and I pick up the phone, in its box, and hurl it at him.

His reactions are quick, I will say that for him. He catches it, which is fortunate, I think, as I stomp out of the shop, because otherwise he could get me prosecuted for assault. He is not short of information about me to give to the police if he can be bothered to piece the forms back together.

I regret my rage the moment I step out of the shop. How do I expect to manage without a phone? There may be another phone shop in Dover but I don't know where it is, and I have missed the bus and there won't be another until four-thirty. I could weep. There are plenty of closed shops around here. It is tempting just to sit down in a doorway and wait for the night to come, when I might, with any luck, be carried away in the gentle arms of hypothermia. On the other hand, people might toss coins at me, which would be embarrassing, and despair is a bad habit to get into at the age of fifty. I have a better idea. There is a question I want to ask Eva. I intended to phone her when I'd got my new phone but, instead, I shall go and see her.

It takes twenty minutes to walk to the hospital and that gives me time to justify my phone rage, to consider the possible pleasures of the phone-free life and to resolve to behave better on this visit to Eva than I did on the last one. By the time I get to the hospital, I am quite cheerful.

There is nothing in the hospital shop that Eva wouldn't shudder at so I buy her a really terrible-looking murder mystery, which might make her laugh, and find my way to her ward. She is looking much better than she did three days ago. She is sitting in a chair beside her bed, looking perfectly *soignée* in a silky dressing gown and full war paint. Her hair is in its smooth silver coil and the dressing on her head has been replaced by a smaller plaster. In spite of my last visit, she actually seems pleased to see me.

'This is a flying visit,' I say, kissing her. 'I won't wear you out, I promise.'

'I'm delighted to have the company,' she says, putting on her glasses and examining the book's lurid cover and unpromising blurb.

202

'I thought it might give you a laugh,' I say. 'Better than chocolates, I thought, and the toiletries in the shop were well below your standard.'

'It will get me through this evening nicely,' she says. 'And they are releasing me tomorrow.'

'Will you be able to manage at home? It's surprisingly difficult to manage with one arm. I sprained a wrist once and I couldn't even pull my knickers up.'

'Lesley has kindly invited me to stay with her. Peter will be away next week so we shall live quietly.'

'She'll want to feed you up,' I warn.

'And I shall indulge her for a day or two. The food here has been quite inedible.'

'Will you be nervous?' I ask. 'After what happened to you?'

'Nervous? No. I don't think I am in any danger.'

'You don't think your attacker might want to keep you quiet?'

'I don't think that what I experienced was an attack. More of a... collision, I would say.'

I lean forward, coming in with the question I really want to ask. 'Eva,' I say, 'I know you didn't see anything and I know this is an odd question, but did you smell anything?'

She looks at me with her old, shrewd eyes under their wrinkled, cosmetically green lids and she says, 'Oh, yes. I did. And it was the same both times.'

'Both times?'

'Yes.'

'I don't underst —'

'You will,' she says.

'But what was the smell?'

'That,' she says, 'is my affair.'

Tea comes round after that and I am amused to see that she has trained them to bring hers black. I leave soon afterwards and spend the bus journey home reflecting on *the same both times*. When I am stalled there, my mind wanders to the first lines of *Medusa*, highlighted in the book on the beach:

A suspicion, a doubt, jealousy
grew in my mind,
which turned the hairs on my head to filthy snakes,
as though my thoughts
hissed and spat on my scalp.
My bride's breath soured, stank
in the grey bags of my lungs.
I'm foul mouthed now, foul tongued,
yellow fanged.
There are bullet tears in my eyes.
Are you terrified?
Be terrified.

And now I know.

Chapter Nineteen

LAST ORDERS

Sunday 23rd February 2014

Paula

DI Paula Powell came out of interview room two and stood leaning against the wall with her eyes closed. She was an hour into her interview with Matthew O'Dowd and she still could not decide whether he was very stupid or very clever. This was his second interview. They had brought him in the previous evening and he had seemed annoyed rather than guilty or fearful. He had had a bit of a rant about officers searching his mum's house again when she had only just got it straight after the last time, but he did not seem to be worried about what they might find. Otherwise he had been quite ready to answer questions. Aaron Green had led the initial interview, just to soften him up, and, in spite of the duty solicitor's demand that they charge him or release him, they had kept him in overnight, justifying his detention by evidence from his phone and computer that his relationship with Kelly had been unstable and aggressive.

She had left him to stew for most of the morning and then, ducking out of family lunch at her sister's on the grounds of an emergency, she had come in to question him herself. Asked about the attack on his girlfriend the previous year, he admitted to it although she had not, in the end, given evidence against him and he could have taken refuge behind that. Instead, he said he had been stupid and learned his lesson and claimed that he was focusing on his sport now, and getting through his English exam, and was hardly drinking at all. Asked about his relationship with Kelly Field, his answers were so unappealing that she thought they had to be true. With Kelly it was just sex, he said. After her morning swim, Kelly liked a quick shag (sorry about his language but that was what it was) and he had no objection. He didn't see her otherwise – they didn't go out or anything. She was annoying, really. If their relationship was aggressive, it came from her. He was an easy-going guy when he wasn't drinking but he was never good enough for her. She kept comparing him with some boyfriend she'd had before. No, he didn't know the boyfriend's name. He wasn't sure there had really been one, actually. He could have been all Kelly's fantasy. If he was so great what would he have been doing with Kelly, because Kelly was a bit of a dog, to be honest.

Paula had fought down her dislike and asked him about *The World's Wife*. How was it, she asked him, that two of the books that had been returned to the library had his fingerprints on them? He looked at her with his guileless, flat, blue eyes and said he had handled Kelly's copy, which he had taken back to the library, and he was pretty sure he had picked up Gina's, which had been lying around on the coffee table when he went for his coaching. No, he couldn't tell her anything about the poems. He wasn't into poems and, anyway, it was women's stuff, wasn't it?

It was at this point that she had come out for a break, sunk in gloom. He was all testosterone, swagger and a good candidate for a knee in the balls but he was also, she was pretty sure, telling the truth. He was a big, healthy, stupid boy without a gram of sensitivity or sympathy, but he didn't care enough to have killed Kelly. In all the text and email exchanges on his phone, the heat came from Kelly. She was the one raging and demanding, while he sent the briefest of replies, hardly bothering to disguise how little he cared.

Paula opened her eyes. They would have to release him though there was still a question mark over the fingerprints on a second book. She had always believed that the book on the beach was Gina's, stolen by Farid or by Matt. Still, other books were missing, so who knew? Who knew anything, actually? They seemed to be back at square one, though that wasn't an expression she liked – it suggested that this was a game. Well, it wasn't. Whatever Kelly Field's faults, she had been a healthy young woman with a life ahead of her and she had been brutally killed. Finding the man who did it was as serious as it got in this job.

She straightened her back and returned to the interview room. 'You are free to go for the moment, Matthew,' she said, 'but don't go anywhere. We may want to talk to you again.'

He stood up. 'And what about my mum's house?' he asked. 'Who's going to clear that up?'

'How about you?' she said. 'Celebrate your homecoming.'

She watched him walk along the corridor with Aaron Green and then went to her desk. *Trust Gina's instincts,* David had told her, and in the absence of any other direction to go in, she decided to go back to the book group which Gina thought lay at the centre of everything. Paula did not buy the Agatha Christie model of the book group members being picked off one by one by some crazed hater of literate women, but the book on the beach was some sort of signal and a second look at the women themselves would do no harm.

She had hardly called a list up on her screen before Aaron Green arrived, panting and brandishing an evidence bag.

'Handed in at the front desk a few minutes ago,' he said. 'The woman who found the body – Gina Sidwell.'

Paula took the bag. Clipped to it was a note in large, bold letters.

Found this among
Lily Terry's books.
Have not investigated it.
Over to you
Gina

She looked at Aaron Green. 'What do you reckon?' she asked.

'Well,' he said, 'it's an iPhone.'

'It is. And what we would like would be for it to be Kelly Field's missing iPhone, but it was found among Lily Terry's books – she's the young woman who fell off a ladder and died in St Martin's just before Kelly was killed. Gina – Mrs Sidwell – has always claimed that she was actually killed, too. So it is possible that this is Lily Terry's phone and she has sent it to us because she thinks it will have evidence on it about Lily Terry's death.'

Aaron Green looked puzzled. 'We could just look at it,' he said, 'I mean, rather than speculating…'

'And we will.' She opened a desk drawer and took out gloves. 'But this isn't the first time Gina Sidwell has been involved in a case of mine. I'm just preparing myself for the possibility that she's right.'

She switched the phone on and waited, with Aaron Green hovering behind her.

'Don't loiter, Aaron,' she snapped. 'You must have stuff to get on with. I'll call you if there's anything.'

He backed off, looking wounded, and she focused on the screen, turning first to the email inbox – nothing much there – and then to the sent box, which she rolled through, hardly breathing. Only when she moved on to sent text messages did she start to mutter 'Oh my God!' until it became a mantra and she stopped and closed her eyes. 'She was stalking him,' she whispered. 'And then Lily – and then – Jesus!' She went to the inbox. Just the one message back from him in all that time. Just the one, dated 13th February, and just one word, *Medusa*.

She turned, realising that Aaron Green was sitting across the room watching her.

'Get the team in, Aaron. Whatever they're doing. I need them here. First two to get here go with us to the house. We arrest him if he's there, and we search the house. Why did we never do that? What made me rule him out?'

She stopped. Why was he just standing there gawping at her? 'Don't stand there with your mouth open,' she shouted. 'Go on! Scoot!'

He turned and picked up the phone. 'Are you going to tell me where we're going, boss?' he asked.

'What? Cliffe Cottages. Number Six. Where else?'

Chapter Twenty

THE REMAINS OF THE DAY

Sunday 23rd February 2014

It is completely dark by the time the bus drops me off and the wind has got up, carrying sleety rain. Still reeling from my Damascene moment on the journey I forget to be nervous as I put my head down and hurry past Simon's door. When I get to my own door, though, I know something is wrong. For a start, in the pale glow of the street lamp, I see Ariel crouched on the scaffolding that disfigures the empty house to the left of mine. She looks like a cartoon of a scared cat, wild-eyed, with her fur on end in the brisk sea wind. She yowls at me, an eloquent expression of fear and outrage. I open the front door cautiously and am assailed by a smell of burning, an acrid, chemical smell. I almost trip over Caliban, who is standing, whimpering softly and staring through the open doorway to the sitting room, from where a faint light leaks. I stand, frozen. If Simon has got into my house and is intent on burning it down, why isn't Caliban savaging him? What is keeping him here, grizzling?

I step into the room and make out a man, so intent on his work that he doesn't hear me, kneeling by my logburner, pulling smouldering objects from it. I switch the light on.

'I can see why you might want to burn the books, Jack,' I say, 'but why in my stove?'

He glances at me once as the light goes on but then goes back to his task.

'Not the time of year for a bonfire,' he says. 'And not many people have real fires.'

'How did you get in here?' I ask. 'I'm sure I took the back door key out.'

'Latch on your back window's loose,' he says, still not looking at me, focused on the job in hand. He is beating the smoking books on the hearth now, sending sparks flying. Although he is wearing his thick, window cleaner's gloves, I fear for his hands, as well as for my rug, where sparks are beginning to smoulder. 'Lotta play in that latch,' he says. 'Easy to slip it up.'

'Spot all the weak spots, do you,' I say, 'cleaning windows? I suppose that's how you got hold of the books.'

'Got to tear these up,' he says. 'They won't burn like they are. Nearly put the fire out.'

He starts ripping pages from the books and, though it goes against the grain of forty years and more, I let him do it.

'Didn't you feel bad,' I ask, 'breaking into our houses? Stealing from us? Getting us suspected by the police?'

'It was almost like old times,' he says, almost smiling. 'Used to do a bit of pilfering back when I was a bad boy, before Lil.' He gives an extra tug at the pages of the book he is holding and crams them into the fire.

'I don't mind the paper so much,' I say, 'but the plastic smells disgusting when it burns.'

'Sorry about that,' he says.

I sit down on the arm of the sofa, trying to look relaxed, but poised to run if need be. Caliban sidles into the room and stands beside me, hackles up, looking from Jack to me, wondering what happens next. *No idea,* I tell him in my head. *Making it up as I go along.*

'So, it was Lily's book on the beach with Kelly, wasn't it?' I ask. 'And Lily highlighted the poem about Medusa. She liked highlighting – I've seen her school books.'

'She said it could have been written about Kelly, that poem. I didn't get it, but I could see the thing about her hair – the snakes.'

'And Kelly was jealous of Lily. I'd never have thought of that. She was years older than you. What made her think she could have had you?'

He shoves a plasticised book cover into the stove, where it shrivels and burns, sending out another belch of foul smoke.

'I had sex with her,' he mutters, coughing in the smoke. 'I was fifteen. I'd been drinking cider and I was off my head. She took me down on the beach and we did it. My first time. And then there were a few more times. When you're fifteen you'll take anything that's offered. I never told, though. And I made her swear not to tell. I'd never have lived it down with the lads.'

'Why?' I am genuinely interested. 'Wouldn't they have been impressed at you having sex with a grown-up woman?'

'Gotta be a better-looking one than Kelly,' he says. 'She was an ugly old slag.'

For a moment I am filled with rage. It flows into me like molten lava. How dare they, these boys? How dare they, these pimply, sweaty, grubby adolescents? What do they think gives them the right to pick and choose – thumbs up or thumbs down – *wouldn't mind getting into her knickers* or *ugly old slag*? I didn't like Kelly. She wasn't likeable, but she never had a chance to be. It's easy to be likeable if you've got good skin, shiny hair and a white dazzle of a smile. If you're plain, it takes real character to be likeable, and the chances are you'll still get disregarded. Kelly decided that if she couldn't be wanted then she would make sure she wasn't ignored, and just for the moment I admire that.

'And then you dumped her,' I say. 'And she didn't like that.'

'You could say.'

'Did you ever think about how she might be feeling?'

'Didn't need to. She made sure she let me know. Phone calls, texts, emails, all the time.'

'What did you do?'

'Nothing. Well, I tried talking to her at first but I just got abuse so then I just blanked her. After a while it stopped. Then I got together with Lily and it all started up again.'

'And Lily knew about it?'

'Oh, yeah. She was sorry for her at first. You know Lil – all heart. But then the bitch started on her – threatening her – and even she was pissed off in the end. When she read that poem, she started calling her Medusa.'

'What sort of threats did Kelly make?'

'All sorts. But knocking her off her ladder was favourite.'

'And you think that's what she did?'

He has only one book left now and he stops his ripping and sits back on his heels. For the first time, he actually looks straight at me.

'She was there,' he says, 'at the pub. When I heard the ladder crash, I had to get down my ladder and run round there. Time I got there, Kelly was beside her. Then George came out, but Kelly was there first. Said she'd been using the toilet there – the outside one at the back – and heard the noise. Bollocks she did.'

'You told the police about the threats?'

'No point. They were dead set on it being an accident.'

'But the threats – didn't Kelly leave any voicemails or text messages on Lily's phone?'

'She's a good liar,' he says, starting on destroying the last book. 'No point.'

'So you decided to keep it simple and just kill her?'

'I didn't care what the police thought. I didn't want them charging her, to be honest. What would she get? A few years inside? That wasn't enough for Lil. I needed her dead.'

'Why leave the book on the beach? What was that for?' I ask.

'That was for Lil. It was the closest I could get to Lil being there to see it. '

'And then you realised that if Lily's book was missing, suspicion would be bound to fall on you, so you decided to confuse things by pinching some of the other books. And being an expert at breaking and entering, you took them from our houses, but you couldn't get Lorna's because it was at the library, nor Dora's because she kept it in her briefcase. I should have seen that. It was stupid of me not to.'

He doesn't answer. All the book pages are burning now and he is sitting with the last cover in his hands.

'Is that why you hid Kelly's phone among Lily's books too – keeping Lily involved?'

'Not really. It was just a place where no one would look…'

'Except your sister.'

'Yeah.'

'And why attack Eva?' I ask. 'What was that about?'

Suddenly he is animated. 'I never attacked her,' he says. 'I didn't mean her harm. I'd been thinking about the books and I thought suppose they look for fingerprints and there wouldn't be one with Lil's prints on, so best wipe them all off. Then I heard someone coming and did a runner and over she went. But I went back. I gave it a few minutes and then I went back – looked after her, called an ambulance. She was a nice old lady. I didn't mean her harm.'

'She knew it was you who knocked her over,' I say. 'She recognised the smell of you. It's distinctive – a mixture of window-cleaning detergent and all those joss sticks Lily used to have around. They're in your clothes, your hair. But she won't say anything. You're safe there.'

He doesn't respond. I'm not even sure that he has taken in what I said. I draw a deep breath. 'The thing is, Jack,' I say. 'Now I know the truth, I will have to say something. I'm going to have to ring the police.'

He turns to look at me and the firelight glints in his eyes. For the first time he actually looks malevolent.

'No, you're not,' he says, 'cos you haven't got a phone. I saw your phone in pieces there in that box of rice.'

'But where do you think I've been,' I bluff, 'if not into Dover to buy a new phone?'

He laughs. 'So where is it then?' he asks.

I look at myself, perched here, still in my coat and so obviously without the bag and lavish packaging that accompanies a new phone. For the first time, I feel a prickle of fear. He gets up from his crouch by the fire and comes over to me. He stands looming above me and he is positioned between me and the door. His voice is wheedling but his body language is not.

'Look,' he says, 'you loved Lil, didn't you? You wanted her to make a good life. Kelly took all that from her. All her future. You don't really think I did wrong, do you?'

I have a flash of déja-vu. It wouldn't be the first time I let a murderer go free. But this is different. He had the evidence of Kelly's obsession on his own phone. The police would have investigated, they would have found Kelly's phone and her messages to Lily. The law would have taken its course. He might not like the outcome but grief doesn't trump everything. And though I've told him Eva won't give him away, I'm still not sure that he might not panic and want to silence her. I am really sorry the killer turns out to be him. I'd have been much happier seeing Simon go to prison, but there it is. However much I don't want to, I am going to have to knock on somebody's door and ask to use their phone.

I am not at all sure, though, that he will let me. I adjust my position for flight while giving a sigh of what I hope sounds like acquiescence. 'Well, maybe you're right, Jack,' I say, and I get up. 'I'm going to make us a cup of tea – clear all this smoke out of our throats – and we can talk about it.'

I pat his arm in a motherly sort of way and dodge past him. He follows me down to the kitchen and I fill the kettle and get down the biscuit tin. 'Chocolate biscuit?' I ask brightly.

He says nothing, but stands, blocking the kitchen door. I say, 'Do me a favour, Jack, will you? Just go and make sure there's nothing smouldering in my hearth rug. Don't want to have to call the fire brigade.'

My voice sounds pretty unconvincing to me but he turns and goes. I clatter mugs for a moment, until I'm sure that he is back in the sitting room, and then I make a dash for the front door. I am, fortunately, still wearing my coat, but there is no time to pick up my bag or Caliban's lead. He is right behind me, though, and we tumble out into the dark.

In the short time I have been indoors, it has turned into a vile evening. There is a drenching, icy rain, which is being blown about savagely by the wind. Where do I go now? There is no chance of being given refuge by Harry or Simon and I expect Jack to come barging out of my house at any moment. Caliban has his own answer. A creature of habit, he heads across the road and down the steps to the beach and, for want of a better solution, I follow. I don't, frankly, feel any safer down here. It is, after all, the scene of Jack's original crime, but I do cling to a hope that, away from the house, Caliban's more savage instincts may reassert themselves and he may protect me.

I am not equipped for the weather, dressed as I am not in my dog-walking anorak but in my proper coat, put on for my visit to the police station. I am wet, cold, scared and – for once in my life – completely without a plan. And then the cavalry arrives. I am aware of flashing lights above me, approaching down the road from Dover. I scramble up the steps and see one – two – police cars which scream to a stop outside Jack's house. Police officers jump out of the first car. One of them is Paula.

'Hi, Paula!' I call.

I can see her because she is illumined by the car lights, but I am in darkness. 'Gina?' she asks.

'Yes.' I start to cross the road towards her but she holds up an arm as if to ward me off.

'Go back!' she shouts. 'Keep away. And take that dog with you.'

And thank you, Gina, for bringing me the evidence that nails our killer, I mutter almost audibly as one of the officers with her leans on Jack's bell and calls through the letterbox.

'The thing is,' I call, 'he's not there. He's actually in my house, destroying evidence.'

'What?'

She turns from looking at the house and strides across the road to me.

'He's burning the stolen books,' I say.

'You warned him? You've been helping him?'

'No! I came home and found him there. He'd broken in.' I am having to shout over the noise of the wind and the continued banging on Jack's door, but I'm also shouting because I want to.

'He's trying to put suspicion on you?'

'I don't know.'

'Why didn't you stop him?'

She shouts this right into my face. She is no better equipped for the weather than I am. She is wearing her nice wool coat and her hair, like mine, is plastered to her face and head.

217

Caliban, however, finds this no excuse for her threatening behaviour. He has been feeling for some time, I suppose, that he ought to be attacking somebody and this is his moment. He leaps up, pressing his filthy paws against her coat, and seizes her sleeve in his teeth. Startled and taken off balance, she steps back, slips and falls to the ground. I bend down to help her up but find myself grabbed from behind, my arms twisted in a most uncomfortable way.

It is all hubbub now. The three police officers have all sprinted across the road: one to grab me. as, I suppose, the directing mind of Caliban's attack, one to check on Paula and one to approach Caliban with something that may possibly be a taser. Caliban has now completely lost it and is snarling and barking like a beast ready to take on all comers. I take a deep breath and, in a tone I have not used since I taught trainee criminals in the D stream of a Marlbury comprehensive, I command him to lie down. I have no real confidence that he will obey, but he – glad, I suppose, of some certainty in a bewildering world – sinks instantly to the wet ground with only the merest whimper of residual defiance. If only the trainee criminals had been so easily subdued.

'I'm sorry about your coat, Paula,' I say, 'and the answer to your question is I didn't stop him because he's bigger than me, and he had flaming books in his hands and this dog thinks he's his friend.'

Paula signals to my captor to release me. 'You, stay!' she says, and I'm not sure whether she is talking to me or Caliban. Then she heads off across the road. 'Come on,' she calls to her officers, and they push past me to cross to my front door. I stand, hesitating, and DC Aaron Green looks back and says, 'I'd go round to a friend if I were you. This'll be a crime scene. You won't be able to get back in tonight.'

'Right,' I say. 'Thanks.'

He follows the others into my house. I stand outside

and hope that, in it all, somebody checks my smouldering hearthrug. So, where to go? If I had my handbag I could go to a B&B for the night, but not with Caliban. In fact, I can't think of anywhere that a wet and filthy dog would be welcome – certainly not Lesley's or Lorna's neat, civilised houses. If I had a phone, I could be truly pathetic and ring Ellie and ask to be rescued, but I have no phone and I'm rather glad that I don't have to resist that temptation. There is no let-up in the rain, which is, if anything, getting sleetier. So here I am, homeless and friendless, hampered by a dog I don't much like and without so much as a toothbrush with which to face the night ahead.

Except. Except there is somewhere. I peer at my watch. It is not yet six o'clock. It will still be open. It has a loo, a sofa, a kettle, biscuits – even cup-a-soups in the cupboard, I believe. It has heat and light and entertainment to keep me occupied through a sleepless night, and I am confident that I can blag entry for a dog. I look at Ariel, who has come lower down the scaffolding and taken shelter under a piece of tarpaulin. She peers out and gives me another yowl. Well, when it's all over, she'll be able to get into the house through the cat flap, won't she?

'Sorry, cat,' I say. 'I can't take you with me. I'll be back in the morning. In the meantime I'm afraid it's a case of *Sauve qui purr'*. She doesn't show any sign of appreciating my pun, but I smile at my own wit as I loop my wet scarf through Caliban's collar and stride off towards the library.

Chapter Twenty-One

STAYING ON

Sunday 23rd March 2014

I have not slept in my house since it was turned into a crime scene a month ago. This is not because the house burned down. Oddly, Jack did go back and stamp out smouldering sparks as I asked him to, and he was still there when Paula and her troops burst in. So once the forensics had been done I could have gone back, but I just didn't fancy it. Hanging out there with just Simon and Harry as neighbours felt grim beyond words, so I found us other accommodation.

Caliban and I spent a cosy couple of nights at the library but after that Lorna started to get edgy about my settling in there, living on cup-a-soups and biscuits and reading my way through the children's section. Identifying a lack of a functioning phone rather than post-traumatic stress as the cause of my sudden inability to make plans or manage my life, she drove me into Dover and sat with me while I entered into a solemn and binding agreement to love and cherish a phone. The process was no easier or faster than it had been the previous time but at least I knew what to expect now, and Lorna damped down sparks of incipient hysteria on my part with a brisk and bracing *Now, now* so that we got through to the finish. She was quite right. The phone put me back in charge. Enquiries at local kennels led me to the conclusion that for hardly more than the price of housing Caliban in kennels and me in a B&B, we could both stay in comfort in a dog-friendly country house hotel. So that is where I have been. Ellie came and collected Ariel, who is adjusting to town life and to Nico, who likes to squeeze her, and Freda, who still hopes for demonstrations of her magic powers. Caliban and I, meanwhile, are at Upton Court, a charming, stone-built house, dating from the sixteenth century, about twenty miles inland from Dover. It has beams and fires and lethally uneven floors and views of the downs (but no hint of the sea) and delicious food. It took me a few days, in fact, to adjust to the richness and plenty of the food, after my period of subsistence living, but I am acclimatised now. It is not surprising, I suppose, how quickly one adjusts to spending money. That's why it has to be all or nothing. Once I started shifting money out of my savings account, there seemed to be no reason to stop. That is what happens to embezzlers, I imagine. Anyway, I'm embezzling only my own money and I'm not sure whether I feel guilty or liberated but I have decided not to ask myself the question. And while I'm not asking, I have bought some dazzling new clothes (which won't fit much longer if I continue eating like this) and I have had a very expensive haircut, including elaborate colouring, so that my hair has turned, like Lady Harbury's, *quite gold from grief.* So this is the new me. The inhabitants of St Martins-at-Cliffe could pass me in the street without associating me for a moment with the scary dog walker who haunted their shore for a year or so.

I did invite Lesley and Lorna over for lunch and it was fine. We talked books and they talked about their campaign to recruit new members for the book group. The original group has dwindled to a mere three – Lesley and Lorna plus Eva, who has made a stalwart recovery from her fall and is, I gather, very cross with me for shopping Jack to the police.

Dora has dropped out of the group, citing too much A level work as her excuse, but really, I think, it's because I'm no longer there to bully her into staying. *So you three are the three weird sisters,* I quipped when I saw Lesley and Lorna but they didn't laugh. They're tired of the witch joke, I gather, and are thinking of changing the group's name. I hope they do, really. It might help to wipe out my embarrassment at being so paranoid and getting things so wrong. There was no plot against us, no deranged anti-feminist serial killer. I was a bit miffed that Paula never thanked me for solving her case for her but, on the other hand, she never pointed out my wrong-headedness either.

So, I'm out of the book group and I've given up the coaching. I felt a bit bad about abandoning Dora and Matt but, actually, Dora did well in her mocks in spite of everything else that was going on, so she doesn't need me any more, and Matt has opted for plan B. He has taken over the village shop. It turns out that Kelly's father didn't own the shop, as I assumed he did, but only leased it, and Matt has persuaded his mother to lend him the money to take on the lease. *Cheaper than a student loan* he said when I rang him to bow out of our coaching sessions and found him full of plans. He may actually be quite good at this, and his long-term plan is to take over the pub when George is eventually felled by a lifetime of alcohol abuse. I do wonder how he will fit in his sporting activities around the job but I suppose he has thought of that.

So, my ties with St Martin's are almost undone. My house is up for sale though it is attracting zero interest at present. Simon, I gather, is staying put in his house but there are no new tenants in Jack's and Lily's house yet. They were never promising looking, Cliffe Cottages, but they must look very sad now. I wouldn't buy a house there. I may have to give mine away.

Jack appeared in the magistrates' court and pleaded not guilty. I hope his lawyer can do something for him, though I can't see it will make much difference. There is no chance of a happy ending for Jack. I wonder what the defence case will be. Manslaughter or diminished responsibility? I have tried asking Andrew about it but criminal law is not his bag. He has, however, played a blinder as far as my asylum seekers are concerned. They are another aspect of the St Martin's life that I have had to give up since nothing short of a taxi each way would get me to Dover from my hotel and even in my current spendthrift mood that seemed to be verging on the eccentric.

Before I left them, though, I brought Andrew to see them and he spent two hours talking with each of them in turn. The results have been startling. It is amazing what public school and Oxford confidence can achieve (and yes, all right, he is quite bright and probably knows what he is doing as well). Anyway, one of his main achievements so far is to get leave to remain for Zimbabwean Ivy, and to get her husband released from the IRC. If they are glad, it is difficult to tell; the ghosts of their dead boys are in their eyes and get in the way. With the other students, it is less a question, he tells me, of how good their case is than of how much our government minds upsetting theirs. On this basis, Soraya should be all right, since we don't much mind upsetting the Iranians, but poor gay Hani will probably be sent back to our partners in peace in Saudi Arabia, and Jing Wei won't get much help either, now George Osborne has his eye on China as the UK's new best friend. For Yaema and Aminata, in flight from geriatric husbands, there is no hope and Andrew has told them so. The money they stole to fund their journey here was their own dowry money, true, but the dowries were not actually theirs, of course. So they are wanted for a crime and will be sent back for punishment. Except they won't. Once they grasped what Andrew had to tell them, they disappeared. The others think they are in London, where the only way they will be able to make a living will be as prostitutes. Will they think that's a better deal than the marriages they ran away from? Perhaps they will.

And then there is Farid. Andrew descended like the wrath of God on the police and the Border Agency, claiming wrongful imprisonment, corruption and much else besides. Farid was out of the IRC the same day, and Andrew has no doubt that he can get him leave to remain for the duration of his medical studies. The question is whether remaining is what he wants. I have had a letter from him. Courteous as ever, he thanked me for my help and for Andrew's intervention but stopped short of committing to staying. *My experience of being incarcerated is burned into my soul,* he wrote. *I don't know yet whether those burns can heal.* I was impressed by the extended metaphor. I can see why Dora loves him. Whether he stays will, I think, depend on Dora, who is proving unexpectedly resourceful. If he stays and if she does well enough in her A levels in the summer, she will see if she can pick up a place at one of the London colleges so they can be together. Her father, I assume, has not been apprised of this plan. There is another act of this drama to come.

So Andrew has done well, as has Lavender, who urged him to ring me on his return from Argentina, almost before he had his coat off and certainly before telling him about the problems with the dishwasher and the need to look for a new au pair. This is why, for the first time in fifteen years, Andrew is invited to my birthday party. Lavender is invited, too, of course, as are Ellie and Ben and Annie and Jon. And Freda. I have warned her that this will be a dinner party at my hotel and that we shall be sitting round the table for a long time talking about grown-up things but she is quite confident that she is up to it. It will be my fifty-first birthday, not one to make a fuss of but I spent my fiftieth on my own, drinking leek and potato soup and rereading *The Mill on the Floss*. I was thoroughly miserable and I can't remember now why I thought it was a good idea. I shall make up for it this evening with overpriced champagne and a new dress.

I am wearing the dress now, sitting in the bar, waiting for the others to arrive. Annie's boyfriend, Jon, is not coming. He is working, apparently, but Annie sounded worryingly flat on the phone and I shall be glad of a chance to have a good look at her and see if she is all right. In fact, I think I need to keep an eye on her. I have let her slip away because it was what she seemed to want and because it was easier. If I were in London, would things be better between us? This is not just idle speculation actually. In my bag I have a letter inviting me to an interview for a job at the School of Oriental and African Studies in London. SOAS is El Dorado for an English Language teacher; it is full of very bright, highly motivated students from all over the world and one would feel in the very heartbeat of the global future there.

It is also in Bloomsbury, which I find unreasonably romantic and exciting, and I have already trawled websites to see whether my huge fortune from the sales of my house and my mother's flat would buy me a broom cupboard there, and it turns out that I could get quite a comfortable studio flat just minutes from the British Museum. Since I have dispossessed myself of almost all my belongings, a studio would suit me very well. I am absurdly excited about the prospect and desperate to get the job. I panicked when I first got the interview letter, feeling that the past two years had left me horribly out of touch with current theory and practice, but since then I have spent three solid days in the wonderful SOAS library, braving the rolling stacks and genning up. Now I feel ready to dazzle my interviewers.

I must not count chickens yet but I can't help thinking

about a London life. I missed it terribly when I was first marooned in Marlbury but over the years the town expanded to fill my life and I forgot about it. Perhaps it is the cultural starvation of the past eighteen months that has made me suddenly hungry for London all over again. Perhaps it is the need to be near Annie (and I could keep an eye on Dora and Farid if Dora's plans work out). And, yes, perhaps I am also thinking that David is in London. I have no idea if he wants to see me but he did tell Paula to trust me, and that is not nothing. And I have his phone number. Paula gave it to me; my grudging reward for services rendered. I haven't used it yet; no point if I'm not going to get the job. But if I do, well…

Chapter Headings

The chapter headings here are all titles of novels which have won the Booker/Man Booker prize in the past 47 years and have been popular choices for book groups.

The Sea	John Banville	2005
The God of Small Things	Arundhati Roy	1997
Offshore	Penelope Fitzgerald	1979
Bring Up the Bodies	Hilary Mantel	2012
The Gathering	Ann Enright	2007
Something to Answer for	P.H. Newby	1969
In a Free State	V.S. Naipaul	1971
Troubles	J.G. Farrell	1970
The Inheritance of Loss	Kiran Desai	2006
Disgrace	J.M.Coetzee	1999
The Old Devils	Kingsley Amis	1986
The Blind Assassin	Margaret Atwood	2000
The English Patient	Michael Ondaatje	1992
Possession	A.S. Byatt	1990
Rites of Passage	William Golding	1980
How Late it Was, How Late	James Kelman	1994
The Ghost Road	Pat Barker	1995
The Sense of an Ending	Julian Barnes	2011
Last Orders	Graham Swift	1996
The Remains of the Day	Kazuo Ishiguro	1989
Staying On	Paul Scott	1977